"A vivid portrait of Pre-Raphaelite glamour and the
perils of beauty, desire and independence."
Anna McKerrow, author of *Crow Moon*

"Love love LOVED *Following Ophelia*. Brilliantly done."
Catherine Johnson, author of *The Curious Tale of the Lady Caraboo*

"Sophia has conjured up a world as alive with colour and texture and
beauty and rebellion as the paintings that she references."
Perdita Cargill, author of *Waiting for Callback*

"A dreamy, romantic novel about a young woman becoming embroiled in the
Pre-Raphaelite art scene... I'm very happy to learn that this is the first in the series,
as ... there's so much more I want to know and see through Mary's eyes."
Melinda Salisbury, author of *The Sin Eater's Daughter*

"This is Bennett's first historical fiction title, and she does a wonderful job
with the glamour, scandal and dresses of the period."
Fiona Noble, *The Bookseller*

"The pomp. The flair. The excess. The detail.
Nothing was missed and it made for such an enthralling read."
Behind on Books

"*Following Ophelia* paints a vivid tapestry of the world of the Pre-Raphaelite
Brotherhood... (Mary) holds her own in a new and intimidating world of
flamboyant, talented men brilliantly... I can't wait for the next book in this series!"
Lauren James, author of *The Next Together*

"Atmospheric and evocative *Following Ophelia* by @sophiabennett
has all the right ingredients and leaves you wanting more."
Rhian Ivory, author of *The Boy Who Drew the Future*

"In a story filled with glamour and excitement, Bennett paints her own
portrait of 1850s London, its fusty interiors and filthy streets, describing
Victorian clothes – her own passion – in particularly wonderful detail."
Andrea Reece, LoveReading4Kids

"Sophia Bennett's familiar tone means that this would be a fantastic start
for fans of contemporary who are looking to try something new. The writing
is beautiful and slightly decadent, rich with research and passion."
The Bee's Princess

"Adored it.  want more.)"

Unveiling Venus

To E... ...Ton. Happy ever...fter.

⁓⊱⊰⁓

STRIPES PUBLISHING
An imprint of the Little Tiger Group
1 Coda Studios, 189 Munster Road, London SW6 6AW

A paperback original
First published in Great Britain in 2018

ISBN: 978-1-84715-825-3

Text © Sophia Bennett 2018
Cover copyright © Stripes Publishing, 2018

A CIP catalogue record for this book is available from the British Library.

Printed and bound in the UK.

2 4 6 8 10 9 7 5 3 1

Unveiling Venus

SOPHIA BENNETT

Stripes

PART I

SERENISSIMA

Chapter One

My dearest Persephone,

Oh, how you must curse me, and how sorry I am! I haven't written to you in an age. All I can say is I have been so busy! And I have much news. More of which in a minute...

But meanwhile I've heard so much about you. Even here in St Petersburg (yes, that's where Mama has brought me) news travels, if it is worth travelling. And now it is all news of magnificent Persephone Lavelle of Mayfair, who is much admired and is sitting for Millais himself, I hear. Is that really true?

You must be wondering why I'm in Russia. Mama and Papa brought me here to meet a young gentleman they have been in contact with for a while. Indeed, I used to know him as a child. His name is Lord Arthur Malmesbury and he is very grand. His father is a duke (!!) but I always thought of little Arthur as my partner in crime when I *was a girl in pinafores. How strange to think that now he is twenty-three, a diplomat flitting about Europe for the Queen, and eminently dashing.*

Have you guessed? Mama and Papa were hoping that I would like grown-up Arthur, and that he would like me too. He has heard all *about me. Much of it good, apparently, because, dear ~~M~~ Persephone, he wants to marry me! And he is so enchanting. Of course, I hardly ever get to see him here in Russia because Mama will not go out in the snow, and I must wait until he calls on us and then it is only for half an hour each day… But half an hour is enough, because he is as handsome as Prince Albert in his youth, and charming and courteous and … oh, I mustn't bore you. But I am so happy. And I have told him all about you. He loves the sound of your adventures as much as I do (isn't he a delight?) and he can't wait to meet you.*

Soon we depart for Venice, where dear Arthur (may I call him 'dear' yet? I think I shall anyway!) has a mission for the Prime Minister, and has invited us all to come too. How I long for you to join me there! Oh, the larks we could have! Think how much more enjoyable your company would be than that of dear old Aunt Violet, or Mama, who gets seasick and won't even ride in a gondola! If only you weren't so busy in London I would positively insist that you come.

Be happy for me, Persephone. As I am for you.
À bientôt. I kiss the paper and send fond wishes.
Your loving
Kitty

Mary risked wearing out the soles of her silk slippers as she paced the carpet of her drawing room, reading Kitty's letter for the hundredth time. Since it arrived over a month ago she had opened it so often that she had worn holes in the folds. Daylight shone through, underlining certain phrases.

dear ~~M~~ Persephone, he wants to marry me!
How I long for you to join me there!

The crossed-out 'M' was telling. When they first met in the spring, she was Mary Adams, scullery maid. But with Kitty Ballard's help, Mary had transformed herself into Persephone Lavelle, the newest, brightest Pre-Raphaelite artists' muse and the talk of London. Still, Kitty had not heard *all* Mary's news. As autumn turned to winter, London had become a place Mary was desperate to escape.

The city contained Felix Dawson, the only man she really wanted to be with. But thanks to a dark bargain she had made, he was the one man she must never see again.

3

Saved by a young admirer called Rupert Thornton she was now, at seventeen, a kept woman with a rich protector, a wardrobe of fine silks and a broken heart.

Though she had lived there less than a year, London was full of shallow gossip and memories that chafed like grazes on her skin. By contrast, Venice glistened exotically in Mary's imagination. She had written back instantly, offering to visit Kitty as soon as she could. But that had been in November and now Christmas was approaching. Kitty must have received her note ages ago but still there was no reply.

Mary retrieved the letter from its hiding place each morning. Last summer Kitty had been her fondest companion, the society girl who enjoyed the company of an artists' model. Then Mary's life had unravelled. Professor Aitken and his wife, for whom she worked as a scullery maid in Pimlico, had discovered her secret artistic assignations and sacked her on the spot. With nowhere else to go she had been taken in, against all propriety, by Rupert. And Kitty had gone silent. After weeks without contact, Mary had assumed the worst. What well-brought-up, rich Mayfair girl would stay loyal to such an outrageous creature? But the letter had made it clear – Kitty *was* loyal, and merely busy with her own love story. Mary had been wrong ever to doubt her.

So, Kitty was to marry a duke? Or at least the son of one. Was he the eldest? She didn't say. Dear, sweet Kitty who was caught up so much in the romance that she neglected to mention whether or not she was set to become a duchess one day.

Mary was so lost in her thoughts that she didn't hear footsteps on the stairs. The sudden knock at the apartment door startled her. She was about to slide the letter back in its usual spot – between the pages of a book of Shakespeare plays – when her housekeeper appeared.

"Mr O'Bryan, ma'am."

Mary relaxed. She had no secrets from Eddie O'Bryan. His big sister Annie had been her fellow maid in Pimlico. Despite the fact that he had once tried to blackmail her, he was now her favourite visitor. A 'lady', she reflected, did not receive young gentlemen unaccompanied. But Persephone Lavelle was no 'lady' and had no reputation to defend. She may as well take advantage of it.

"Show him in, Mrs Howard."

"Yes, ma'am." Mary suspected the housekeeper disapproved but she didn't show it.

Eddie strode into the parlour with his usual swagger, dressed in natty tweeds whose cut and style belied the fact that they were cheap and second-hand. Following Annie, he had come to the big city from Ireland to make something of himself. He was still working on it, scraping a living as a bare-knuckle boxer and in various jobs Mary didn't want to enquire about too closely. He bowed so extravagantly low that he brushed the floor with the cap clutched in his hand.

"Milady."

He was being ironic, as usual. Eddie still thought it funny to see the girl his sister used to boss around in the scullery now dressed in coral silk, with turquoises in her ears. Mary smiled and shook her head. "Don't tease me."

"That wasn't teasing! I am the soul of politeness, I think you'll find. And how are you, this fine morning? Ah. She has a letter. She clutches it to her bosom. It is from her long-lost lover…"

"Eddie! Stop it!" Mary couldn't help laughing. Eddie knew the miserable state of her love life, yet still he mocked her. "You know who it's from."

"Not Kitty Ballard?"

Mary nodded.

"The same note as last time?"

"Yes, the same." Mary looked down, embarrassed. "I haven't received another."

"Would this be of interest, by any chance?"

She glanced up at him. Eddie was holding out an envelope between two extended fingers. He must have been concealing it behind his back.

"For me?" she asked.

"Who else? I passed the postman on the steps outside. Told him I'd save him the trouble. It's fancy writing. A lady's script, I'd say…"

"Eddie O'Bryan! Hand it over this minute!"

He faked a wounded look. "I was only being helpful." He grinned as she snatched the letter from him.

Seconds later she was sitting at her writing desk, sliding a silver opener through the paper with shaking hands. It *was* Kitty's handwriting. A more tactful man might have withdrawn and left her to it but Eddie stayed and watched while she raced through the close-packed lines.

"So? What does she say?"

"Shh. I'm reading."

"Come on! I can see it's good news. Tell me."

Mary put down the letter and looked up. "She's already there, in Venice. It took an age to get my reply – it arrived in Russia just as they were leaving. She's thrilled I said yes. She wants me to come as soon as we can arrange it."

Eddie laughed and Mary realized her voice had gone up an octave. She was breathing fast.

With Eddie looming over her shoulder, she read the rest. The Ballards had taken *"a rather decrepit-looking palace on the Grand Canal"*, rented from an impoverished Venetian aristocrat they'd met in St Petersburg. Now, with her father's help, Kitty would organize Mary's journey for her. And there would be plenty of space for her to stay in the rented palazzo, *"if you don't mind the damp and the songs of gondoliers beneath your window"*. No, Mary didn't mind. She really, really didn't. She thought the whole thing sounded idyllic.

The only worry was Kitty's brother. Mary had not parted with him on good terms. But neither of Kitty's letters mentioned Roly. Perhaps he had not travelled with them? In fact, Mary was sure she had heard reports of him being in London.

"So you're going?" Eddie asked, as soon as she put the letter down.

"Of course I am! How long do you think it takes to get there?"

"You're asking a boy from County Cork. As if I'd know. Days, I should think. Weeks, perhaps?"

"Surely not? I'm right to go, aren't I?"

She paused, her green eyes huge against her freckled skin as she gave Eddie a look of serious hesitation. When she needed it, the one man who had helped her was Rupert. He paid for this apartment and everything in it. She owed him more than she could repay, and already she was planning her escape.

Eddie shrugged and smiled. "Oh, you'll go. You'll go whatever the rights and wrongs. There's no holding you back."

"You make that sound like a bad thing…"

"Not me. I happen to think it's very good. You don't suit life in a gilded cage. There's nothing for you here right now but tittle-tattle. Let it calm down for a while. Go and amuse yourself with the Italians, why don't you?"

"So you agree!"

"It's hard to disagree with you, Mary."

There was a ruefulness about his smile that made Mary rub the side of her thumb with her nail. It was a habit she had got into recently, since she had stopped scrubbing floors and grates, and started to grow long fingernails again. She did it when she was nervous about something, or embarrassed. It wasn't the Italians but thoughts of her relationship with Rupert that made her feel this way.

Eddie held her gaze. "Nothing's changed, has it?"

Mary shook her head. She was friends with Rupert. She enjoyed his interests and conversation, but he didn't make her heart race. Though she had tried to turn her gratitude into love, it hadn't worked. He had agreed to wait, and three months later he was still gallantly waiting. Half of London assumed she was his mistress, but London gossips were not always as accurate as they liked to pretend.

"Promise me one thing," Eddie said.

"What?"

"Tell him to his face. Treat him decently. He's done as much for you."

Mary nodded. Then Eddie was all grinning

playfulness again. His teeth flashed white. He really was a handsome man, she reflected, for one who made a living being punched in the head. And it was amazing he had any teeth at all.

"Ha! Imagine!" He laughed.

"Imagine what?"

"If anyone knew what a good girl you are, behind the scandal!"

She faced him, unsmiling, and played with her hair, which hung loose to her waist and glowed like fire against the light. "No one will ever ask, and no one will ever know, and no one will ever care."

"I know. I care."

"You don't count, Eddie. Now you'd better go. You're not helping my reputation by staying here so long."

"Ah, but as you say, I don't count, fine lady. Nobody would picture the likes of you with the likes of me."

He bowed and left with another flourish of his hat. Mary listened thoughtfully as his boots clattered down the stairs. *Not true*, she thought. *People think anything of the likes of me, and if they saw that glint in your eye, who knows what they'd think of the likes of you?*

Chapter Two

Rupert was due to dine with Mary that evening. The time had come to tell him everything. So far, she hadn't mentioned Kitty or Venice because she felt disloyal to him even thinking about going away. It was why that first letter had ended up hidden in the pages of Shakespeare. But now plans were afoot and she couldn't keep them secret.

However, at the last minute he sent a message to say his parents had important guests to dinner and he was obliged to attend. Rupert lived off a generous allowance from his father. He did as he was told. Mary ate alone.

The next day, he was sent on business to Chatham in Kent, where one of Mr Thornton's ships was having problems in the docks. By now he hadn't seen her for a week. She began to feel rather neglected.

"He'll be back soon, no doubt," Mrs Howard said,

noticing Mary staring glumly out of the drawing-room window at the dull, leaden skies.

As two more days went by, she wondered whether Rupert's father was acting deliberately to keep his son busy out of town. Mr Thornton, she knew, disapproved of his son setting her up in this apartment. The situation was never openly discussed, but the way Rupert flushed whenever he referred to his parents made it all too obvious. The issue, she suspected, was not morality but money. Since mixing with the upper class, she had learned that the lives of women born outside it were not valued much, but property and inheritance were taken very seriously. These furnished rooms would be considered a waste of funds; her presence in them somewhat incidental.

Mary distracted herself by going out. She had various requests from artists who wanted to sketch or paint her. She had to be careful where she went, as most of the artists she knew also knew Felix Dawson and if she saw him, there would be desperate consequences. She liked to sit for Dante Gabriel Rossetti, but her most regular patron was John Millais, who was doing endless studies of her head, hair and hands, drawing her as a disembodied, ethereal beauty.

While she posed for Millias she updated his wife, Effie, on the new letter. Effie was thrilled. She had once been married to John Ruskin, one of Venice's greatest admirers, and though the marriage had been unhappy, her honeymoon there with him had been enchanting. She talked little of the man but her eyes lit up when she thought of the city.

"You'll love it, my dearest! St Mark's … the Grand Canal … the strange little alleyways. They call it *La Serenissima*, you know. Isn't that beautiful? It will be winter, of course, so cold and damp, but there is nothing like Venice in the mist…"

La Serenissima? The words alone made Mary shiver with anticipation.

When she got back that evening, rosy-cheeked and refreshed from her walk across Hyde Park, there was a new letter waiting for her in that familiar handwriting. It would be hard to guess that Kitty Ballard, a willowy, nineteen-year-old beauty, should also be a master of cross-continental administration. But so it proved. The paperwork was already under way and a date was set for Mary's departure. She must worry about nothing – it was all taken care of. She would join the Ballards in their palazzo in January.

So far, the furthest Mary had ever travelled was from her childhood home in Kent to London, and that was ten times as far as anyone in her family. She reread *The Merchant of Venice* in anticipation of the trip, and some translated stories from Dante, which she had thought would be set in Italy but which turned out to be set in Hell and Purgatory. She would have given up, but the stories were very good.

By now, Christmas was only days away and telling Rupert had become an urgent necessity. To her frustration, he sent another apologetic note saying he could not visit over the holiday – his mother demanded absolute attendance at home.

However, my dearest, I think of you always. I enclose these trinkets as a token of my devotion. Happy Christmas, from one who loves you more than words can say...

The package contained two large gold bangles. They looked expensive, even for a young man on Rupert's allowance. Mary cursed them as they glittered on the desk in front of her. What kind of man sent *bangles* instead of risking his mother's wrath to keep her company? She was not made for such a life. She could have written to explain her plan but she had promised Eddie to do it in person. She would just have to wait.

On Christmas Eve Mrs Howard left to visit her family in Essex. Mary dreaded spending Christmas Day alone. She briefly considered going home to Kent but the thought of her father put her off the idea completely. If Pa ever found out how she was living – and somehow, he would – he would beat her beyond endurance and she had vowed she would never let him touch her again.

Effie and John Millais were away, and Mary didn't know her other artistic friends well enough to invite herself to stay. Besides, Felix might be with them. Eddie and Annie had gone to see a sister of theirs in Liverpool. There was, however, one person she could count on for company: her cousin Harriet, who worked as a laundress in Chelsea. Mary sent a boy along with an invitation, and he came back with a note brimming with gratitude.

With the ground two inches deep in snow that morning, she sent a cab to collect Harriet and her baby. Mary waited in her bright parlour, picturing it pulling up at the big grey house, set slightly back from the King's

Road, where Harriet worked. The house belonged to Mrs Lisle, a patron of the arts who had set up Felix in his studio. It was she who was entirely responsible for Mary's ruined reputation and broken heart.

When she fell in love with Felix, Mary had hardly spared a thought for the widow who paid for his paints and clothes. She should have done. Mrs Lisle had turned out to be a jealous woman and a brilliant adversary. *Far cleverer than me*, Mary thought bitterly.

While Felix painted Mary with increasing obsession over the summer, Mrs Lisle must have sensed his growing attachment to his muse. Patient, cold and calculating, she had waited to discover the one thing that could tear them apart. Then Harriet was thrown out on the streets, pregnant with the child of the son of the house who had seduced her. Mary knew that if she did nothing her cousin's fate would be the workhouse or the river. If she was to be saved she needed a place to stay, food – the basic things – all of which required money. First Mary turned to Kitty but her friend had no funds of her own to give. When no man would help – not Roly Ballard or even Felix – Mary had run without thinking to the rich widow. She was generous. She was a woman. She would understand.

Mrs Lisle understood perfectly, in fact. And so she had made her pact. She would take Harriet and her unborn child into her home, and in return Mary must agree to give Felix up instantly and forever, and never speak to him again.

Harriet was safe. It was done. No point in raking over the ashes.

Shaking herself out of her sad reverie, Mary set about arranging the dining table with a feast of festive treats for her cousin. She filled the prettiest china bowls with fruit and gilded walnuts, and hung garlands of popcorn and red berries from the candle sconces on the wall. It seemed only a few minutes before she heard the wheels of a hansom in the street outside.

Mary flew downstairs to find Harriet standing on the doorstep, clutching a parcel tied with string. After a brief, close hug, Mary led her up to her apartment. Once inside, Harriet looked around with eyes on stalks. Mary guiltily reflected that this was her first visit here.

"My goodness, your furniture! Which chair do you sit on?"

"All of them!"

"And who polishes this floor?"

"I have a housekeeper," Mary admitted, embarrassed. "Where's Aileanna?" she asked. She had hoped to spend today doting on her little god-daughter, but there was no sign of her.

"Mrs Lisle wanted to look after her," Harriet said with a wobbly smile.

"On Christmas Day? Without you?"

Harriet nodded and chewed her lip. "There's a wet nurse who feeds her. Mrs Lisle insisted. My own milk is poor." She looked down at her plain black dress, which hid a slim body back to its usual shape only two months after the birth, or thinner, even.

"You hardly look like you have the strength," Mary said, observing the collarbones sticking through her cousin's shabby clothes.

"I'm perfectly well – the better for seeing you. And that table. It's positively laden with delights. We can't possibly eat them all."

Mary sensed that Harriet didn't want to talk about the baby, so she led her cousin to the table instead. After some chicken and jellied eels, Harriet brightened and Mary saw a glimmer of the girl she used to know.

They drank a little beer and exchanged presents. Each had embroidered handkerchiefs for the other. Mary had also made her god-daughter a matching dress and cap, smocked with thousands of impeccably fine stitches.

"She'll look like a princess!" Harriet grinned.

Mary shook her head modestly, though she privately doubted that any child at Buckingham Palace had clothes better made. It was one of the advantages of all those evenings spent alone.

The afternoon ended on a jolly note, even though Mary admitted it might be months before she saw Harriet again.

"I'm glad," Harriet said, with spirit in her eyes for once.

"Oh, really?"

Harriet laughed. "Not for me – for you. You need this trip to feed your soul, Mary. Go and have a wonderful time in Italy and don't think of England once."

"I can't promise that!"

When Harriet was gone and the apartment was quiet again, Mary was surprised how much she missed her. It had been like going back to their childhood days for a few hours. She promised herself that someday, when she could, she would entertain her cousin in such style again.

Chapter Three

By the end of the first week of January, the paperwork Mary needed for her travels was complete. The journey was to take a week, passing through France and Switzerland. Her accommodation along the route was arranged. She would leave the following Tuesday.

She sent a message inviting Rupert to dine with her on Monday night. He had visited once already since Christmas, but that evening had quickly descended into petty argument after so much time apart and he left before she could tell him anything.

Tonight he was due at seven. She wore his favourite dress: a luscious olive-green velvet one she'd made herself, which he said reminded him of Rossetti's favourite model, Lizzie Siddal. Was the dress a good idea or a bad one? She didn't know, but she wore it with the bangles he had sent and hoped it would put him in a favourable mood.

Mrs Howard had cooked a roast beef dinner with treacle tart to follow. The apartment smelled invitingly delicious. There was red wine on the table and two pots of sweet-scented lily of the valley that she had bought from Covent Garden. Mary wanted to make the evening as pleasant for him as she could. A bitter pill should come in sugar-coating.

Rupert took off his coat and hat, and threw them on a chair. The memory of their last, brief meeting seemed to have gone, thank goodness.

"You look divine," he announced, running his fingers through her hair. He dipped his head to kiss her on the cheek and she tried not to stiffen at his touch.

"You look tired," she said. "Was your day enjoyable?"

"Enjoyable? Ha! Father insisted on sending me to the docks again this morning. He wants me to learn every last detail about loading procedures. Can you imagine? Shipping is the most boring business on earth."

Shipping, Mary noted, paid for her clothes and this apartment. To her, it seemed full of risk and adventure. As so often, she found herself privately disagreeing with her protector but her role was to entertain, not criticize. She smiled. "Can I pour you some claret?"

"Please do. A lot."

She waited until the meal was over and Rupert was chasing the last spoonful of treacle tart and custard around his plate. He was happy and slightly drunk, which suited her perfectly. She took a breath. *See, Eddie? I shall keep my promise.*

"Rupert. Dearest. I have some news. It's about Kitty."

"Kitty who?"

"Kitty Ballard. You remember?"

"What? Pretty Kitty? I thought she'd gone to India to meet some dashing suitor. That's what the talk in the club was."

Oh, Rupert. Why hadn't he *told* her this? It would have saved her a lot of heartache two months ago, when she thought her friend had abandoned her. "Not India. Russia," she said mildly. "But now she's in Italy."

"Italy, eh? Why?"

"Her suitor's working there, as a diplomat."

"And she's following him around the globe? Like a lovesick pup? Poor Kitty."

Mary hadn't thought of it this way. Surely it was romantic? "They're keen to spend more time in each other's company. She's with her family but she needs a chaperone. She'd like me to join her."

"You? *You?* You'd be the worst chaperone in the world!" Rupert threw back his head and laughed.

"What d'you mean?"

"Admit it. An unmarried girl? Not yet eighteen? Kept by a dashing…" He didn't finish the sentence. Lover? Not that. But still. She felt the familiar flush creep up her neck.

"Not chaperone exactly," she conceded. "Companion."

Rupert laughed again. "Kitty Ballard always had the strangest ideas! I remember when she let that intolerable brother of hers take her to the races. The *races* of all places! No sign of a chaperone then – except Roly himself, who's a reprobate of the highest order. So who is this brave young knight who wants to take her on?"

"Lord Arthur Malmesbury."

At this, Rupert's bushy eyebrows shot up. "Arthur Malmesbury, by God? You must be mistaken. He's one of the biggest toffs in the country."

"Yes, she said."

"And he wants Kitty? Kitty Ballard? How extraordinary. He must be one for a pretty face and not mind the reputation."

Reputations were a sensitive subject in this household. Mary pushed back her chair and stood up, trying to stay calm. "She needs me. Lord Malmesbury is busy and she's lonely. I've told her I'll go."

"To Italy? You can't."

"Why?"

"My God. You're serious." So far, Rupert had been leaning back in his chair, grinning at her story. But now he paled and stood up too. "Don't be ridiculous. You can't suddenly go halfway across Europe on a whim."

They were arguing again but she couldn't help it. "It's not a whim," she said fiercely. "It's a serious invitation. I've accepted."

"Without asking me?" He was astonished. "I forbid it. You can't go without my permission."

"I have another man's." She glared at him.

"*What?*" Rupert stepped back in such shock that he knocked his chair over. A candle fell out of the candelabra on the table, spilling hot wax on the mahogany.

Mary realized how her words sounded. "It's not what you think. He's an older gentleman." She meant Kitty's father but she had suddenly decided to give Rupert no more details. Anything she said might be used to stop her and she could not let that happen. "It's too late," she said. "Everything's decided."

Rupert took two steps towards her. His breath smelled of red wine. For a moment, fear flickered inside her. But his anger melted away as swiftly as it had come.

"Please don't go," he said softly.

"I must."

"I've neglected you. I'm sorry."

"It's not just that…" she murmured. "I can't depend on you for everything."

"I don't mind."

"I do."

He shook his head as the news sank in. Taking another step closer, he put his hands gently either side of her neck, under her hair. His eyes scoured hers for hope. "Think again. Please. I… I come into money soon. I won't be so dependent on my father. I can spend more time with you. Give you more money for dresses."

"Oh, Rupert! I don't need more dresses."

"Art lessons, then. You love those. Piano lessons… What do you want?" Mary prised his hands away and stepped back, losing a bangle in the process. It rattled on the floorboards. He looked across at her. "Please, Mary."

"I'll come back," she said, glancing down at the remains of the dinner on the table. But they both knew she was lying. Once she had tasted her freedom she would be gone for good.

He stood there for a while, breathing deeply and trying to master himself.

"I know what you think of me," he murmured. "You think I want your gratitude and we both know what that means, but I don't. Not necessarily. You're so beautiful, Mary. I just want to make you happy."

"This is how," she said with a catch in her voice.

His shoulders slumped. She felt more tenderness for him then than she ever had. She wanted to rush over to him and comfort him but that would only make it worse.

"I'm sorry," she whispered.

He shook his head. "Don't be." Summoning what dignity he still had, he called for his coat and hat, and walked out without trying to kiss her goodbye, or even to right the fallen chair.

Mary stayed where she was, listening to the sound of his feet on the stairs and his carriage pulling away into the street. To her surprise she was shaking so hard that Mrs Howard had to wrap a cashmere shawl round her and lead her to an armchair to sit down. She could only watch as the housekeeper quietly cleared the table and cleaned up the melted wax.

She wished Rupert had stuck with his sudden, imperious rage. It would have made it easier than the pitiful sadness of letting her go.

She was certain she had never loved him and never could. She wasn't even sure that he loved her, exactly. He loved the look of her, and wanted to please her, but can you really love someone just because you think they're beautiful? She didn't think so but it didn't make her guilt any easier to bear. He had saved her from the streets, and she had repaid him like this. She hadn't even managed to tell him how soon she was leaving.

There must be flint in my soul, she thought. But a mind knew what it knew. A body felt what it felt. She had loved Felix. And what she felt for Rupert was not enough. However guilty she might feel, she would be gone by morning.

The coach to Dover was due to pick her up at dawn. Mary packed by gaslight, after Mrs Howard had gone home for the night, and agonized over what to take with her. It felt like stealing to take any of her new possessions acquired through Mr Thornton senior's funds.

In the end the trunk was very light. First in was Little Miss Mouse. After that, she packed only the dresses she had made herself, her toiletries, the anthology of poetry that Felix had given her, her sewing box and the watercolours Rupert had bought her for her art lessons. She hoped he wouldn't mind her bringing those. She left behind all the jewels and trinkets he'd given her, which she wouldn't miss, and her dancing shoes, which she would.

Before she left, she sat at the desk and wrote him a letter in the looped handwriting she'd learned in the village school. She thanked him excessively for everything he'd done for her, and finished as kindly as she could.

I thank you too, dear friend, for all you did not do. For your reserve and respect, which was more than I deserved and which I treasure.

Forgive me for what I must do. My coach leaves soon.

Your affectionate

Persephone

She spent a full minute considering the signature.

Rupert usually called her by her real name, but she felt that she was changing in a new and irrevocable way. Mary Adams had been a country girl from Kent with no education and no future. Persephone Lavelle was a mysterious, risk-taking adventuress. It was the name written on the passport Mr Ballard had acquired for her in Italy. Goodness knows what information he had given to get it, but there it was.

I am Persephone Lavelle. I am no one's plaything. I go where I please.

Next to the envelope, she left Rupert a sketch of herself that Millais had given her, with her long copper mane swirling sumptuously around the page like liquid fire. It was her hair that Rupert had noticed first. She hoped he would be pleased that Millais had done full justice to it.

The coach came at first light. Persephone left London shrouded in early morning fog, unable to see the streets beyond the carriage window or hear anything except the muffled clop of horses' hooves. But as she sped down country lanes towards the coast, the sun came out to create a glistening blanket of light on frosty fields.

Persephone cast her past off like a cloak, and let it disappear down the road behind her.

Chapter Four

The journey across the Continent, which Persephone had looked forward to with such high hopes, was thoroughly miserable. It drizzled in France for three days solid, and teemed down even more bleakly, if such a thing were possible, in Switzerland. The interior of each new diligence smelled of wet wool intermingled with cough elixirs. Though the passengers changed on each leg of the journey they all shared the same rheumy-eyed, glum expression and the same cold. The food in the wayside inns was awful. Persephone didn't know what half of it was, and couldn't eat it.

By the fifth evening all she could face consuming was red wine, and the next day on the road was by far the worst. Her head promised to explode at every pothole in the road and now they were in Italy, and Italy was made of potholes. She had thought she would spend the journey either consumed with guilt for leaving Rupert or mad with joy at the idea of seeing Kitty again. Instead, she was simply hungry, cold and unwell.

Finally they reached Milan, and from here Kitty had arranged that the last leg of the journey would be by train. It was not much faster, and the damp was merely replaced with steam and soot, which hung heavy in the acrid air. But each hour brought Venice closer.

At first Persephone sat in the middle of a bench seat, squashed between a priest and a nun. The priest tried and failed to engage her in conversation in Italian. Then he stood up and bowed, pointing to the spot he had just vacated. "*Prego, prego,*" he insisted.

She didn't know what the words meant, but realized that he was offering her the window seat with its view of the Italian countryside. She smiled her thanks as she took it. He blushed and smiled back, like a schoolboy. Could priests really blush in this country? Truly, she was in a foreign land.

Looking out of the window, she began to notice properly how different the landscape had become. Hills had a softer shape and fields grew different crops to those in Kent, marking them with unexpected shades of brown and green. Inside, the language spoken by her fellow passengers sounded like bright, fast music, trilled expertly and energetically by adults and children alike.

Persephone pulled her shawl about her for warmth and eventually she slept, sitting upright in her seat. She woke to the sound of the people about her trilling at each other even more vigorously than usual. They were looking out of the windows, where there was ... nothing!

Persephone pressed her face to the glass and looked out more closely. The 'nothing' was water, far below, choppy and grey. They must be travelling along a narrow causeway over the lagoon. Their destination was out there ahead of them, through the mist.

La Serenissima.

She didn't know what to expect, but as the train finally ground to a stop Persephone found herself in a busy railway station full of smoke and grime. She jostled her way through the disembarking passengers, her trunk clutched tightly in her hand, and fought off the attempts of various porters to take it from her. All around her was noise – mostly words she did not understand. For a few moments, she felt afraid.

And then, among the throng of people waiting to

greet the new arrivals, a small, moustachioed man rushed toward her.

"*Signorina Lavelle?*"

She nodded.

"Ah! I thought it be you. *Benvenuta!* Welcome. I take you. My name is Nico. Come." He took the trunk and led Persephone outside.

"Oh!" She stopped in her tracks. Suddenly, her world was transformed.

Nico looked back anxiously. "*Signorina? Problema?*"

But there wasn't a problem at all. She was simply blinded by the light that bounced off the water ahead of her. The mist was lifting and a whole new world was emerging through it.

They approached some steps that led down to a wide canal, as busy as Piccadilly, where boats of all shapes and sizes crowded together to ply their trade. Boats! Persephone knew, of course, that Venice was built on water, so it would not have roads in the normal way. But still, the reality of travelling everywhere by foot or boat was astonishing.

Venice had long been a shimmering fable in Persephone's head. She knew it slightly from oil paintings she had seen on the walls of various collectors' houses. But the rich colours and strangely shaped buildings of those pictures had not seemed real or possible. And yet it was all true.

The city ahead of her was different from everything she had ever known. Effie had told her about the sleek black-lacquered gondolas that worked the water like hackney carriages but she didn't say how beautiful they were. Even simple rowing boats, piled high with jewel-coloured fruit and vegetables, were joyful. The air smelled of brine and rang with shouts from boat pilots on the water and vendors on the shore. Not understanding a word made it all the more exciting.

"We go?" Nico asked. He indicated a large bright red rowing boat tied up among a group of peeling poles.

Persephone took in one more breath of strange sea air. "We go," she sighed happily.

The journey down the Grand Canal, past ancient buildings that looked like a child's drawing of exotic palaces, was so crammed with beauty that she could hardly believe it was real.

Nico rowed, clearly at home on the oars. He guided the boat strongly and smoothly through the choppy water, adroitly avoiding the steam boats, gondolas and cargo vessels that ploughed up and down all around them, changing direction without warning, just like carriages on a busy road.

Meanwhile, he proudly described every building they passed in an accent so thick she only understood the words ''ouse' and ''istory'. But she didn't care. Nico's love of his city was obvious in every exaggerated syllable. In a strange way, she felt as if she were coming home, to a place she had always dreamed of.

As they navigated under a large stone bridge with shops built along its edges, she turned to Nico.

"What is that?"

"The Rialto, *signorina*."

She knew the name from *The Merchant of Venice*. A bridge from Shakespeare! And they were rowing underneath it! Soon after, as they finished rounding a bend, Nico pointed out a building slightly taller than the rest further down on the left-hand bank. "*Ecco*." He smiled. "Here we are, *signorina*. Palazzo Colleoni."

Persephone drank it in. The palazzo had a long river

frontage, three storeys high, with tall, arched openings on the lower floor and Gothic-shaped windows above them framed by delicate white-stone tracery. On the first floor, an ornamental stone balcony added grandeur. On the second, a smaller wrought-iron one gave hints of romantic views. The façade was several shades of pink, faded with time. The windows were unevenly spaced, as if the architect kept changing his mind about where to put them. She instantly fell in love.

Nico must have seen the look on her face. He grinned. "*Bella*, no?"

Persephone nodded. She knew only two words in Italian: *Serenissima* and *bella*. Beautiful. Yes, it was.

❧❧

Nico pulled up to a little pontoon in front of a great arched doorway and skilfully tied up the boat. He helped her out and guided her through the gloomy entrance and up the stairs to the grand first floor. There stood Kitty, eagerly waiting for her in a dress of oyster silk that seemed to emanate light.

"Persephone! You're here! I can't believe it. Thank you, thank you!" she cried, rushing forwards.

"I should be thanking *you*," Persephone said, throwing her arms round her friend. "You saved me!"

"Don't be silly. You've saved *me*. Mama is out visiting and Papa is shut up in his study, so we're alone. Let me show you the palazzo. It's very old – falling apart in places, you'll see. But the position is good. Come on."

Kitty grabbed Persephone by the hand. Persephone flashed a smile at the local girl in a maid's black skirt and white apron who had been standing dutifully at Kitty's shoulder. By 'alone' Kitty meant 'alone apart from the many servants who make the house run smoothly', she assumed. Having been one of them herself, she did not find maids as invisible as her friend seemed to do.

But Kitty was already off, pulling Persephone behind her. Gold rooms, silver rooms, red rooms... So many that Persephone could not take them all in. She saw sumptuous silk and velvet, frescoes on the walls, paintings on the ceilings, and flashing views of nearby buildings undulating through uneven glass.

"Is it all like this?" she asked, breathless after a rapid tour of the first floor.

"Some of it's worse." Kitty sighed. "Mama says it would take a year to fix it up properly. Some of the furnishings are held together by a thread and a prayer. And the damp! It's worst in winter, of course. We have the fires lit all day long. Let me take you up these stairs. My bedroom is here, and Mama and Papa are down there. Your room is along this corridor. It was supposed to be Aunt Violet's but thank the Lord she took one look and decided to go back to London. Mama tells me I'm ungrateful and I am. I love Aunt Violet dearly but the thought of her sitting at my elbow every waking moment... Here we are."

She flung open a carved wooden door and Persephone found herself in a symphony of green and gold. The bedroom overlooked a side canal and another ancient patchwork building just beyond. The walls were lined with damp-stained jade-green silk. The bed had an ornate gilded wooden headboard, painted with images of little cherubs under billowing clouds. A gold-silk coverlet, frayed at the edges, trailed on the floor. The wardrobe and the chair were painted to match the walls, and shaped in sinuous curves.

"This is mine? Really?" Persephone marvelled.

"There is a bigger one along the corridor," Kitty said dubiously, "but its damp patches are bigger too." She bit her lip. "Will it do? After you've come all this way?"

Persephone didn't know how to express her feelings, beyond hugging Kitty again. "It's perfect in every way. Even the damp patch."

Kitty giggled. "You are silly. How I've missed you."

"Not as much as I've missed you. Now, tell me all about the man who has brought us here."

Sitting on the golden bedcover, Kitty cheerfully made a list of her suitor's qualities. Lord Malmesbury was the only son of the Duke of Bristol, he had several sisters, both older and younger, he was 'very attractive', he had 'nice eyes', he was 'very kind to Mama' and wore 'the most exquisite uniforms to balls'. It was not entirely satisfactory. Persephone felt she learned more about his diplomatic dress than she did about the man. Unfortunately she would have to wait a few days to meet him in person as he had just gone away on business – some errand on behalf of the Prime Minister.

"But don't worry, we have so much to do while we wait," Kitty assured her. "Venice is full of art and history, and Mama and I have only seen half of it."

❧ ❦ ❧

The thought of 'Mama' made Persephone nervous. She had tried to put off thinking about Mr and Mrs Ballard ever since Kitty's letter had first arrived. They had been away when she had visited their house in Mayfair with Kitty. True, they did not seem to mind their daughter spending time with her in London, but that had been before Rupert took her in. What on earth would they make of such a scandalous creature?

She did not have long to wait. That evening, dressed in all their finery for dinner, they welcomed her like a long-lost child.

"Kitty has been so excited! She would not stop talking about you!" Mrs Ballard said, clasping Persephone by the hands.

Catherine Ballard was as pretty and golden-haired as her daughter but covered in more flesh, like Kitty wrapped in a quilted coat. Her greatest desire was simply to see everyone in the family happy, it seemed. Her husband was harder to gauge. He was short and grey-haired, with a gruff face sticking out above a high stiff collar, but his eyes twinkled when he smiled. He did not speak much, but did not need to; his wife spoke easily enough for both of them.

Persephone's reputation as a muse did not seem to repel them. If anything, they were bedazzled by it. And no mention was made of Rupert, or how she had lived these past few months. They had been out of town, away from the worst of the gossip, she remembered. She was certainly not going to enlighten them.

"Tonight you must go up early," Mrs Ballard said. "I'm sure you are tired after your journey. Aren't trains dusty? I cannot bear it. I notice you didn't have much luggage. How sensible! We can get you whatever you need here, and of course you can borrow anything of mine – or Kitty's. Can't she, Kitcat? I have a spare fur cape you might find useful in this weather, with a matching hat. And tomorrow we thought you might like a little tour around the Rialto. Nico can take you and Kitty together. He's so good at explaining, when you can understand him. I'm afraid we only brought two servants from London; my maid and Frederick's valet. The rest are looking after Balfour House. But you can usually make yourself understood to the Italians if you speak slowly and clearly."

Over the meal, conversation turned to Kitty's brother, who was definitely still in England, much to Persephone's relief. She still could not forgive Roly Ballard for the way he had treated her cousin Harriet. Without him, life with the Ballards would be infinitely easier.

After a lavish dessert of syllabub, candied fruit and cake was served, Frederick Ballard excused himself from the table. He managed his many property interests in London through a series of messengers, and one of them was waiting for him downstairs. As talk between Kitty and her mother drifted to various new acquaintances, Persephone felt her concentration begin to lapse.

"Dear Persephone!" Kitty teased. "If your head hangs any lower it will be resting on the cherries. Come – let me take you upstairs. Will you excuse us, Mama?"

Soon Persephone was lying in her nightdress, in her green-gold room, listening to the sound of gently lapping water in the canal. At her head, cherubs gazed up at painted clouds. *Surely this must be heaven?* she thought. A minute later, she was asleep.

Chapter Five

For the next two days, Persephone's head was a whirl. Accompanied by Nico and armed with a small red leather-bound guidebook, Kitty took her to a dozen churches and nearby houses, pointed at a hundred paintings and sculptures, called out the names of a thousand points of interest and generally bewildered Persephone with every step.

Everything was gorgeous, but there was almost too much to take in. Venice was a labyrinth of alleyways, half of them made of water. She never knew exactly where she was. She loved the sense of constant surprise, but wondered if she would ever make sense of it.

In the afternoons, joined by Catherine Ballard, they visited ladies of note. The hostess on the second day was a rich American lady, Mrs Stewart, whose house overlooked a square on the other side of the

Grand Canal. In her sunny upstairs salon filled with treasures, the conversation flowed among little groups from English to French and Italian, with occasional exclamations in German. Some cosmopolitan women seemed to speak every language, while others, including Kitty and her mother, stuck to English and joined in when they could.

Persephone might have followed the topics better but she was still recovering from the shocking beauty of everything she had seen in the morning. And she needed her wits about her for those moments when the conversation turned to her.

"Ah! *Dear* Miss Lavelle… So you know Rossetti?"

"A little. That is—"

"I was friends with his father. A great Italian scholar. Do give him my fondest wishes when next you see him. So he painted you as Persephone? The goddess, I mean."

"No. Felix Dawson did."

"It must be *heavenly* to pose for John Millais. I can't *imagine* it. You lucky creature! Does he paint you very often?"

"Only sketches. I—"

"It was you, I gather, who posed for his famous painting of *Ophelia*."

"No. That was Lizzie Siddal."

"Oh yes. Ah. Lizzie. Are you not her? I'm confused!"

The ladies were indeed confused and so was Persephone. After two hours in their company she began to feel she knew less about the Pre-Raphaelites than she did before.

As she sipped her lemon cordial and struggled to concentrate, she overheard her hostess and another lady talking about Titian. At last! Here was something she could hold on to. In her early days in Pimlico, working for Professor Aitken, Titian was the artist who had opened her eyes to the glory of art. She vividly remembered the moment when she had first seen a reproduction of one of his paintings. She had been enraptured by the crimson and gold of the picture, the pearls in the model's hair, the velvet cloak that pooled at her waist...

She turned to the ladies, smiling. Mrs Stewart noticed and asked, "Are you a follower, my dear?"

"Of Titian? Oh yes! He's my favourite artist."

"He is buried just round the corner from here, you know, in the Frari. You should see his monument. And his *Assunta*. It's behind the altar. Huge. Magnificent."

"As-sunta?" Persephone asked, pronouncing the word carefully.

"Yes. *The Assumption of the Virgin*. Many say it's his masterpiece."

"Thank you. I will."

In an instant, she recovered much of her lost energy. A Titian masterpiece? Round the corner? Why had Kitty not told her? Titian's art was one of the many reasons she had wanted to come to Venice. She sought out her friend in a far corner of the salon, where she was chatting to two elderly women in tiers of papery silk and lace. She did not want to interrupt but Kitty saw the excited look on her face.

"What is it? Something marvellous has happened, I can tell."

Persephone explained about the painting, and Titian's monument, and her need to see them. Kitty's face fell. "Oh. But I saw them last week with Mama. We'd have waited if we'd known. They're very nice. But I must say God looked rather like a vulture in the painting." One sighting of a Titian with a vulture-God was clearly enough for Kitty.

"Don't worry," Persephone reassured her. "You don't need to come with me!"

"If you're sure…"

Kitty sensed Persephone's urgency and took pleasure in arranging for her to go that very moment. At Kitty's insistence, their hostess arranged for a maid to accompany her to the church of Santa Maria Gloriosa dei Frari, which was less than a five-minute walk away.

As soon as she got outside, Persephone felt better. To be in the fresh air and not be in a rush… To be able to appreciate the colourful canal-sides and squares without dashing past them… She felt slightly disloyal to Kitty for not missing her company just this once, but actually it was more enjoyable to see the city without the tyranny of the little red guidebook.

The outside of the Frari was massive and imposing. In England, one might almost have assumed its red-brick walls would house a factory or a workhouse, but once through the open door she found herself inside an enormous, vaulted, church-like space. The maidservant beside her said something in Italian. Persephone caught the words 'a casa'. She nodded vaguely, but to her surprise, the woman bobbed a curtsey and quickly left her.

"Hey!" There had been some kind of mistake. Persephone hadn't looked precisely where she was going, assuming the maid would take her back, but the woman obviously didn't intend to wait. Persephone hesitated for a second. Should she follow? But if she did, she might never see Titian's painting and his monument. And surely she could easily find her way back again?

Shrugging off her worries, she ventured down the pink and white chequered marble floor. This whole church was pink and white, and full of light. Much of it came from a vast Gothic window at the far end, behind the altar. Persephone found herself drawn to it, hurrying along past worshippers and tourists, eager to appreciate it from close to.

As she approached, her attention was drawn instead to the painting in front of the window. It was enormous, set into an elaborate arched stone frame, and lit by the many glass panes on either side. She stopped and stared. At the bottom of the picture, a group of larger-than-life-sized men looked up towards the heavens. One of the men had his back to the church, but Persephone was drawn to him by the aching gesture of his reaching arms, and through him her eye was carried upwards to two winged cherubs who seemed to be holding up the clouds above. And then she realized what she should have known from the start: *this* was Titian's masterpiece. *The Assumption of the Virgin*. Of course.

Above the cherubs a woman stood with her feet on the clouds, holding out her arms in worship. Persephone always thought of the Virgin as a simple girl in blue and white, as she appeared in the pictures and statues she knew at home. But this Virgin was Italian. She wore a stunning rose-pink robe with a dark contrasting veil and cloak – not simple at all, but richly dressed and glamorous. Above and around her, the sky was gold.

This was Titian. These were his gorgeous colours. She knew them so well, but before they had been in the pages of books. Here the colours looked as fresh as if the master had painted them yesterday. Persephone felt herself getting lost in them: bright vermillion, malachite green and lapis blue.

And Kitty was right! God, floating above the Virgin and the golden heavens, did look a little like a bird of prey. It was the clever way He had been portrayed – horizontally, with His head closest to the viewer and His dark cloak billowing out behind. They called it foreshortening. Persephone was learning how to do it and it was remarkably difficult. Titian made it thrilling.

Her eye travelled around the painting from top to bottom, and up again. Good art always did that, she found. Your eye could not rest, because there was always something new to see and understand. And those colours!

They reminded her of Felix's work. He painted with bolder colours than anyone she knew. If he were here, how he would adore this picture. She could imagine the two of them standing together, soaking it in for hours. And as she thought of Felix, and glanced away to try to suppress the memory, she noticed that the sunlight filtering through the Gothic window had changed and dimmed. Was it getting late? Had much time passed?

Looking at her pocket watch, she realized that more than forty minutes had gone by. How was such a thing possible? Panic began to set in. Would Kitty and her mother still be at the American lady's salon? What was the woman's name again? And her address? She remembered nothing!

With one last snatched look at the painting, Persephone ran out of the church. She had not even seen Titian's monument. She would have to come back another day. On she ran, past the tall brick wall. Over this canal bridge, then down this alleyway and she would be there. Or was it that alleyway? Both options now suddenly looked the same. She tried first one and then the other. Both seemed wrong.

She could not ask directions because she could not think of the name of the house she had been visiting. Only that its square was called a *campo*. But when she bravely stopped a passer-by and said, *"Campo?"* they pointed in what she was certain was the wrong direction. Several minutes went by and she did not believe it was possible to get so thoroughly lost. She could still see the Frari roof above the houses. But lost she was. And getting more lost by the minute.

A new idea came. *I shall just go back to the Palazzo Colleoni. It's not too far from the Rialto. If I can get to that bridge, I think I might know where I am.*

She asked three more people for directions. They all seemed to understand 'Rialto' but all of them pointed in opposite ways and said the same thing. It sounded like *'Sempayd ritter'* but she had no idea what it could mean. Perfectly panicked now, she sought someone who could speak English. In the end, an orange seller, working out of his boat on a small canal, gave her slow and careful directions. "Ten *minuti*," he said encouragingly and pointed down the canal.

Persephone nodded gratefully and set off. She needed to follow this canal, turn right over the next bridge but two, then turn left at the next one. Apparently she would see the Rialto from there. The light was fading fast. The air was colder and she regretted not borrowing Mrs Ballard's cape. Pulling her shawl around her she hurried on, counting bridges.

But as she reached the one she needed to cross, she found her way blocked by a crowd. It was full of young men shouting and laughing. Peering past them, she saw that in the middle of the bridge two men were fighting. They were stripped to their shirtsleeves and punching and wrestling each other with no mercy. Then one threw the other into the dark water. There was a shout and a huge splash, and the crowd roared. Money changed hands – had there been a bet? – and the young men began to go on their way.

Just as Persephone thought it was safe to carry on, one of them noticed her.

"*Ciao, bella!*"

She pretended not to hear him.

"*Ey! Signorina! Bella! Come stai?*"

He would not leave her alone. Others heard him shout and spotted her too, and quickly a crowd started to form around her. They were still excited from the fight. She was so close to the canal that if they came much closer they might push her in it as well.

"*Scusi! Signorina!*" A shout came from behind her.

Turning round, she saw a gondola slowly approaching. It was one of the smarter ones, new and shiny, with a raised cabin covered in black-wool felt. The gondolier stood at the stern, but another man stood in front of the cabin. He wore a small red and green chequered mask and a top hat, and seemed dressed for a ball.

"*Che succede?*" he asked, getting closer.

"I'm sorry!" Persephone called back, close to tears with fear and frustration. "I don't understand."

The gondola slowed to a stop and the man gracefully leaped out of it on to the path beside her. "English?" he asked.

She nodded.

"Please." He indicated his boat, as if she should climb

into it. But she dare not. Go off with a stranger? Never.

The crowd of men was drawing closer. She was terrified now, but the masked man didn't seem remotely afraid. He stood next to her, brandishing his ebony cane at them and shouting a string of what sounded like choice Italian insults. A few men shouted back, but nevertheless they retreated. He yelled some more, hardly pausing for breath. They hesitated but now they looked angry, as if any one of them might rush forwards at any minute.

He sensed it too. "Quick!" he said. "Into the gondola."

It was her only hope. He leaped back into it and held out his hand for her to join him. It took quite a jump, but with his help she made it safely. The gondolier kicked off from the wall with his foot and the boat lurched forwards.

As it did so, the masked man grabbed Persephone by the waist and pulled her down sharply beside him.

"Hey!"

She was too shocked at first to think, but as the gondola sailed under the bridge, almost brushing its underside with the roof of its cabin, she realized he had merely been saving her again. Had she stayed standing, she would surely have been knocked out of the boat. As they emerged on the other side, she sat up, giggling with relief. "Thank you."

He smiled at her. "I'm sorry for that. Please – come inside. It's more comfortable there. Where can I take you?"

Though grateful, Persephone was deliberately vague. Best for this stranger not to know exactly where she lived. "Near the Rialto," she said, projecting more confidence than she felt. "I can find my way from there."

He called back in a long, complicated sentence to the gondolier and ushered her into the curtained-off cabin. "I'm Arturo Fioravante Iuliano, by the way. May I ask your name?"

But she hardly heard him. She was too absorbed by her new surroundings to answer.

This was Venice as she'd never seen it before. From outside, the narrow cabin looked makeshift and plain, but inside was another matter. Though small, it was richly carpeted, with red-velvet cushioned seats and windows with louvered blinds that cut out most of the light. Instead, a little hanging lantern gave a gentle glow. The closed-in dimness was luxurious and calm.

Through the slats in the blinds, Persephone could just see the boats and houses gliding by outside. For the first time since she arrived, she truly felt she could sit back and relax.

"Thank you," she said again.

"It's my pleasure."

He sat down beside her, and she noticed his long legs in tailored trousers and expensive, handmade boots. Turning to look at him more closely, she guessed he was quite young from the firm look of his jaw and the full softness of his upper lip. But it was hard to tell precisely, because his silk hat and the chequered mask he was wearing covered his cheeks, nose and brow.

He saw her staring and his mouth twitched. "Excuse this." He touched the mask lightly. "Tonight I am Harlequin." He noticed the puzzled look on her face. "He's a character they like to play here. A comic servant. It's for a little soirée I'm going to."

"You speak remarkably good English for an Italian," she observed.

He grinned at her. His eyes sparkled behind the mask. "Thank you. But let me ask: what on earth was a beautiful young woman doing out on her own in Venice at dusk? Did you *want* to encounter half the youth of the city?"

She flushed. "Not at all. I just wanted to see a painting."

"Oh?" He looked surprised. "Which one?"

"The *Assunta*." She pronounced it carefully, in Italian, in honour of his country. "By Titian."

He laughed. "I know the one. What did you think of it?"

She drew in a breath. It was almost like a gasp. Just thinking back to the painting gave her pleasure – especially here in this warm dark floating cabin, a world away from ordinary life. "I could hardly take it in. The colours... The rose-pink of her dress... The way she seemed to glow against that golden sky..."

He gazed at her keenly. "You're fond of Titian?"

"Oh *yes*! Though I hardly knew him until today. Not like this. Mostly from books. But he was the first Old Master I truly fell in love with." She stopped and held her breath. What a ridiculous thing to say to a stranger! And how wrong it felt to talk of love in this boat, alone with him.

As she berated herself, a flurry of emotions seemed to

flash behind his eyes. Puzzlement, curiosity, and then finally, certainty.

"Aha! I know who you are. You're Persephone Lavelle. That hair... I should have guessed. You know your art, and your artists. You're the girl who sat for Felix Dawson, whom I must say I admire very much. The loss of *Persephone and Hades* was a tragedy. You arrived three days ago, I think."

She felt breathless. "How can you possibly know that?"

His smile was slow and lazy, like a cat unfurling. "It is my job to know everything of interest that happens in Venice. And now I know where to take you." He raised the louvered blinds and called out to the gondolier again in fast-flowing Italian. Persephone made out the words '*lento*' repeated, and 'Colleoni'.

"You're magic!"

"Not magic, *signorina*. Merely well informed. As I say, it's my job to know." His eyes were fascinating. She couldn't tell their exact colour in the darkness, but they seemed to dance with the promise of enjoyment. "You're surprising too. Tell me more about Titian."

He leaned on one elbow against the velvet cushions and gazed at her. As the gondola travelled smoothly on,

Persephone found herself telling him things she thought she would never tell anyone. Perhaps it was the dark snug cabin interior, or the way he had rescued her from harm. Perhaps it was just the calm she sensed behind his mask, but she felt as if she had found a kindred spirit, and someone who could keep her secrets.

And so she found herself admitting how she was working as a maid when she discovered the *Venus with a Mirror* in one of her master's books. How the painting was a revelation, with its gorgeous use of red and gold, and lustrous skin. It was the moment she had first seen Rupert too – but she didn't mention that. She preferred to think about the picture.

Venus was a goddess Persephone held in particular affection. She had read about her in some classical stories the professor had let her borrow. Venus's origins were vague and uncertain – like Persephone's own. She seemed to have been born of the sea. She was the goddess of love and beauty, among other things, and with Mars as her lover she was the mother of Cupid, who held up the mirror for her in Titian's painting.

Titian had depicted her half-undressed, sitting in the folds of her fallen cloak, in all her bare-fleshed loveliness. Persephone swallowed and looked away as she remembered how long she'd gazed at the Venus's neck and naked breast. When she looked up, she tried to wipe the memory from her mind and the glorious shock of it from her face. But the Harlequin's eyes danced brighter.

"Ah yes, the *Venus*," he said. "You must go to Florence and see his *Venus of Urbino*. It's very special."

Persephone nodded and felt a flush bloom on her neck. She had seen an illustration of that painting in Felix's studio. It put the *Venus with a Mirror* in the shade. The young goddess in the *Urbino* painting was naked completely. She lay on a bed, starkly pale against the dark background of her chamber, looking knowingly at the viewer as if to challenge him to stare back at her. She was a vision no stranger should see, and yet so achingly lovely...

The Harlequin's face suggested he was picturing it too, and the gondola was quiet for a moment. But when he spoke at last, it was to change the subject. "So you were a maid, you say?"

"I was," she admitted, grateful to talk about something else. "A drudge, in the scullery."

"You washed the dishes?"

"I cleaned everything that didn't breathe."

He laughed and gesticulated with Italian gusto. "And now you are a traveller. A connoisseur."

Was he teasing her? She sensed laughter in his voice, but the way he looked at her was openly admiring. The bloom on her neck crept higher. "What's a conny-sewer?"

"A *connoisseur*. A man who appreciates the finer things in life. Or woman, in your case. I suppose that might make you a *connoisseuse*. Anyway, you know what's good. Few English people really do, despite what they say. The last Englishman who truly felt Venice's bones was Ruskin."

"Oh!" Persephone smiled.

"Do you know him?"

"No, but I know Effie, who came here as his wife. She told me how he would just stop and not talk to her for half an hour, admiring the carving on a window."

The Harlequin smiled again. "Of course you know her! Persephone Lavelle knows everyone who matters. And understands the mystique of a Venetian window."

His repetition of her name reminded her that she

couldn't remember his – only that it was complicated and Italian. She was about to ask him to repeat it when she felt the gondola shudder, slow and turn. The Harlequin popped his head outside the curtains, then back in again. "We've arrived. Too soon. You are the most fascinating creature, Signorina Lavelle. We must continue this conversation."

It sounded like a promise. For now, he held out his hand. She was grateful for his strong grip as he helped her out of the cabin and on to the bobbing pontoon. She recognized the arching row of windows ahead of them and saw, regretfully, that she was home.

Once they were both standing in the misty half-light he bowed low. "Your current address, I believe."

"Yes." She shivered.

"It's cold. I'll call for a servant to let you in."

She thought suddenly that she might never see him again. "How do I find you? To thank you."

He grinned – that slow, lazy smile. "I'll find you, don't worry."

Stretching out an arm, he pulled the bell at the water entrance. But before the ringing had finished echoing inside the palazzo, he had run to the gondola, leaped aboard and disappeared inside the black-felt cabin. Persephone didn't have time to say a word. At his command the gondolier moved swiftly off into the flow of traffic on the Grand Canal.

She watched the boat disappear behind a barge and was still watching as the door at last opened behind her, casting a warm shaft of yellow light across the pontoon.

Chapter Six

"Oh Lord!" Kitty exclaimed, rushing down the stairs behind Nico, who stood at the open door. "Never do that to me again! We thought you were dead!"

"I'm so sorry! I got lost in Titian's painting. Then *really* lost outside the Frari."

"That was hours ago! And miles away. How did you get home?"

"I had the most wonderful adventure," Persephone said, unable to suppress the laughter in her voice as she took off her shawl and handed it to the waiting Nico.

"Well, at least you're safe. Nico, get someone to let Mama know. She was about to send out a search party. She already sent a servant back to the Frari, but you'd gone."

Kitty led Persephone upstairs to the salon on the first-floor *piano nobile*, whose multiple windows overlooked the Grand Canal. Above them was a ceiling painted with blue skies and soft clouds. The walls were gilt and mirrors.

Kitty loved nothing better than adventures. "I don't know how you do it," she said half-smiling, half-pouting. "You could pop out to buy a match and exciting things would happen to you."

"Not like today," Persephone assured her. They sat on shabby silk settees in front of a low table where cakes flavoured with almond and orange had been set out for tea. Kitty had saved a few for her friend, should she make it back alive. Outside, lights flickered on the water through the gathering darkness.

Knowing how much Kitty would enjoy the tale, Persephone emphasized every exquisite detail: the danger of her situation, the sudden arrival of her saviour, the beauty of the Harlequin's face below his mask, his bravery, the luxury of his gondola, his amazing intuition as to who she was.

"I don't believe it! You're making it up to please me!"

"Every word is true, I swear it."

"But who can he be? We must find out." Kitty had a determined look in her eye. "There can't be *that* many rich young spies in Venice. He must be a spy, don't you think? He seemed to imply it. And not many Italians can speak English quite so well. I'll ask Arthur. We'll find him. Then we can all go about together."

For a moment Persephone pictured herself and Kitty side by side, two girls in silk dresses with their glamorous *beaux*, strolling through a smart Venetian square. It was a lovely image, but impossible. As Persephone Lavelle she could be Kitty's unconventional companion, yes, but surely never her equal?

There had been something magical and otherworldly about the gondola, as if its canopy enclosed a private theatre where she could live out a fantasy. He had felt it too, the Harlequin. It was as if they had briefly shared a dream. Something deep inside her told her that she would not see him again, or if she did, he would be quite different in daylight, on the land.

❧☙ ❧☙

The next day dawned bright and clear. It was as if the City of Water had never known mist or fog. The sky was a blue so intense Persephone wondered if she had ever seen it such a colour above the fields of Kent.

It certainly was never like this in London.

The sunlight seemed to bounce off the water and into the breakfast room. Through the mottled windows, the sky threw the eccentric shapes of the buildings opposite into sharp relief. Red-tiled roofs were topped with fantastical chimney pots. Their outline was punctuated by spires and domes and gleaming bell towers. Everything shone today.

Kitty, when she eventually appeared at the table, was in a mood that, even for her, was exceptionally sunny.

"He's back! Mama has had a note from Arthur. He returned from Rome last night and begs to visit us this afternoon. You will be here, won't you?"

"To see Lord Malmesbury? Of course."

"Oh, Persephone, I'm so happy. I've missed him."

Kitty's eyes took on a dreamy look. Persephone reflected how lucky her friend was that the man her parents had chosen for her was someone she could so quickly love. A few months ago Arthur Malmesbury had been merely a distant childhood memory for Kitty. Now her face lit up at the thought of him.

Persephone grinned. "I've missed him too, and I haven't met him yet!"

"You'll love him, and he'll love you. One can quite see why he's a diplomat. He's so debonair. All the ladies are fond of him."

The morning was spent in another flurry of sightseeing, but Kitty's mind was elsewhere, and she was a skittish mixture of nerves and smiles. After lunch, she spent an hour working out what to wear. She swept off to her room, dragging Persephone behind her.

"You must come. I need your advice."

"I can't advise you!" Persephone laughed. "Nothing could make you look lovelier than you already do."

"My feelings exactly," Mrs Ballard called out after them. "You put it so well, Persephone."

But Kitty wouldn't be persuaded. She tried on almost every day dress she possessed, while her maid helped her with the corsetry and sleeves, and Persephone positioned the long glass. The pink silk was 'too showy', the lilac 'too dull', the forest-green 'too narrow'. In the end, Kitty settled on a bodice and skirt of pale blue satin stripes over a crinoline of such extraordinary magnitude it would hardly fit through the doorway. A row of pearl buttons from neck to waist drew attention to her sculpted chest. With the addition of a French lace collar, suggested by Persephone, she found it acceptable.

"I'm not sure how many are coming today," she remarked, picking up an aquamarine earring and checking in her dressing-table mirror for its effect. "Between ten and twenty, I should think."

"So many? I thought it would just be Lord Malmesbury."

"Oh no. Not if we're receiving. Dear me, I thought London was busy for visiting but Venice is another world entirely. You saw it at Mrs Stewart's yesterday. And everyone's so grand. I feel quite ordinary in their company. So does Mama."

"Well, soon you'll be a duchess!"

"Not for a while." Kitty sat at her dressing table to apply her earring. "First I shall be a viscountess. Arthur is Viscount Malmesbury until his father dies, and I shall be Lady Arthur."

Persephone frowned. "Not Lady Kitty?"

"No. That would be for our daughters, or Arthur's sisters. As his wife, I take his name."

"It sounds very complicated." *And bizarre*, Persephone thought.

"Perhaps." Kitty smiled, fixing the other earring into

place. "But it all makes sense when you're used to it."

"How many sisters are there?" Persephone had meant to ask this earlier.

"Six." Kitty counted them off on her fingers. "Lady Elizabeth, Lady Cecily, Lady Emma, Lady Anne, Lady Caroline and Lady..." She paused to think, humming as she sought to remember. "Ah yes, Lady Carlotta. Arthur is the eldest, after Lady Elizabeth. She's very grand, he says. More like a duchess than her mother. I can't wait to meet the others... Oh, and Lady Elizabeth herself, of course."

Kitty gave a quick, reproving glance at her reflection in the mirror. It made Persephone smile that she was obviously keen not to slight the family in any way, even by accident in the privacy of her bedroom in a foreign country.

"And where will you live?" she asked. "Does he have a castle?"

Kitty missed her playful tone. "He has two. Well, his father does. One in the West Country and one in... I don't remember. Possibly Scotland. There's also an estate in Norfolk for shooting and a good house in London near the park."

Persephone assumed she meant Hyde Park. There were many parks in London but all the richest people tended to live in the vicinity of Hyde Park, where they could ride. "Will you live there?"

Kitty pouted slightly. "Yes, I imagine. Though of course it's up to Arthur. And I mustn't think too far ahead. He's discussed marriage in general terms with Papa, but hasn't *officially* asked me yet."

"He will," Persephone said, marvelling at the perfect healthy pinkness of Kitty's cheeks and arresting periwinkle-blue of her eyes. Aside from being so pretty, Kitty was sincere and affectionate – and besides, the deal was already decided with her father and that, surely, was the hardest part. "How could he not?"

Kitty came to stand beside her in front of the long glass, and they examined their combined effect. Unlike Kitty, Persephone was pale and freckled, with a challenging straight nose and deep-set green eyes. Her hair fell loose in a copper cloud around her. And she dressed like no one else outside artistic circles.

Today's gown was crimson velvet, worn with a silver belt. Persephone had created a whole wardrobe inspired by the first dress Felix designed for her. Her clothes didn't need corsets, hoops or frills, relying instead on rich fabrics and clever seams to form their flowing shape. With high necks and low waists, they were reminiscent of medieval ladies' costume, and in London they made her stand out as a bohemian curiosity. She hoped they would have the same impact in Venice.

One advantage of their simplicity was that it took Persephone a fraction of the time it took Kitty to get dressed. Another was that she did not feel the need to compete with her fashionable friend. She grinned at her now and Kitty finally agreed that she was ready.

 ❧⤜⤛⥿ ⥾⤚⤝❧

By three, the curtains in the mirrored salon were half closed to keep out the low rays of the winter sun. The room itself was full of talk and laughter, the rustle of silk, the clink of porcelain teacups and the echoing noise of river traffic from outside.

As before, the visitors were mostly female, of every age and nationality. Persephone could hardly tell one from another, but Kitty had assured her there would be Russian countesses, French baronesses, Italians of every aristocratic rank, merchants' wives from

Flanders and Sweden, rich tourists from America and a sprinkling of English visitors. There were even a few gentlemen, most of them quite old, who seemed to have nothing better to do than drink tea and compliment the ladies on their dress.

Catherine Ballard stood near the door, smiling hard and breathing fast. She loved the company of good society and yet it made her anxious. In London she had generally avoided large gatherings, to Kitty's horror, but now Kitty's future was in the balance she was ready to do whatever it took. Knowing this, Persephone went over to give her hand a reassuring squeeze. Her hostess squeezed back gratefully.

"My dear Persephone, I had no idea our little *salon* would be quite so popular. Look at them all. So kind to come. I do believe everyone in Venice is here!"

Persephone smiled at the thought of this select little group being 'everyone in Venice', just as Kitty called out to her from halfway across the room. "Persephone! Sephy! You must come!"

Sephy. A new nickname. Kitty hadn't used it before. She was thinking about how much she liked it as she made her way through the throng to Kitty's side. There, she found herself face to face with a tall, serious-looking young man in immaculate afternoon attire. Persephone quickly took in the style of his high starched collar and the confidence of his canary-yellow cravat, held in place with a diamond pin.

She smiled and curtseyed. Looking up, she thought she recognized the gentleman's soft mouth and solid jaw. *But...*

"Lord Malmesbury, may I introduce my friend Miss Lavelle?" Kitty said excitedly.

Persephone's mind went into a spin. It was as if a picture in her head had turned into a puzzle and the pieces were falling apart. Could it be possible? This was the face she had seen below the chequered mask in the gondola. She was sure of it. Yet Kitty was beaming at him with proprietorial fondness.

His eyes looked back at her with the blandest of polite curiosity. Her smile vanished.

The Harlequin was Arthur Malmesbury? If she was right, surely he must know her too? Why didn't he show it?

Instead he bowed low.

"Miss Lavelle. What an honour it is to meet you."

He straightened. "I've been looking forward to it."

The voice was the same. It was him. It was *him*. Now she could see his whole face, unimpeded by the mask, he was even more handsome than yesterday. He had gently curling hair the colour of wheat, a broad brow and sharply angled cheekbones above those sensuous lips. His complexion was elegantly delicate. His eyes – green like hers but paler – glittered.

Persephone was too shocked to respond. Images flashed across her mind of the *Venus of Urbino*, and the two of them together in the little cabin, and she thought she might faint. Luckily, before the silence grew embarrassing, Mrs Ballard came bustling along.

"My dearest Lord Malmesbury! How kind of you to come today! We've missed you! How was Rome?"

"Deadly, madam. I couldn't bear to be without you. I raced back as soon as I could."

"You're too kind." Catherine Ballard blushed. "I must tear you away from my daughter for a moment. Come and talk to the Contessa dell'Agua. She's been longing to see you again."

He gave Persephone one last, lingering look as his hostess led him away, leaving Kitty glowing with delight and Persephone trying to keep her balance.

"Isn't he perfect?" Kitty grinned.

"Yes … yes of course."

"I was never sure about him when he was a boy, but … look at him now."

"I… Yes," Persephone said vaguely, thinking of the chiselled cheeks, the glittering eyes.

"And he liked you, I can tell."

"Oh no!" Persephone flushed. "I doubt that."

"He did. Trust me. I always know when Arthur likes someone. For example, look at him chatting to that contessa." Kitty nodded towards the far side of the room. "He's not interested at all! He's only talking out of politeness, but he's so charming she'll never know. Tell me, what did you think of him?"

Persephone swallowed. "I thought him … very tall."

"Oh, Sephy!" Kitty chided gently. "That's not enough and you know it."

"I liked his cravat."

Kitty grinned as if her friend were teasing. Persephone smiled back but inside she was panicking. What would he say to Kitty about their meeting? And why hadn't he said it yet?

The next few minutes – or many minutes, Persephone lost track of time – passed in idle conversation about subjects she soon forgot. Somehow, as she went to get a fresh cup of tea from an adjoining room, Lord Malmesbury was by her side and they were all but alone. From his confident grin, she sensed that he had engineered it that way. He looked at her with perfect recognition this time. Furious, yet equally relieved she wasn't going mad, she turned on him.

"You hid your real identity. You used me!" she whispered angrily.

"Not at all. You used *me*, remember? Without me, you'd still be lost in San Polo."

"I thought you were Italian!"

"You chose to think so. I am Italian, a bit. My grandmother was born in Lombardy – hence my exceptional grasp of the language. Admit it, I'm good."

Those eyes. How they danced.

"You said your name was…?"

"Arturo Fioravante Iuliano. My own name, my middle name – from my Italian side – and my grandmother's surname. I like to travel here incognito when I can. It has its uses."

His smile was *wicked*.

"You were supposed to be in Rome."

"Trieste," he amended. "Just along the coast. I came back yesterday, but young Kitty's mother is very ... *sociable* ... don't you find? Her company is so intensely delightful that a man needs a break from it once in a while. Or indeed often."

He was so blatant, so honest, that Persephone couldn't help but smile. "You're a fiend," she protested.

"Tut tut. I'm your beloved friend's near-betrothed. Be nice to me. I shall certainly be nice to you. In fact, you'll find me nice to everyone." He turned to the lady who had just walked in to get some tea. "Ah, my dear Mrs Gardner, how is New York this winter? Do come and join us. Have you met Persephone Lavelle? Isn't she a *stunner*?"

He was brilliant and dazzling. As Kitty had promised, he charmed the room. He didn't stay long, but made every woman in it feel like a princess, every man feel that he alone could talk politics with any weight, and Kitty feel more than ever like Cinderella at the ball. Persephone sensed that he was playing with each of them. That his charm, which came so easily, was simply a game.

It was clear he intended to keep their first encounter a secret. She was still furious with him, but after all, wasn't she as much at fault as he was? Under his spell, she too hadn't said anything to Kitty just now. She was no more immune to that charm than any of the women here. Worse, she still tingled at the thought of the looks and conversation they'd shared in the gondola.

At least yesterday she was not to blame for her feelings. She did not know any better then, though he did. He had kept his promise to find her again – and most devilish it seemed to her now. Perhaps it was best to pretend their meeting had never happened. Then she remembered Kitty's promise to find him for her. She wished she had never mentioned the Harlequin.

Chapter Seven

The Ballards had tickets for the opera that evening.

"La Fenice's one of the best houses in Europe," Kitty said, consulting the guidebook before they left. "You say 'Fay-nee-chay'. It means phoenix and it's well named because it's been burned down twice and risen from the ashes." Kitty looked up. "Everyone loves the opera here. Of course, the locals understand it, which must help."

Everyone, Persephone assumed, was everyone rich. But when she heard gondoliers singing snatches of opera tunes as Nico steered them to their destination, she chided herself for being cynical. The music carried on the night air, sad and lovely, matching the mood of the city. She rather liked the way she couldn't understand the words. It seemed to make each song more atmospheric. She huddled in her borrowed furs and wondered if any other place in the world could be as beautiful as this.

Kitty sat next to her as they glided down narrow dark canals. Now was the perfect opportunity to smile and joke and tell her everything. Friends didn't keep secrets from each other. But each time she breathed in to make a remark, she breathed out again in silence. She rehearsed the conversation in her head.

Ha ha, guess who the Harlequin turned out to be?

Kitty, on learning the truth: *Why didn't you tell me this afternoon?*

No answer.

Kitty: *You pretended not to know him! You made me look a fool!*

However Persephone imagined the scene, it couldn't end well. She bitterly regretted her excitement in describing the mysterious stranger. She hadn't meant to mislead Kitty but with every minute that passed it became more impossible to tell the truth.

And so her thoughts twisted and turned, like eels under the water; a silvery, slithery nest that never fully resolved itself. Until the boat arrived at its destination and it was too late to speak anyway.

The opera was in Italian, by a German, and was apparently funny, though none of the Ballards or their party knew when to laugh. Persephone admired the extravagant costumes, all creams and golds, and the high ladies' voices that trilled endlessly above the orchestra, but was too distracted to get any sense of the plot.

It wasn't until Kitty nudged her that she noticed how many people in the audience were glancing up at the box where she and Kitty sat.

"Who do you think they're looking at, you or me?"

Kitty said it with a giggle but Persephone knew that in her heart she wanted a serious answer. For someone so pretty, Kitty was oddly lacking in self-confidence these days. Once Persephone could have assured her in all honesty that Kitty's blue-eyed, golden beauty outshone everyone – but she had found this last year that her own unusual looks had a certain attraction in some quarters. So she was not entirely truthful when she said, "Oh, you, dearest, of course." But she did it convincingly and was pleased when her friend blushed and smiled. Most of the admirers probably had been looking at Kitty anyway.

In the interval, Mrs Ballard cooled herself vigorously with an ivory fan.

"I must say, it is well done, isn't it, Frederick?"

"Oh? Yes, of course," Mr Ballard grunted, trying to catch the eye of a waiter behind them circulating with champagne glasses on a tray.

"Very well done and very pretty. I do find it complicated, though."

"Do you? Mmmm. I'm sure you're right."

"Oh, so do I!" Kitty agreed heartily. "If only Arthur were here to explain it. He knows all the operas. He did in St Petersburg too. Even the Russian ones."

"Well at least you'll see him tomorrow," Mrs Ballard said. "He's so kind to spend so much time with you when the Prime Minister has given him such important duties. The whole day!"

"And you'll come with us too, Mama?" Kitty asked.

"Of course."

"Oh good. I want him to take us to St Mark's and San Giorgio Maggiore."

Mrs Ballard paled. "That church on the island? By boat?"

"How else?" Kitty laughed.

Mrs Ballard went green.

Persephone knew that she hated boats because it was

one of the first things Kitty had told her. She would never have come to Venice if it hadn't been to secure this match. Why was Kitty so set on this itinerary?

"It sounds like an interesting day," Persephone said with a curious glance at her friend.

"It will be!" Kitty agreed.

"Oh dear," Mrs Ballard said. She was fanning herself harder than ever.

Kitty looked as if a thought had just struck her. "Mama! You don't *need* to come on the boat. You can go home after St Mark's if you prefer. Sephy can keep me company. And I'm sure Arthur can look after us."

"I don't know…" Mrs Ballard looked to her husband for advice. She was torn between her strong desire to spend as little time on water as possible and the need to protect her daughter's reputation. "What do you think, Frederick?"

Mr Ballard was not listening. He was admiring the décolletages of three passing society ladies, which were somewhat unavoidably on display. "My dear?"

"What do you think? Shall I come home tomorrow or stay out with Kitty?"

Persephone marvelled at how Mr Ballard had become

a master at understanding what his wife really wanted without ever paying her much attention. He heard the unspoken plea in her voice. "Oh, come home, my dear. Don't you think? I'm sure it will be all right."

At this, Kitty looked Persephone triumphantly in the eye and Persephone grinned back. The plan was a work of mastery. She knew she wasn't a proper chaperone for the young couple but Kitty's engagement was as good as announced. What harm could it do?

Persephone steeled herself for the day ahead. Now she was over the shock of meeting Lord Malmesbury in his true guise, she would be a model of decorum. Distant but polite. Devoted to Kitty. The perfect friend.

This wasn't mere loyalty to Kitty. What she had felt for the Harlequin in that gondola had been a rush of admiration that had made her dizzy, but that was all. He had been, as she suspected, an impossible dream. Her heart was still Felix Dawson's, to do with as he pleased, and she ached for him.

After the interval, the opera shifted from comedy to romantic disaster, and Persephone let the tears flow freely down her cheeks. *This* was the love she knew: impossible and broken. Kitty was welcome to the happy kind.

Chapter Eight

The ladies were to meet Lord Malmesbury in St Mark's Square the following day at ten thirty. Nico led them on foot down a series of narrow alleys, through little squares and over bridges, until a vast space opened up suddenly in front of them.

"*Ecco!*" Nico said proudly, as if he had built it himself. "*La Piazza San Marco.*"

It was the most stunning space Persephone could possibly imagine. She felt overwhelmed from the minute she walked into it. The sun was shining again today and the light dazzled. Stretching away from them, the sides were lined with colonnades. At the far end, crosses mounted high on several oriental-looking domes rose above golden mosaic arches. There was a long, low building next to it, pink and white, with stonework like fine icing. The square itself was thronged with people and birds and trinket stalls and noise. Kitty somehow spotted Lord Malmesbury in the middle of it all and ran to him. Persephone trailed behind, trying to take it all in.

"Arthur! You're so punctual!" Kitty laughed. "I do admire you."

"How could any man be late for you?" he asked with a gallant bow.

Kitty blushed. Today she had chosen a black and white walking dress with a black velvet jacket edged in golden sable from Russia. Her fur-trimmed bonnet was set at a jaunty angle. Lord Malmesbury was dressed to match in a frock coat and fur collar, with an elegant ebony walking cane. Persephone recognized it as the Harlequin's.

"How delightful … to see you," Mrs Ballard puffed, struggling to catch up with them.

"And indeed you, my dearest lady. My day is not complete until we have met." Lord Malmesbury smiled, bowing again. "Hello, Persephone," he added, as an afterthought. Despite her determination to be distant it made her heart race for a moment, as if his indifference was a private joke between them. To cancel it out, her curtsey was deep and formal.

"So here we are." Mrs Ballard sighed. "St Mark's Square. What does Murray say, Kitty?"

Kitty consulted the little red guidebook, which Persephone had by now learned was known as Murray, the authority on all things Venetian. "*Napoleon*," she quoted, "*called it the most beautiful salon in Europe*." She looked up. "I can't think why."

Persephone could. It was like a crowded room open to the sky. All around them voices from groups of tourists sounded in a cacophony of different languages.

"That building at the end is St Mark's Basilica," Kitty said, nodding towards the distant domes, "where the body of St Mark himself is buried."

Mrs Ballard peered at it through the crowd. "It's a bit of a hodge-podge," she said, frowning.

Persephone took in the arches and columns of different shapes and sizes, the pointed Gothic flourishes, the flags and spires… Her eye flew from one marvellous, exotic feature to the next.

"It lacks symmetry," Kitty agreed. "Though I quite like it. It stands next to the Doge's Palace – look – there, Mama, the pink one – and dates from the eleventh century. Goodness!" Kitty turned over several pages in the guidebook. "There's an awful lot to see inside. I think we may have to do the shortened version."

"Let me guide you," Arthur said. "I assure you, I've been a hundred times and I can make you fall in love with it in twenty minutes and still have time for coffee."

"Arthur! You are a wonder!" Catherine Ballard said gratefully.

He was as good as his word, striding purposefully through the crowds, scattering children and match-sellers out of his way. Once inside the vast golden building, he pointed out key mosaics and explained the history of the Basilica. Persephone missed most of it. She was too busy looking around, overwhelmed by the glittering light and colour, the shapes and symbols she had never seen before, and the chattering of all their fellow tourists. Kitty and her mother treated each place they visited as a shopping list of sights to be admired and crossed out. Persephone couldn't work that way. Her eyes hurt. She wondered if there was something wrong with her.

Back outside, Lord Malmesbury found them a table at one of the cafés and ordered much-needed drinks. After a short trip to buy photographs of the view from one of the many shops around the square, Mrs Ballard announced herself quite ready to go home. Nico appeared as if by magic to accompany her there.

"And now we are free." Kitty grinned, waving her mother off. "Isn't it exciting?"

"Absolutely," her suitor agreed.

He caught Persephone's eye and she was forced to look away.

❧❧

By the time they set off for the island, Persephone already felt full to the brim with culture and quite fatigued. It would take weeks to appreciate the beauty of every artefact and vista in St Mark's Square, she thought, and they had taken precisely ninety minutes, including the coffee.

According to Kitty, deep in her Murray, "*The church of San Giorgio Maggiore was designed by Andrea Palladio in 1566.*" She looked up. "We must admire the classical references of the façade, apparently." But Persephone didn't want to admire anything. She wanted to go home and sleep, and dream about what she had already seen. At least the view of the Grand Canal back the way they had come was glorious. She reclined in the gondola and focused on that, and the gentle splash as the boat carved its way through the waves.

Kitty put down the guidebook. "Oh, Arthur! I've just remembered. You can help us."

"Can I?" Lord Malmesbury said politely. "Your wish is my command."

"You need to find someone for us. Someone special."

Persephone sat up quickly and tried to catch Kitty's eye. But Kitty was grinning at her suitor.

"Go on," he said. "You intrigue me."

"Sephy had the most extraordinary encounter the day before you arrived. It was so romantic."

Whoosh. Persephone's neck, always the source of her blushes, felt as if it was on fire. Remembering all the ridiculous things she had said, she pulled her cape around her and wished herself a million miles away. Lord Malmesbury caught her eye again. There was no doubt that he knew what Kitty meant. His mouth twitched with anticipation.

"Romantic? Really? Persephone, how exciting."

"No – not at all..."

"Oh, it *was*," Kitty insisted. "She was in terrible

danger, out on her own in the city, but she was rescued by a masked young man, a Harlequin."

"I see. And what was he like, this Harlequin?"

"I hardly remember," Persephone muttered with a desperate glance at her friend.

"Yes you do!" Kitty encouraged. "He was very handsome and dashing, you said, and tall with flashing eyes. He spoke excellent English, though obviously he was Italian, and he knew all about art – which Sephy adores, Arthur, as you know. There can't be so many young men like that in Venice, can there?"

Reflected light from the water played on the young aristocrat's face. He assumed an expression of mock seriousness, but his dancing eyes gave him away. "Handsome and dashing, you say? And impeccable English, though *obviously* he was Italian…?"

"Promise me you'll find him?" Kitty pouted.

He reached out to take her hand. "I promise."

Persephone sensed it wasn't Kitty he was addressing with that teasing smile. She regretted every lavish word she'd used to describe him. From then on, she couldn't even glance in his direction, though she sensed he was willing her to. She had never been so mortified.

When they got to San Giorgio, Persephone wandered around disconsolately and hardly noticed it. Each time they reached a flight of stairs, Arthur offered to take her hand to help her up and down. She refused to let him, at great cost to her safety, as her skirts and petticoats threatened to trip her at every step. He would occasionally ask her for more details about the dashing Harlequin – "to help with my research, you know." But eventually he changed the subject and discussed instead the strange preponderance of cats on the island. It seemed he was finally taking pity on her.

Back in the gondola, he opened a basket that seemed to appear from nowhere and offered them bread, wine and meltingly soft salami for lunch. Persephone ate greedily. She wanted to be dainty and refined for Kitty's sake, but she was starving after so much walking. Afterwards, a soporific feeling overtook them all. They sat back and said little, watching small watercraft come and go around them, while larger ships sailed grandly towards the docks.

Eventually, Kitty suggested heading back. Refreshed, Persephone sat up to admire the city from this new perspective across the water. It was beautiful from wherever one viewed it. She should be used to it by now, but each new vista took her by surprise. The rest during lunch had helped. Her eyes were ready to see and admire once more.

As they drew level with St Mark's again to the east, a huge white building loomed towards them on the western side. Its large pale dome sat above archways and pediments of different heights and styles, with a smaller dome and teetering bell towers behind. Catherine Ballard would have called it a 'hodge-podge' but Persephone thought of it as a challenge to her imagination. It was as if it had been brought about by accident, by someone dreaming of a half-forgotten country, washed of colour.

"The church of La Salute," Lord Malmesbury said quietly, leaning forwards and following the direction of her gaze. "I know what you mean." He spoke as if she had said something, but she was sure she hadn't. How could he know what she was thinking? She wanted to ask, but she still wasn't talking to him. He didn't seem to mind. "It was built to celebrate the end of the plague in Venice. One of my favourite places. It has some Titians. Three, I believe."

Persephone felt her neck flush again.

"We could go inside," Kitty said, chewing her lip. "But I don't want to stay too long. I must buy a new headdress before tonight's dinner."

"Then we must rush on," her suitor said decisively. "*Gondoliere – avanti!* Art can be postponed for another day. Headdresses never can."

Persephone thought she would mind missing the Titians, but she didn't. It wasn't art today, but architecture that moved her. She was content to sit back on her cushions and admire La Salute from the water. As they pulled away, it seemed to shimmer against the winter sky, as if it were about to disappear.

This time they arrived at a new landing post, further up from St Mark's. As usual, they were met by an impossibly confusing arrangement of alleyways and canals but Lord Malmesbury knew exactly which turnings to take. They soon found themselves in a busy thoroughfare, lined with artisan shops of all descriptions. There were shops for books, for exquisite hand-printed paper, for maps and photographs and shoes and knick-knacks made from coloured glass. Eventually they found the hat shop Kitty wanted and she happily set about choosing the perfect headdress for the evening. Persephone soon found, though, that despite her best efforts her brain had no room left for brims and ribbons. After ten minutes, Kitty noticed her listlessly trying things on.

"You go outside, Sephy. I have plenty of help here. I'll see you shortly."

Persephone gratefully left her to it. Lord Malmesbury had taken refuge in the street already. He smiled at her as she joined him, but didn't speak. She was grateful for that too. She simply looked up, and up, at the brightness of the blue above them. It was a while before she noticed her companion's polite cough. She shook herself out of her reverie and looked at him.

"What does a girl think about, when she stares up like that?" he asked.

"Nothing really. I was trying to understand the colour of the sky."

"Ah." He smiled slightly. "The Italians have a word for it. They say *celeste* for a pale blue sky, but one like this, a deep one, is *azzurro*."

Persephone tried to repeat it the way he'd said it. "Add-*zoo*-rrroh." She rolled the 'r' on her tongue. It made them both laugh. "Is that azure?"

"We stole the word from them. The English like to think they invented everything, but the Italians have an eye for colour, don't they?"

"Yes." She breathed the word. *Azzurro. Azzurro.* The way her tongue rattled somehow seemed to capture the sharpness of the colour, the sense of space beyond it. *Azzurro.* Like *Serenissima.* "I think I might like to learn Italian."

"I think you should."

"That reminds me. When I was lost..." She glanced away. There was so much she should not remember about that day. Especially with him. "...I was trying to get to the Rialto. Everyone seemed to point me to *sempayd ritter.* Do you know where that is?"

He stared for a moment, then threw his head back and laughed. "Yes! Yes, I do. *Sempayd ritter,* you say?" He laughed again. "It's *sempre dritto.* It means 'straight ahead' in Italian. To Venetians, every journey in the city's so obvious it feels like a straight line. But of course, that's impossible. After ten paces, you are faced with an obstacle and an impossible decision. I've suffered that way too, many times."

They shared a smile. He slipped his arm through hers, as if to wander off together, but quickly remembered himself, withdrew it and apologized. For a moment, thinking of her ease with the Harlequin, she was sad. This was a different, softer Arthur Malmesbury from the one who had teased her on the island. It would be nice to walk arm in arm with such a man through Venice, get lost perhaps, and practise new words in Italian. But that was for Kitty.

They waited awkwardly outside the shop until eventually Kitty appeared, piled high with boxes that she quickly handed to Arthur to carry for her. Persephone watched with admiration as he looked at the stack of purchases, called to the nearest street boy and made a quick bargain for him to follow them as their porter. Everything he did seemed effortless. She thought of how elegant Kitty's life would be with Arthur easing it for her at every opportunity. It wasn't often she truly envied her friend, who was always so generous and kind to her, but for a moment, she did.

Chapter Nine

My dearest Harriet,

You are probably wondering how I am…

Persephone sucked the end of her pen and looked across at Kitty, who was writing diligently at the other end of the table. Lord Malmesbury was away on government business and Kitty had endless correspondence from her friends to catch up on. Persephone had written to Effie and Annie. This was her last letter.

Venice is a constant whirl, and while I think you'd hate the damp streets and shabby houses (though they are grand too), I am very happy here…

In half a dozen lines she had described the opera and St Mark's. Two more took care of the food and the comfort of her green-gold bedroom. She could not possibly mention her adventure in the gondola for fear of questions she could never answer. So she signed off affectionately and marvelled at how Kitty's hand continued to fly across the page, leaving a neat trail of ink on the paper.

Kitty always found a lot to talk about. In Arthur's absence, she had been constantly busy. There were new dresses to commission and more social visits to make. Churches had to be seen and ticked off the list of Murray's 'essentials', and photographs purchased as gifts and souvenirs.

Some but not all of this involved Persephone. In her free time these last few days she had happily done little, wandering the nearby streets with her sketchbook and watercolours, often getting lost regardless of which map she consulted and suddenly finding herself by the Grand Canal when she thought she was half a mile away. She copied Lord Malmesbury's trick and used a little money to pay for a boy to carry her folding stool for her. Then she could sit wherever she liked and sketch.

She found the city hard to write about, but magnetic to draw and paint. Every palazzo façade begged to be captured. There was hardly ever any symmetry. Walls suddenly stopped where history decided a new building should emerge out of an old one. Windows were circles, where in London they would be rectangles – or better still, trefoil flowers. Gothic arches created patterns unique to the city. No two balconies were the same.

And then there was the water. It pooled and flowed and sparkled. It was sometimes dark as pitch and sometimes bright turquoise in the sun. Persephone tried and failed to conjure its mercurial qualities many times and never tired of it.

When Lord Malmesbury returned a few days later, the three of them resumed their walks. While he and Kitty led the way, heads bent in conversation, she often fell behind to marvel at a piece of carved stone, or a view of gondola stands sticking up like fronds through the water, or a row of washing hung out to dry against a medieval wall. She didn't mind if the sun was shining or the mist was rising from the marshes. Venice tore at her heart with its loveliness however it looked.

This gentle way of passing the time seemed set to last indefinitely, but after not much more than another week the Ballard household was utterly disrupted by the arrival of Roly.

"He should have joined us ages ago," Mrs Ballard explained the night before, over cards. "But there was a problem with paperwork. It's taken far longer than he expected."

Persephone's heart sank, but Kitty's raised eyebrow at Mrs Ballard's little speech intrigued her too. When they were alone, she asked, "So what's really been keeping him?"

Kitty grinned. She adored her wayward brother. "He wrote to me last week. The 'problem with paperwork' was an assignation with a lady friend in Sussex. He is utterly incorrigible. I can't wait to see him. Venice has been so dull without him. Oh!" Her hand flew to her mouth. "I didn't mean..."

"I'm not offended." Persephone laughed. But she was surprised. Not for her own sake – girls tend to take other girls for granted – but for Arthur's. Surely Kitty didn't think him dull? True, Persephone found the two of them quite staid together, politely chatting as they walked. But she assumed that was just how Kitty wanted it. Arthur was the Harlequin, after all. If it was excitement Kitty was after, she knew no one better who could offer it.

She pondered on this when she was alone, getting ready for bed. Something wasn't quite right and yet how could anything be wrong when Kitty had found such a perfect partner? However, her thoughts soon turned with some trepidation to Roly Ballard, who was a more immediate concern.

Persephone had known Kitty's brother for several months now, and he was anything but dull. By impersonating his own great aunt with theatrical gusto, he had helped Felix work the ruse to get her out of Professor Aitken's house so she could pose for him in his studio. They had spent plenty of time in joint pursuit of pleasure too. Roly was funny and gregarious. A party wasn't a party without him at it. But after he had refused to help her with Harriet, she had hardly spoken to him. She practised being gracious in the mirror.

Roly, how lovely to see you again.

Not, *Roly, if you had had your way my cousin would be dead in the river, and her baby never born.*

❧❧

Roly must have been practising too.

"My dearest Persephone, what a delight! You look *charming.*"

They stood at the waterman's entrance, ready to greet him as he arrived at the pontoon. Catherine

Ballard had just released him from a hug that looked set to last all winter.

"I'm so lucky to have her," Kitty insisted, with her arm round Persephone's waist. She smelled of warm figs and cinnamon, having been tasting cakes to celebrate his arrival. She looked even happier than when Arthur had first appeared. "I have so much to tell you, Roly. You really mustn't go out with your friends until we've had a proper chat."

Kitty took his hand and led him upstairs.

"What friends?" he asked as he followed. "I know no one in this godforsaken place."

"What? No! You'll know everyone, I promise. You always do, Roly. Besides, the Edwardses are here."

"Oh?" He nodded. "True. I know them."

"And the Blakes."

"Ah! Charlie Blake? Good man. Haven't seen him since Oxford. I must call on him tomorrow."

"You see? And now I'm in danger of never seeing you myself. I take it all back. Nobody's here. Just Mama and Papa and Sephy and me. Come and tell us all about London. Do they even remember me there?"

She took him into the mirrored salon, where the

cinnamon cakes were served with coffee, and from then on the chatter didn't stop. Persephone was pleased to see the family so lively and happy and together, but equally relieved that nobody seemed to notice she wasn't talking. The only thing she and Roly had in common now was their fondness for Felix – and as far as Roly knew, she had abandoned him. He didn't mention his friend once, and merely gave her a couple of cool glances across his coffee cup.

❧❧❧

At Kitty's suggestion they went out *en masse* for dinner at the Hotel Danieli, where Lord Malmesbury was staying.

Kitty's thoughts, as usual, were on her outfit. "Do you think I've gone too far?" she asked as they prepared to leave the palazzo. "I want Arthur to be proud." Tonight, under her furs, she was wearing lace from shoulder to ankle – tiers of it that cascaded in cream ruffles, caught by satin bows. Her tiny waist was emphasized by a satin sash and her hair was curled and coiled and caught with little butterflies made of mother of pearl.

"If he doesn't love you like that he never will," Persephone assured her.

She had meant to be encouraging, but instantly regretted the words she'd used. They had another, darker, echo that she didn't intend. Kitty's flickering frown of concern suggested that she too had sensed their double meaning. She spoke little during their journey down the Grand Canal.

The Danieli was the most famous hotel in Venice, housed in an ancient palazzo beyond St Mark's Square. A procession of great people had stayed there, including Ruskin and Effie, who'd talked nostalgically about its magnificence. Persephone had looked forward to the evening, and had worn her best amber velvet in its honour, but from the start it seemed to go awry.

First, it was hard work to be continually gracious to Roly, though she tried. Second, she noticed Lord Malmesbury trying to tell Kitty about the hotel's famous origins, and Kitty not really listening. She longed for him to talk to Kitty about her new hairstyle instead, and for Kitty to say something interesting about the architecture of the ancient building. They both looked bored. The word 'dull' came to mind.

Dull *here*? Dull *now*? How was that possible?

Third, Roly – being Roly – had already seen three young men he knew among the gathered diners and two of them had joined the Ballards' table. One was French and focused mainly on the food. The other was English and somehow managed to squeeze himself into the seat next to Persephone. His name was George something – Persephone had not caught his surname – and he was deeply annoying.

"I must say, you look so stunning with your hair … like that," George began. It was loose, as usual, falling in waves to her waist. "You really are a stunner!" He laughed at his own joke. "Is it actually that colour?"

"What?" she asked.

"Your hair. That red."

"Yes." How could it be otherwise? Did he think it was a wig, perhaps? Or that she stained it with carrot juice?

"I say, this food is good, isn't it? What is it? Fish? Chicken? What d'you suppose? Are you having more? I think I will."

Persephone glanced down the table. Roly, who looked as his name suggested, was heartily partaking of several dishes at once while talking to the woman next to him.

Kitty and Arthur seemed to have run out of things to say to each other. Kitty was talking to her mother.

"...vellum. Is it vellum? It's so clever." Beside her, George was talking again.

She turned back to the annoying young man. "I'm so sorry. What's vellum?"

"Your dress."

"Do you mean velvet?"

"Ah, yes! Vel*vet*. Ladies' wotnots. Ha! It looks a bit like the one you wore for that thing."

Persephone frowned. "What thing?"

"By that artist. I saw the exhibition. Roly took me. Hey, Roly!" He waved across the table. "Who was that artist? The one with the thing? The painting that got stolen."

"Not stolen, lost," Roly called back. "You mean Felix Dawson. *Persephone and Hades*."

"Yes! That!" George smiled triumphantly to Persephone. "Awfully good. Lots of trees. Your hair all ... like that. I remember it perfectly."

"I see you do." Persephone smiled politely. *Oh Lord, please make him stop!* Why did he have to have seen that painting? The night it was first displayed was the worst night of her life. It was when she had made her pact with Mrs Lisle.

Felix had a new stunner now – one whom Mrs Lisle must have found more acceptable. Persephone had seen him with the girl in Hyde Park. Her curls were honey-blond, not red, but he had looked at her the same way. She imagined them in his studio after a painting session, Felix caught up in his art, then his hands caught in her hair, as they had once been in hers...

"I say, are you all right?" George asked, pausing with a large forkful on the way to his mouth.

"Perfectly, thank you."

It was why she had left London – to escape all this.

Persephone lost her taste for the meal. Her new companion didn't mind. He kindly ate her dessert for her when it came. As she looked back down the table Arthur Malmesbury glanced up and saw her. He held her gaze for a moment, sympathetically. It was as if he knew what she was thinking. Somehow he seemed to understand.

On the way home, it rained. She huddled in her cape, reflecting that she would never be able to follow that long line of famous faces and stay at the Danieli, if she was ever asked. The grand hotel was spoiled for her now.

Chapter Ten

It rained heavily through the night. The relentless drumming of drops on the roofs outside seemed to match Persephone's restless dreams. It was still raining when she opened her shutters the next morning and noticed that the view from her bedroom window was different. Persephone stared at the patchwork wall ahead and the little canal below, but couldn't work out what it was. Nevertheless, she felt unsettled.

The house was full of bustle. Servants appeared and disappeared carrying planks and wooden clogs. One of the maids had a dark stain on the bottom of her dress that almost reached her knees. Everyone was in a bad mood.

"What's happening?" Persephone asked at breakfast.

Mrs Ballard explained. "It's the *acqua alta*. The high water. It happens in winter sometimes. We're lucky to have avoided it so far. Look – see? The pavement on the opposite bank. Gone."

It was. Persephone looked out and marvelled. It was as if the city had sunk two feet. *That* was the difference. Hardy Venetians, wrapped in cloaks against the damp and cold, went about their business, treading their way through alleyways flooded with seawater. Anyone who could stayed at home.

"It comes when there's a high tide," Kitty said. "The servants say this isn't such a bad one. It won't last long. What shall we do?"

In the end, it was decided that they would paint. Persephone took out her sketches of palazzi and waterways and chose a few to turn into watercolours, sitting in an upstairs room above the salon, overlooking the Grand Canal. Kitty worked on a portrait of her mother, who happily sat for her while chatting endlessly about her friends' grandchildren. It was obvious that in her mind she had already moved on from the wedding and was picturing a little row of lords and ladies running around the house in Mayfair whenever Kitty came to visit. Persephone also sensed that Catherine was longing for home. The main 'must-see' items in the little red guidebook had been ticked off her list, the waters were rising and Venice was losing its charm.

Roly Ballard rose late, having returned several hours after the others from the Danieli – and soon left again to meet his friends and play cards 'somewhere dry'. But Arthur Malmesbury dutifully arrived at four, suitably attired in rubber boots, and meekly agreed to Kitty's request to sit for her. Mrs Ballard left them to it. "I'm sure you'll keep an eye on them, Persephone," she said with a wink.

Persephone hated her role as chaperone. She wanted to leave the young lovers alone. How could you grow close without touching, caressing and saying the things that mattered? She was glad that her social status – or rather lack of it – meant no one cared what she did, or who with. She and Felix had shared precious moments unguarded by anyone, and even if they broke her heart she didn't regret them.

She sensed that Kitty had suggested this portrait because she was a very good amateur artist, and it would show her off to her future husband just as well as her French lace collar, or the seed pearls in her hair. Given their history, Persephone didn't particularly want to focus so closely on Lord Malmesbury, but once she had her pencils in her hand she quickly forgot her feelings and focused only on the planes of his face, the pleasing symmetry of his eyes, the generous curve to his lips.

Kitty kept up a running commentary as she drew. "Oh look! I've made your nose too big when really it's so shapely. Do smile slightly, Arthur. You look so serious! That's better. How long will you be in Venice, do you think? Will your business keep you here much longer?"

"Not much. A few weeks."

"How many?"

"Three or four at most. My mission's coming along nicely."

"So few? How lovely! I mean, Venice is wonderful, of course, but *London…*"

Kitty took after her mother, Persephone thought, in so many ways. She found herself drawing a furrow between Arthur's eyebrows. But when she looked up again, he was merely politely curious.

"You don't like Venice?"

"No, of course I do. But London's so much more comfortable, don't you think?" Kitty reddened at this admission, drew something in her sketchbook and rubbed it out vigorously.

"I'm perfectly comfortable where I am," Arthur drawled unperturbed, leaning back and spoiling Persephone's composition. "How could any man not be? I truly declare that I'm deliciously content."

Persephone looked up again to see how to adjust her portrait now that he had moved, and found him looking straight at her, the way Felix used to. She stared back.

That look can't mean what I think it means. I've said nothing, done nothing. I've just been drawing.

After that, her fingers couldn't guide her pencil properly and the resulting portrait was disastrous. Kitty, on the other hand, had done a very creditable job. But Arthur insisted on taking Persephone's sketch as well as Kitty's and holding both of them to his heart. After he'd left, Kitty let out a happy sigh.

"Did you see how he kindly took your picture as well as mine? He knows how fond of you I am. It makes me love him more."

But how fond of me is he? Persephone wondered. For the first time she felt a shiver of misgiving. Then she chided her overactive imagination. Arthur's eyes were always dancing and he was only being charming. The perfect diplomat.

It seemed that Roly spent his days staying as far away from his family as he could, carousing with friends around the city, while Arthur now came daily to call at Palazzo Colleoni, regardless of his duties for the Prime Minister.

"He has the best manners in the world!" Mrs Ballard declared. "He's so in love! I can see it, Kitty. I know it. Trust your mother."

Kitty nodded seriously, as if willing herself to believe it. She was palpably excited, however, by the new thought of home. The whole family, which had been growing somewhat morose over several days of bad weather, cheered up at the prospect of returning to their much more lavish house in Mayfair, where their dogs and carriages and horses and favourite servants were patiently waiting. Plans were made to vacate the palazzo by the middle of February.

The return that so delighted Kitty loomed over Persephone like a thundercloud. Though she would be relieved to be out of Lord Malmesbury's way, she didn't know how she would drag herself away from Venice. She was just settling in! As soon as the waters receded she even managed to recognize little journeys she could make on foot, and started to navigate without getting lost at every turn.

While Kitty and her mother made their final round of visits to the ladies of society, Persephone retraced her steps to some of her favourite vistas of the Grand Canal. It was there one morning that she encountered a young man, not much older than her, painting a familiar view. She stopped to admire the watercolour he made of La Salute church, sitting across the water with his sketchbook on a board on his knees.

"May I...?" She looked at the page, full of greens and blues and greys, and didn't know what she wanted, or how to ask.

He smiled up at her. "You're Persephone Lavelle, aren't you?" he asked with a slight American twang. By now she was used to being recognized as 'the girl with the copper hair'. She smiled and he grinned back. He had an attractive, mobile face under his low wide hat, with bright eyes and an elegant moustache. "I thought so.

James Whistler, from Massachusetts. I know some of your friends in London, though I'm trying to find my own style."

"And succeeding," Persephone said, looking greedily at his painting again. It was more of an impression than an accurate sketch of the church. Kitty, who had been taught everything there was to know about line and perspective, would not have liked it. But it was how Persephone saw the view when she closed her eyes. She loved its insubstantial quality.

He tore out the page carefully, without disturbing the drying watercolour, and handed it to her. "Have it. On one condition."

"What?"

"That you'll sit for me. If ever you come to Paris. I bet you hear that all the time."

"I used to," she admitted. "Except the Paris part. Why there?"

"I live there. I'm heading home soon. Do we have a deal?"

"It seems unlikely," she said with a sigh.

"Oh, you never know what will happen in this world." He grinned. "I have rooms in Saint Supplice. A poor, impoverished artist. The usual kind. Look me up there. *If* you come."

She smiled. "I can think of nothing I'd like better, Mr Whistler."

She told Kitty about him over tea in the salon. Kitty was delighted by the encounter.

"An American? Living in Europe?"

"Yes."

"What a shame it's Paris, though. If only it had been London. He sounds good company. Poor Arthur has had no luck at all with seeking out your Harlequin, I'm afraid. I feel so guilty having the perfect man when you have no one."

"Don't feel guilty," Persephone begged. "I'm happy alone. I don't need a man."

"Oh, what rubbish!" Kitty laughed. "Everyone needs a man."

"What's that?" Roly asked, bounding into the room. "Talking about needing a man? Quite right! Can't do without us! Speaking of which, we need some women."

"Oh?" Kitty arched an eyebrow. "Why?"

"We're going to an island. Tomato? Tortellini? Your duke's arranging it, Kitcat."

119

"Not duke, Roly. Viscount."

"Details, Kitcat. He's got his hands on the best boat in Venice. A launch. Steam-powered. Positively rockets over the water. Mama would die! Ha ha!"

Kitty frowned. "And what does the boat have to do with anything?"

"This island's miles across the lagoon. Takes an age to get there otherwise. But it's very pretty. Like Kent, he says. Trees and fields and so on. We're going for a picnic tomorrow, if it's dry, but we need ladies."

"Well, you have two, at least," Kitty said.

"Good-oh. Can you get the food? I imagine we'll need bread. And pies and whatnot. And wine, of course. For about ten of us. I said I'd do it, but it wants a woman's touch."

Kitty didn't mind being given all the dirty work. She clapped her hands together. "Trust me. It will be wonderful!"

Persephone felt nervous and wasn't sure why.

Chapter Eleven

The island was called Torcello. The boat, which they joined from a landing stage off the Fondamente Nove, was indeed very fine. It sat low in the water, sleek and dangerous, like a predatory animal. Inside every surface of polished teak and brass oozed luxury. The party was jolly. In addition to Persephone and Kitty, there was an American woman, aged about twenty-five, and her mother, and three young Englishmen who were friends of both Roly and Arthur. Rich people seemed to know each other wherever they went, Persephone noticed. Europe was like one big drawing room to them.

The others chatted to each other while she looked out to sea. Kitty, alarmed by the effect of the wind on her artfully constructed hair and bonnet arrangement, remained firmly inside the cabin.

They had been motoring for five minutes when Roly

pointed out an island on the horizon. "By God! We're already there."

Arthur grinned. "By God we're not. That's San Michele. It's where they bury their dead."

Roly laughed. "Ha! Hadn't thought of that. No graveyards in Venice. That place must be full of bones."

"It is. Sometimes, they have to dig some up and secretly get rid of them to make room for more."

"Malmesbury, you appal me! No Englishman would do such a thing!"

No they wouldn't, Persephone thought, with unpatriotic disapproval. Venetians were so much more interesting than Englishmen. In just over two weeks, they would all be leaving this place. She leaned over the boat rail, feeling the spray on her face, soaking up every drop of the experience while it lasted.

It was a long journey after all, though they stopped off at another island on the way: Murano, where the famous coloured glass was made. Half the party bought souvenirs there. Persephone didn't. They reminded her too much of Felix, who had wine glasses from Murano in his studio, and Mrs Lisle, whose rooms in Chelsea hung with red chandeliers from precisely this place.

The cemetery and the thoughts of Mrs Lisle put her in a melancholy mood as they set off again. That was easily done these days. She was already nostalgic for Venice, even though she was still here.

It helped a little that the weather, which had started cloudy, was clearing with every mile they travelled. Arthur came to join her at the front of the boat, clutching two glasses of champagne. He offered her one but she refused. He raised the other towards the sky.

"Soon it will be *azzurro*."

She smiled. She had been avoiding him since the portrait session but here that was impossible. She had forgotten how much she could like him.

"I'll miss it too," he added.

Persephone had said nothing. She frowned.

He grinned. "Oh, I always know what you're thinking."

"I doubt that."

"No you don't. I remember how you looked at La Salute, as if you were dreaming it. You have very expressive eyes. I'm sure you've been told that before." This was true. "Emerald eyes…" he murmured.

No, malachites, she thought. More unusual stones and less obvious.

It was Arthur's turn to frown. "I've said the wrong thing."

"No, no..."

"I have, tell me. You see? I do know what you're thinking."

Reluctantly, she explained how Felix had described her.

"Hmmm. Malachites. I see what you mean," he said. "But I still prefer emeralds."

The way he looked at her made her skin prickle. It reminded her of Felix again. She sensed his urge to touch her.

"How's Kitty?" she blurted.

"Ah." At a stroke, he was calm politeness. "I came to tell you. If she insists on staying in that cabin, she'll get seasick. To hell with her hat. Will you ask her to come outside?"

He bowed and left her. Persephone waited a moment to catch her breath. After that she didn't leave Kitty's side.

❧❧

But the island of Torcello, when they got there, was so lovely she couldn't regret this trip. It hadn't escaped her notice that Roly, quoting Arthur, had likened it to Kent. Did Arthur know she was from there? Had she told him? It was utterly unlike Venice, which was all stone and brick, built up higgledy-piggledy over the centuries. Torcello had been the main city first, but over time it had reverted to its marshy state and now it was dirt paths and tall grasses, copses of trees and quiet open spaces. At this time of year, it was almost deserted.

Kitty, with the help of her mother and a local servant, had bought enough parmesan and fresh bread, cold chicken, beef and soft cheese to feed a small army, and enough wine to make even Roly happy. The Americans had brought blankets and Arthur had arranged for there to be camp stools for everyone, fine china and crystal glasses. The air was by now as warm and bright as a February day could get.

Once they had picnicked on a little patch of grass by the water's edge they made their way inland along a winding waterway, past a few old, crumbling houses. They were heading for the churches and tall bell tower they had seen from the launch as they arrived.

"Some people say Torcello comes from the words for

the tower and the sky," Persephone heard Arthur telling Kitty.

Kitty nodded dutifully, as if learning from a schoolbook. Persephone thought the words desperately romantic. *Why can't he talk to Kitty in a way she understands?* she wondered sadly. *And how can she not be uplifted by the idea of the tower and the sky?* Somehow, she found herself thinking of the *Venus of Urbino* again. She sensed that Kitty's first thought would be to want the girl in the picture to put on a housecoat of some sort, to keep warm. Whereas hers...

When they reached the buildings, Roly, who had eaten well as usual, was accused by one of his friends of being out of breath.

"Not at all," he protested. "I bet you ten shillings I can run around that big church and this small one in less than a minute. Trust the Italians to have two churches where really none would do."

"One's a cathedral," Arthur said, but only Persephone was really listening.

"You're on!" Roly's friend exclaimed. "Race you. And if I win, you're buying dinner too."

They took off their coats and gave Kitty a pocket

watch so she could time them. As they chased each other, laughing, Persephone noticed a family in simple country clothing leaving the larger church. It must be the cathedral, she assumed – though if so it was surely one of the smallest of its kind in Italy. The door was open. Leaving the others to it, she went inside to escape their noise.

The building was ancient and stunning in its stark simplicity. She had the sense here of a thousand years passing and generations being lost and forgotten. This was nothing like English churches, with their complicated carvings and stained-glass windows. Nor was it like the vast pinkish Frari. Here, the floor stood out for its intricate tiled patterns. Above it, plain stone columns arched to the sky.

She found a large mosaic of the Virgin Mary in an alcove, blue against a shimmering gold background. The artists were gone – probably thrown out of their graves by now – but this remained. Made of tiny tiles, it could not match the movement and detail of Titian's *Assumption*, but in its own way it was just as beautiful.

She stood to admire it for a long time, but as she turned to leave she noticed another, even bigger gold mosaic on the back wall. It soared from the floor to the tip of the roof, with the arched doorway running through it.

Persephone, who had been trained to read church pictures before she could read her letters, understood it instantly: it was the Last Judgment. Jesus sat at the top in Heaven surrounded by saints, and below him were all the layers of the living and the dead, until it reached the sinners burning in Hell, where a blue devil sat surrounded by winged and bearded creatures. Stepping forwards, she found herself mesmerized by stacks of skulls of the damned, whose eye sockets were plugged with wriggling snakes. She heard her name being called but couldn't pull herself away.

Arthur stood in the doorway. He stared for a moment, then closed the door and walked over to stand beside her.

"This is the third time I've come here," he said after a few moments' silence. "And I never noticed this wall. Isn't that strange? Those tortured souls."

Like her, he focused on Hell, not Heaven. She felt a momentary kinship of guilty thoughts, though she didn't know what Arthur's sins might be. Persephone had been thinking of the people she had let down, like

Felix and Rupert. Was this what happened to girls like her? "It's hard to be good," she murmured.

Arthur gently took her hand, squeezed it, and brushed it with his lips. "Venice is more interesting with you in it."

Before she could react the door opened and Kitty stood there, her bonnet askew, her fashionable form framed by the light.

"Ah! There you are! Well done, Arthur. You found her!"

Persephone felt her hand being dropped like a burning coal.

"Yes," he said. His voice was calm and conversational. "We were just observing how fascinating this wall is. Excellent use of *tesserae*. Come on, Persephone."

As they all walked back down the waterway together, a boat was coming towards them, accompanied by a band of locals, singing songs.

"Oh look!" Roly called out. "A wedding party!"

The groom walked along the path, surrounded by friends. The bride, with long black hair against a pure-white fur-trimmed cape, stood in the boat that silently glided along the canal, steered by an expert gondolier.

She looked entirely serene. Persephone found her voice at last and called out, "Good luck!" in English. The young woman turned to her and smiled. Once the boat had passed, Persephone couldn't quite believe the vision had been real. The whole day was starting to feel like that.

She ran to catch up with Kitty, who was walking on ahead with Arthur and Roly.

"Did you see her?" she asked.

"Who?"

"The bride!"

"Oh yes. But my dress will be much nicer."

Kitty flushed. She wasn't supposed to talk about such presumptuous things, especially in front of her suitor.

Roly let out a huge guffaw. "Oh, Kitcat! You slay me!"

Arthur, who might have been offended, was nothing but smiles. Persephone wondered at him. She realized with increasing certainty that he didn't love her friend. Yet he continued to court her. And what did he mean, exactly, about Venice being more interesting with Persephone in it? Suddenly she felt out of her depth in this marshy place.

Chapter Twelve

Lent was starting soon. The Italians liked to celebrate the lead-up to it in typical Continental style – with great excess. They called it *Carnevale*. 'Carnay-varlay'. Persephone rolled it around her mouth the way one of the maids had taught her to say it.

Under the rule of the Austrian Empire, Venice had been forced to ban most forms of frivolity, but the Venetians still had *Carnevale* running in their blood. Though no public balls and processions could take place, parties were held privately – small ones in merchants' houses, and grander revels in the palazzi of the aristocracy. Their friend the Contessa dell'Agua was holding one and as a special concession to Kitty on her last night in Venice, her mother had agreed that all the family would go. Arthur would be there of course, and 'everyone' they knew. Now all talk was of what to wear and how to impress. At least, *almost* all the talk was.

"What do you think of this wig, Sephy?" Kitty asked as a professional costumier visited the palazzo to create appropriately splendid outfits.

"Stunning. You must wear it."

Kitty gazed at the pompadour construction and laid it aside. She looked up to catch Persephone's eye.

"I have something special to ask you," she said.

"Anything. It's yours," Persephone answered without thinking.

"Oh good. It's a big request, but you just promised. Remember that."

"Of course."

Kitty grinned. "We have got on together, have we not?"

"Certainly." Persephone was confused and a little concerned now.

"Do you have plans for when you return to London?"

"No." Persephone sighed and put down the mask adorned with bells that she had been considering. Once back in England her plan was to disappear as quietly as she could. She had nowhere to go and should probably look for another servant's situation. The shilling an hour she earned from modelling was not enough to live on. As soon as she could, she would check the advertisements, looking for places that provided board and lodging. But she could not bring herself to think about it too closely after sharing this world with Kitty.

"Well I'm glad," Kitty said. She stuck out her chin. "I have plans for you."

"Oh?" Did she know of a situation at a grand house in London as a maid or governess? How humiliating. Persephone's heart couldn't help but sink.

"Yes. I want you to come and live with us."

The shock of it made Persephone gasp. "I'm sorry?"

Kitty was slightly embarrassed and talked in a rush. "It won't be for long. Only until I'm married, which will probably be in the summer. Assuming Arthur asks me, of course. But until then, I can't think of anything nicer. We never run out of things to do or say. I've always wanted a sister. Roly is adorable but he can be a pest, as you've seen. And he's hardly ever at home these days. Balfour House is awfully large. There's plenty of room. I've asked Mama and Papa and they say please come. You fit so nicely into our family. It wouldn't be the same without you."

She hardly paused for breath. Persephone struggled to take it in. The costumier, standing nearby, coughed to bring their attention back to his exotic wares but they both ignored him.

"*Live* with you? As your friend?"

"What else?"

"I couldn't possibly."

"Why? You do it here." Kitty frowned.

"Because … it's too generous. Too much."

"Don't be ridiculous! If that's the only reason then it's settled. Papa always said what's the point of having a big house if people can't live in it. Mama loves your company. I shall introduce you to all my friends and they shall love you as I do. There is only one condition."

"What?"

Kitty smiled again, confident. "That you continue to be Persephone Lavelle and have adventures. I'm so ordinary compared with you…"

"You aren't, Kitty! Don't be silly."

"Yes I am. But I shall shine in your reflected glory."

"Oh, Kitty, you're the maddest, kindest girl in the history of the world." Persephone did not know what to do. She shook her head and laughed, and nearly cried, and ended up hugging her friend and almost squashing the valuable mask between them.

Moving back to London so soon would present its problems but she had little choice and couldn't bear to refuse so kind an offer. Also, she was starting to feel deep concern for her friend. Arthur Malmesbury did not behave in any way like a devoted suitor. His behaviour in the cathedral had been improper. In fact he seemed much too interested in the girl he had met one heady day in a gondola, and not nearly enough in the one he would be married to for life.

For this reason, since Torcello, Persephone had studiously avoided being at home when Arthur came to call. Was this how aristocrats behaved? She wanted to talk to Kitty about it, but did not know how to frame her questions without seeming disloyal. Still, she tried.

"Have you talked to Arthur about how your life will be?" she asked quietly, while the costumier's presence was required elsewhere. "After you're married?"

Kitty gave her a confused smile. "I've read all the etiquette books. I think I know my duties."

"But I mean … when it's just the two of you."

"There's not much to discuss. Arthur will run his estates. I'll bring up the children. With a nanny's help, of course. And we'll have dogs. You must come and visit often. Are these feathers too excessive? I can't decide."

Persephone sensed Kitty hadn't thought about life after marriage much. Her answers were always affectionate but vague. She never mentioned love. The wedding itself was the pinnacle of her dreams and everything else was simply a matter of recreating the life her mother had made.

The costumes were gradually completed. Kitty would look spectacular as a seventeenth-century French princess in silver satin, with a high lace collar, a white wig sporting ostrich feathers two feet tall and a mask adorned with pearls.

Persephone gave up her typical medieval look in favour of a Columbine costume, ready-made. It was the simplest to wear and most common type to find. Columbine was a maid, the costumier explained in thickly accented English, and one of the characters from the *Commedia dell'arte,* which was the traditional Italian pantomime. These were the costumes generally used in *Carnevale.*

Kitty wanted her to choose something else, but Persephone liked the maid idea. She didn't regret her choice as she put on her costume the night of the party and admired herself in Kitty's mirror. Here she was, a real maid, become a muse, dressed as a carnival character in a familiar white apron and mysterious black mask. Truth and artifice intertwined. The dress was red, in cotton tiers, with satin shoes and a neat red jacket. The costume also included a white cotton ruff, which made her feel historical. Anyway, shouldn't a princess have a maid? As a couple, she felt she and Kitty worked well together.

Besides, she did not care too much about her looks tonight. She had one object: to avoid Arthur Malmesbury and get through the evening. That was all. There must be no more talk of emerald eyes.

Chapter Thirteen

Nico arranged for the Ballards to be transported from Palazzo Colleoni in two covered gondolas. Persephone found herself sitting with Kitty and Roly, watching the city float by through the slatted blinds. Despite the siblings' chatter, it was impossible not to remember travelling like this with the Harlequin. She pictured every look and word. The silence after they started to think about the *Venus of Urbino*...

"I say, this is dashed comfortable," Roly observed, drawing out a bottle of champagne from under his cloak. "I wish hansoms had so many cushions. Do you like my mask, Kitty?"

"Its nose is rather long."

"I'm a plague doctor, apparently. I keep forgetting I have this beak. I leaned in to say something to Mama as we left and nearly skewered her wig. Mind you, it will be excellent for a do in Sussex next month. Thank God we'll be back in time. Will you have a sip? I've brought glasses."

Persephone listened to them vaguely, watching golden light from a host of windows pool and fracture on the waves. They had turned off the Grand Canal and were floating down a narrow side street under low stone bridges. Ahead, a waterside palazzo was lit with burning braziers. A queue of gondolas jostled to find space to moor outside. The sound of Mozart was carried on the evening breeze.

Kitty grabbed Persephone's arm as they alighted from the boat and joined up with her parents.

"I'm so excited! Aren't you? I think I might die from it. Have you ever seen anything like it?"

In fact, Persephone had. The gaggle of costumed arrivals ahead of them reminded her of a party at Little Holland House in London, where everyone was dressed in 'Exotic Araby'. Kitty had not been allowed to go that night, but Roly had been there and had escorted Persephone around the rooms, dressed as a Nubian water carrier. She missed the rapport they had then, but friendship shows its true nature when it is tested.

She followed him inside now but was not disappointed when his dark cloaked figure disappeared ahead of them into the crowd.

The palazzo was ancient and unpredictable with several floors of rooms opening off a central courtyard. Costumed guests milled around on stairs and balconies. It was like being in a play. Their masks ranged from simple affairs that covered the eyes, like hers and Kitty's, to vast creations with bells and feathers. Swathes of silk enveloped some guests from head to toe. It was impossible to know who anyone was.

"How will I ever find Arthur?" Kitty complained, looking up at the balconies. "He could be any one of these tall men in cloaks and hats! Why didn't I think of that? We should have had a signal of some sort."

"Perhaps the anticipation and uncertainty is part of it," Persephone suggested. Despite her misgivings about the night she liked the thrill of mixing with so many revellers and not being sure who was who. Her pulse beat faster.

They soon lost track of the other Ballards as they ventured further inside. The noise in the grand salon was overwhelming. Glasses clinked. Chattering voices and loud laughter competed with the music from a band on a platform at one end, while shouts from the water outside filtered through the open windows.

"Shall we go on?" Kitty asked. She had to shout. "I can't see him anywhere."

Persephone nodded. They squeezed past women dressed as fairies in gold gauze and a thousand multicoloured silk flowers. Eyes peeped out of masks. Mouths grinned beneath them. Daring décolletages revealed soft, plump female flesh, glittering with bright jewels.

Behind the salon, a corridor gave way to an interior small courtyard, with a spiral staircase leading up several floors. It was lit with hundreds of candles in waxed paper bags, weighted with sand, which flickered from every windowsill and balustrade.

"Oh!" Kitty sighed. "How lovely!"

And suddenly, there he was, striding towards them down a narrow walkway. Persephone gasped. Kitty hadn't noticed him yet, but Persephone saw him instantly – Arthur was the Harlequin again. He was wearing the same chequered mask, this time with a tight-fitting jacket in red, white and green, and matching skintight breeches. They showed the slim outline of his body in stark detail. Persephone nudged Kitty, who frowned and stared as he stopped in front of her.

"My lady." He bowed, took Kitty's hand and kissed it.

"Ah!" she gasped. "I don't... Oh, *Arthur*! It's *you*!" She beamed, faltered for a moment, then grinned again. "You look wonderful. So colourful."

"I could never look as magnificent as you, my dear." He paused for a beat. "Persephone." He said her name in dutiful, clipped tones and bowed briefly. Persephone curtseyed back. What game was it tonight?

"But..." Kitty's smile had faltered again. "You are Harlequin, yes?"

"Yes indeed."

"Forgive me, wasn't he...?"

Arthur seemed relaxed. "...Persephone's mystery *beau*? Indeed. I thought I'd wear this costume in honour of that stranger. Indulge me, Persephone. He seemed like such a *fascinating* creature. And you never did find him again?"

Persephone shook her head in shame and discomfort. "No."

"He's quite the best character from the *Commedia dell'arte*. A servant, but a romantic hero. A bit of a devil sometimes. And did you know –" Arthur smiled, offering each of them an arm – "that Columbine is traditionally his companion?"

"Oh no!" Persephone groaned. "I had no idea."

"I love your serendipity. Yes, a Venetian maid. Although of course no maid could ever match the unattainable beauty of a princess. I assume that's what you are, Kitty, my dear. Either that or a courtesan."

"Arthur! *Really!*" Kitty blushed to her very core. "How you tease me!" She was shocked to be compared so casually to a woman of pleasure, but equally flattered by the princess reference.

Persephone saw how Arthur grinned at her reaction. *He's playing with her, like a cat with a mouse. And playing with me too – knowing there's nothing I can do about it.*

These were games, it seemed, that the future Duke of Bristol greatly enjoyed. He was in the best of humours as he guided his almost-future-bride and her not-quite-chaperone from room to room. Gradually masks came to be loosened or discarded. It became clearer who was who, and friends joined together in groups to talk and drink. Music came from the band in one room, a harpsichord in another and a string quartet in a third. Kitty was keen to dance and Arthur whisked her round the floor of the grand salon in lively polkas and mazurkas. She begged him to ask Persephone too and he did so, bowing with stiff politeness, but Persephone refused.

"I will not dance tonight. My costume won't permit it."

Not with you, she thought. *Not ever with you.*

Even so, the Harlequin was the most popular man in the room. Everyone wanted to talk to him and his pretty companions. But as the evening wore on he seemed increasingly distracted.

"Are you tired, dear Arthur?" Kitty asked.

"I never tire, my princess. That's something you should know about me."

Kitty looked wistful. "Would you like to go outside? Somewhere quieter?"

She wants to be alone with him! Persephone realized. She cursed herself for not thinking of it before. This party was the perfect moment for a kiss. Kitty surely must have imagined it.

"I'm thirsty. I must find water," Persephone muttered. Kitty smiled at her gratefully. Without looking back, she moved quickly through the crowded salon, as far away from them both as she could.

Wandering from room to room, she lost track of time. Various men approached and invited her to dance, but she refused them. She went back out to the little courtyard staircase where the air was cooler and looked up to the dark canopy of the starlit sky. By night and day, Venice took her breath away. If Felix were here, how would he paint it? What colours would he choose? She missed his presence with a sudden searing wave of intensity.

As she rested her head against a pillar, she heard footsteps approaching fast. There was a warm hand on her shoulder. She spun round and was astonished to find the Harlequin standing close behind her.

"Columbine?"

"Yes, what is it?" she said sharply.

"I need to talk to you."

"Where's Kitty?"

He gestured to the room where the dancing was at its merriest. "She has a list of partners."

"I thought you were going outside."

"We did but … we came in again."

He did not look like a man who had recently engaged in ardent kissing. Which meant Kitty hadn't either.

"Oh! I should go to her." Persephone headed for the nearest doorway.

"Don't," Arthur commanded, calling her back. "Her brother's there too. She's quite all right. Look, can we go somewhere quieter?" Behind the chequered mask his eyes were serious. "There's something I need to tell you."

"Something about Kitty?"

"No."

"Then I'm not interested."

"You will be, I promise."

And before she could think of a way to resist he had taken her hand and was leading her down the spiral steps, through a darkened passageway and on, further down, until they were in a boathouse at water level. Here the light from the outside braziers filtered dimly through the shutters and the air smelled of salty damp.

Oars and other equipment were stacked against the walls. The floor looked wet and muddy. Persephone paused before she reached the bottom step and hugged her arms around her to keep warm. The Columbine's thin red jacket was no match for the cold here. Arthur noticed and pulled a boatman's jacket off a hook on the wall. He put it around her shoulders, standing on the muddy step below, so their faces were almost level.

"W-what is it?" she asked. "Tell me quickly."

He glanced down. Without looking at her, he said, "It's not something I can just blurt out, I'm afraid. I need to do it justice."

"Then, please…"

He looked up at her but infuriatingly he started to talk in riddles. "You remind me of my Italian grandmother, you know. Fierce and stubborn. Beautiful and rare."

"I'm none of those things. Stubborn perhaps."

"Shh. You're all of them… And so different from everyone else." He was gazing straight up at her now. "I see Venice through new eyes with you. There's something unreal about this city. You feel it. I do."

"I'm sure many people do. Please, my lord, I'm cold."

"Oh, not 'my lord'! Honestly, Persephone. Call me Arthur. I want to hear it from your lips."

"No!" Her unease grew. They were alone, and nobody would look for them down here, and he was talking about her lips and who knew what might—

"Hey, hey! I'm not going to hurt you. I never would. I'm sorry." He reached out a hand to touch her face, just brushing her cheek. He was serious again and gentle.

She watched him guardedly. "I should go."

"You always say that, Persephone. Or you think it. You have no idea how it pains me, but I understand your reasons. You sense how I feel about you and you're loyal to Kitty to your fingertips."

So he *did* feel that way about her. Oh Hell and damnation. Now everything was spoiled.

"I am loyal," she hissed, taking a step up, away from him. "You should be too."

He calmly shrugged. "That kind of loyalty eludes me. But I value it in a woman. Will you kiss me?"

"Of course not! How could I possibly?"

"You wanted to in the gondola."

Had she wanted to kiss him then? Or had he just imagined it? "I didn't know you were practically engaged to my best friend!" she protested. "She's waiting for you upstairs. How can you even think to ask me?"

"Because I love you."

"No!"

Persephone gasped as he tore off his mask, threw it down and stared back at her, pleadingly. It was the last thing she had expected. But she had seen love in a man's eyes before, and she had to admit, it looked like this.

Did he want her to be his mistress?

"I adore you. You must have realized by now. The more I see you, the stronger it gets. I can't hold it back." His voice was low and passionate. His eyes burned into hers. No mask. No games. No embarrassment or shame. She was utterly confused.

"What… What about Kitty?"

"I saw her first, and you second," he said. "Believe me, if you had been in Russia, I wouldn't have looked at her. Must we talk of her?"

"Yes!"

He sighed. "Since you insist. I knew Kitty when I was just a boy and she made no impression on me. Later I heard tales of her in London, dashing around the city. I heard how she spent her evenings with artists and their models…" His lips curled in a smile. "How the old ladies disapproved. I loved her rakishness." He shrugged again. "But now I see that was all down to her brother. Without him she's a china doll."

"Don't say that!"

"Deny it."

"I do," Persephone said hotly, though a part of her was infuriated that there was something doll-like about

Kitty sometimes, porcelain-pure and vulnerable.

He caught the flash in her eyes and grinned. "See? You feel passion, even when you're lying. I mention the naked Venus and I see you sizzle under your cloak. You burn like stars in the night sky. Kitty's an attractive gas lamp."

"But…" Persephone struggled to ignore most of the things he was saying and focus on her friend. "If you think this way about her … you must tell her. You shouldn't marry a woman you don't admire."

"Don't be naïve. Besides, I don't intend to. I *want* to marry a woman I admire intensely. That's why I brought you here. I don't want Kitty. I want you."

The shock of the words hit Persephone like a blow. Not a mistress then. But surely he didn't mean…?

He stared up at her with compelling persuasion. "Can't you see?" he insisted. "We can make each other happy."

"I don't love you!"

"I don't care! You feel something for me, I know you do. I sensed it that first day. Our minds match. Our intellects keep meeting. You wouldn't depend on me, and that makes you so much better for me. I have interests in London and all over the family estates – I'm often away. I need a woman who'll have her own life and not mind."

"Not me," Persephone said, retreating up another stair. "You don't know anything about me."

He followed her. "I know enough. You created yourself, Persephone. Can you imagine how I esteem that? You have your artist friends, your world. I can give you everything you need to be one of them: houses, gardens, tours abroad, extravagantly simple dresses... Then when I come home, you can fascinate me with your conversation. You fascinate me just by looking at the sky. Can I kiss your eyes?"

"No!"

"Just your eyes, my darling!"

He was smiling, cajoling. His blank politeness had completely vanished and he glowed in the aqueous light.

He took her hands in his. "Look, I haven't made my case enough. Money. Land. Servants. I can protect you from the world forever. I know you've seen the gutter and actually so have I. It's no place to be. I don't play by convention. I'll make you my duchess and society will bow to you because I tell it to. I'll drip you with diamonds. Our children will rule lands we haven't yet discovered. I could tell this tale to any woman in England but I'm telling it to you. I want … you."

Persephone let out a sob. The extraordinary thing was that she was starting to believe him. He wasn't asking her for a night of passion. He had nothing to gain from a proposal. And yet he persisted. He stepped back to the bottom of the stairs and sank to one knee in the mud.

"Marry me."

Those words. Those impossible words. This could not be real!

"I d-don't… I can't…"

"You know I'm a fiend, and you're right." Arthur leaned forwards, raising the hem of her dress to kiss it. "But I mean it. Marry me."

She had never felt such emotion. She put the back of her hand to her lips. "Get up! Please!"

He did, dashing up the stairs until his face was close to hers again. He still bristled with uncrushable confidence. "I wanted to give you my grandmother's ring but it's in Suffolk, in the house where she died. If I send for it there will be questions. As soon as you say yes I will, though. Meanwhile, I thought emeralds, for your eyes…"

She looked up at him. What was he doing? In a moment, she felt his hands behind her neck, under her hair, his fingers moving, and something cold against the skin of her neck. Where had he hidden it, in his skintight outfit? She glanced down and caught a flash of green.

"Wear them," he said. "Think of me. Give me your answer soon."

Then he left, running fast up the stairs, and Persephone was too shocked to think or even breathe. She put a hand to her throat. Her fingers rubbed against one enormous stone and then another. There must be at least a dozen of them, each the size of a quail's egg. Her knees gave way and she put out her other arm to steady herself. Outside, she heard the steady *slap slap* of the flowing water, while the band above had struck up another dance tune. Unearthly lights flickered in the gloom. Finally, her head stopped spinning.

If I keep this, I could be a duchess. She held her fingers against the necklace. *And destroy my best friend.*

Then she staggered into a corner, to retch against the wall.

Chapter Fourteen

"Sephy? Sephy? You're miles away! What were you thinking?"

Kitty smiled. Persephone sat opposite her at the breakfast table but she hardly knew where she was. "I'm sorry."

"Wasn't it a lovely evening? The starlight was perfect. I almost thought that Arthur might propose. But I suppose…"

"Yes, I did too, dear," Catherine Ballard said, sitting down to join them with a plate of sausages and eggs from the sideboard. "But perhaps he needs to observe the niceties. The finest ranks of society must not be seen to rush."

"Exactly." Kitty sighed. "I suppose he's waiting until London. Even so…"

"Well he couldn't have been more delighted with you.

You looked enchanting. Didn't she, Frederick?"

"Erm, what? Ah. Oh yes. Enchanting. You really did, Kitty. Well done."

"Thank you, Papa. So did Sephy."

"Ah? Oh. Of course. Not quite so... But very..." He gestured to suggest spectacular versus ... not spectacular, but nevertheless acceptable. Persephone warmed as ever to Frederick Ballard's loyalty as a parent.

"That kind of loyalty eludes me. But I value it in a woman."

She remembered every word. Last night's conversation spun around in her head incessantly.

"We leave at midday, don't forget," said Mrs Ballard. "Make sure the servants pack everything you need for the journey. The rest will follow on. Oh, Samson and Delilah ... how happy they'll be to see us."

Samson and Delilah were her spaniels. This was a household where everyone was treasured, even the dogs. And Persephone had been invited to betray it to its core.

"You will have the blue room on the children's floor, near Kitty's," Mrs Ballard was saying. "Stay as long as you like – even after the wedding. I know Kitty's so grateful for your company."

"Thank you. Thank you so very much. Please excuse me."

She ran to her room and was sick in the commode, and cursed herself for hating the sound of Kitty's anxious voice at the door.

"I'm fine, honestly. I just had too much champagne last night."

"But you hardly drank any!"

"I did when you weren't looking." *Go away, Kitty.* Better to be her drunk friend than whatever Lord Malmesbury had made her.

The emeralds lay in a heap under Persephone's pillow. She went over and lifted the necklace to look at it again. It glowed green like some kind of enchanted reptile, or poison. She wrapped it in a silk scarf, and that in turn in brown paper and string. Best not to make it look too special. She wrote Arthur's name in full on the package, and *Hotel Danieli*, and entrusted the discrete and reliable Nico to deliver it. This was her answer.

Now ... what to tell Kitty?

How?

Where to start?

Kitty was in her room surrounded by two maids, a dozen bodices and skirts, several furs, and too many shoes to count. Her face lit up as soon as she saw Persephone.

"Sephy! Are you feeling better?"

"I think so. Thank you."

"How perfect. I need your help. What shall I travel in? Mama says I can only take two dresses but the trip is several days. I shall look like a beggarmaid."

"Can we talk?"

"Yes please. Which do you think? Wool is warmer but my velvet is much more comfortable."

"In private?"

Kitty looked around, confused. "But we are."

Persephone indicated the maids with a flick of her eyes and Kitty laughed. "They're only Italian. They don't understand a word."

Persephone knew this wasn't true. Having been a maid herself, she well understood that servants listen to everything and learn fast. Also, that it pays for them to pretend they don't.

"Please? Can I show you something in the library?"

Kitty sighed and followed her out. "I haven't got much time, you know."

It was hard to know where to begin, and harder still to make Kitty sit and listen, but once they were finally settled on two little throne-like chairs in the library, Persephone took a deep breath.

"How did you think that Arthur ... was ... last night?"

She heard her voice shake, and hoped that Kitty didn't guess everything instantly, so she had a chance to explain.

"He seemed quite well to me." Kitty's polite frown was both heartbreaking and infuriating. She didn't have a clue.

"Did you know...? I heard..." Persephone hadn't decided exactly how she would say this but forged ahead anyway. "I heard ... rumours of him ... with another woman."

For a moment, Kitty's eyes flew wide. She clasped her hands in front of her. Then she cocked her head to one side and gave Persephone a sad little smile, placing a small pale hand on her sleeve. "Last night? Oh, Persephone! You mustn't believe such things! Do you know, someone said the same thing to me in St Petersburg? It was all a terrible mistake. Arthur introduced me to the woman in question – she was his cousin! He's related to half the families in Europe. What did you hear?"

Persephone faltered. She was not surprised to hear there had been a 'cousin' in St Petersburg. A man like Arthur probably had half a dozen 'cousins'. What she had to tell Kitty was worse. She wished she had prepared more carefully. "I... Nothing ... in particular."

"You didn't see him with anyone yourself, did you? He was with me most of the time, except when he had to take an urgent message from London."

So that had been his excuse?

"N-no."

"People can be so cruel. It will happen in London too, I warn you. Half the young ladies there want him. They'll say anything." There was a sudden new set to Kitty's jaw. Her eyes turned a slightly icier shade of blue. "But I won't let them break us up, don't worry." She squeezed Persephone's arm.

This was Persephone's moment and she missed it. The only way to go on was to admit everything that Arthur had said and done. What would that do to Kitty? There was no way to say it that would not pierce her best friend's heart. She tried and tried to find the words but they would not come.

❦

Frederick Ballard had organized the travelling arrangements. For some reason that his wife did not fully understand they seemed to involve him and Roly going on from Milan by mail coach, which was more comfortable and faster (and quieter, Persephone reflected), while she travelled along behind in a diligence with the girls.

Persephone did not, for a moment, stop thinking about Kitty's predicament. The worst of it was that the poor girl had absolutely no idea what was at risk. Persephone wondered if Arthur would break off their understanding. If so, would he do it kindly? Or would he marry Kitty and keep a mistress? She knew aristocrats did that, but could Kitty – *her* Kitty – bear it? She wanted to forget the whole sorry business for a while.

But Mrs Ballard did not make it easy.

"Kitty, my dear," she said as soon as they were settled in the diligence on their way to France, "I've been thinking about bridesmaids. Your cousin Emily—"

"Too soon, Mama!" Kitty chided.

"Not at all." Mrs Ballard paused to cough. She had caught a cold somewhere between Venice and Milan. "We might as well decide. Emily will certainly want to walk behind you, but she is nearing eight-and-twenty and will look ridiculous in orange blossom and white satin. We need an excuse not to have her."

"Not now, Mama. Really!"

"Then when? It's not my fault Emily remains so obstinately single. However, if you have Maria, assuming she's not married herself by then, and Bee and Uncle Patrick's girls, we can keep it to eight: four big, four small. That's enough, don't you think? And we can tell Emily we are sorry, but there simply isn't the space."

"Yes, Mama."

"And…" Mrs Ballard's eyes flicked uncertainly towards Persephone. "Of course…" She sneezed to hide her embarrassment.

Persephone found this whole conversation Purgatory but didn't know how to make it stop. The last thing she wanted was to feature in it. "Don't worry about me," she said keenly.

Mrs Ballard smiled and took Persephone's hand. "You're so kind. I know you will be a great help to Kitty in your way. Now, Kitty, your trousseau…"

And so it went on. Left to her own devices, Persephone stared out of the window at the snowcapped mountains in the distance and thought back to the chill of the cold stones around her neck.

Oh, Arthur was a fiend! He admitted it. Why couldn't he love Kitty? She was the wife that any self-respecting aristocrat should aspire to. She would be an ornament to the Court. The Queen would surely adore her.

Whereas if he married me, it would be a scandal.

For a moment, Persephone saw it vividly. The shocked looks. The gossip behind gloved hands.

An artists' model! Wasn't she Rupert Thornton's mistress…?

It wasn't true, but Arthur wouldn't have cared. She couldn't help admiring his rebel spirit.

What would her life with him have been? she wondered. Very different from the one Kitty dreamed of certainly. When Persephone was busy refusing him she hadn't had time to reflect on his offer, or wanted to. Now, with little else to occupy her mind, she couldn't help it. He *had* proposed. For a brief moment she had held her future in her hands.

Mary Adams, the basket weaver's daughter from Westbrook, a duchess. Think of it. Of course, it would entail being married to a man like Arthur. But though he might be a faithless wretch, he was not all superficial charm. She remembered the depths of his emotion as he had stood looking at the mosaic in Torcello. He could have taken her to Florence, taught her the Italian words for river and sea and sunset. What *was* the Italian for sunset, she wondered? Or art?

"You burn like the stars in the night sky."

"Persephone? Sephy? Are you all right?"

"Ah? Oh yes, Kitty. Perfectly, thank you."

"You looked distracted."

"No, no."

"Would you like a humbug?"

Persephone took the sweet from the paper twist her friend was kindly proffering and felt thoroughly vile. The vision turned to ashes. The fact was Arthur *was* a faithless wretch. Kitty's happiness was at stake. And she had no idea what she was going to do about it.

PART II

THE RED ROOM

Chapter Fifteen

"And this, dearest Persephone, will be your bedroom. Call for anything you want. *Achoo!* Excuse me. That dreadful journey has poxed me. But now we are in London, I'll be better in an hour."

"Thank you so much, Catherine."

As Persephone stood admiring her new quarters, Mrs Ballard's oblivious generosity made her think back to that mosaic in Torcello, and the special place in Hell reserved for girls like her.

The bedroom was large and square, with tall Georgian windows and wooden panelling on the walls, painted duck-egg blue. The silk hangings on the four-poster bed were embroidered with sea-green fronds and the pillows were edged with creamy lace. It was like living underwater, she thought, which was appropriate after Venice.

Kitty sat on the bed and picked at the bedcover. "Do you like it?" she asked. "Despite that horrid wardrobe and the ancient chair. Will it do?"

"At least the walls aren't stained, I suppose," Persephone said, unable to resist a sidelong glance at her friend. Kitty stared at her aghast. "I'm teasing you, Kitty, honestly!" she relented. "I love it. Change nothing, please."

Even the dogs came to say hello. While they sniffed around, Kitty's maid Winnie stood at the door and bobbed a curtsey, promising to help with anything 'Miss Persephone' wanted. Winnie was one of the few people who knew Persephone's true story. They had first met when Persephone visited Balfour House with Kitty while she was still working as a maid. She wondered if the girl would secretly judge her for getting so far above her station, but Winnie grinned and gave her a heavy wink from the doorway. Persephone smiled shyly in return and assured her she had everything she needed, and more.

⚜

Kitty's first thought was to see her two best friends in London, and made plans to visit them that afternoon. The first, Maria Hope, lived in a large old house on

Portman Square that was even more richly decorated than Balfour House and boasted an onyx balustrade leading up to the ballroom, for which it was quite famous, Kitty said.

Maria was small, with dark intelligent eyes. She rushed over to Kitty as soon as they both entered the gilt-edged drawing room where she was waiting.

"I can't believe I haven't seen you since September! You were cruel to deprive me of your company for so long. Cruel, Kitty, I tell you! But don't you look pretty? It must be love!"

Kitty introduced Persephone to Maria, who curtseyed politely.

"Miss Lavelle."

"Call me Persephone, please."

"I've heard so much about you." Maria gave her a cool, appraising glance. "You look ... artistic."

"Thank you." Persephone sensed it wasn't a compliment.

Maria had recently become engaged to the son of a surgeon, Samuel Muller. She showed Kitty a photograph in which they sat side by side, his hand resting gently on her knee.

"He looks so in love!" Kitty cooed. And it was true, he did.

"Oh, you know Samuel…" Maria sighed, putting the frame back beside a host of others on a table. "But tell me about the delectable Arthur Malmesbury. I gather you've been spending lots of time with him."

Kitty blushed. "He's very thoughtful, isn't he, Persephone? Very generous to us both."

Persephone agreed and willed her neck not to give her away. That was her only contribution to the conversation, however. The two old friends had a lot to catch up on after so much time apart and talked without stopping for an hour.

The second girl they visited was Beatrice Clairmont, known as Bee, who lived the other side of Hyde Park in one of the mansions Mr Ballard was constructing on the Kensington estate. Bee was tall and extremely slender – most unfortunately for a girl of nineteen. She towered above the other girls and had little to fill out the bosom of her bodice. But her graceful face was almost as pretty as Kitty's. She too longed to hear all Kitty's adventures in Italy and Russia, and they sat for ninety minutes without pausing for breath.

"Sephy's been such a joy to me," Kitty gushed, keen to bring Persephone into the conversation. "You have no idea how much fun we had in Venice. She makes everything more interesting. And now we're all together. I'm sure you'll be such good friends."

I'm sure we won't, Persephone thought.

Bee's reaction to her was much like Maria's had been. Their narrowed eyes and fake smiles made their feelings towards her obvious. They did not share Kitty's innocent enthusiasm for her mysterious new friend. They did not trust her. And she did not like them. The unspoken feelings were instant, mutual and powerful.

"Wasn't that *wonderful*?" Kitty said in the carriage home. "I felt as though I hadn't seen Bee for a year. How perfect that she can visit us tomorrow. I'd swear she's grown, poor thing. Did you not love the house? Her mother has decorated it with such style. I must tell Mama they have added a conservatory…"

Persephone smiled politely as she chatted on. Outside the window, London passed by. The city already posed its dangers for her, and she had just found two more reasons to be anxious about surviving in it.

The following morning, Winnie caught her after breakfast. She looked a little flushed and smiled complicitly.

"Excuse me, Miss Persephone, there's a young man as wants to see you. He's waiting round the back."

"Who?"

"His name is Eddie. Says you'd know who he was."

"Where is he?"

"In the mews, miss. Anyone can show you."

Persephone was amused by the effect Eddie could have on a girl. Grabbing her bonnet and shawl on the way out, she followed directions to the mews behind Balfour House, where the family kept their horses. It was hard not to break into a run when she saw Eddie's friendly face.

"Mary Adams! Aren't you the lady?"

He swept his cap low to the ground in the ironic courtly bow he reserved for her.

"And you're quite the gentleman!" she answered. Though in truth he was reassuringly unchanged: still dressed with the swagger of the street fighter and, if anything, more frayed and bruised.

"I'm no gentleman. Quite the opposite. In fact, I've come to ask a favour."

"How did you even find me? How did you know I was back?"

"If it's news, I hear it. The Ballards coming home to Balfour House is news. Look at you now! Next week, I swear you'll be a duchess."

Persephone flushed deeply. This was too near the mark. "I won't," she promised. "What was the favour?"

"Did you miss me? Swear you did."

"To be honest, I hardly thought of you at all."

"I don't believe it. Surrounded by dull Italian lads, with not an Irishman in sight..."

"You'd be surprised who you'd find in Venice. Anyway – what was the favour, for the second time?"

He struck a pose, tipping his cap off-kilter with his right hand and looking at her from under the brim. "Work, to put it plain and simple. Work with horses, if it's possible. You know people who know people. I have debts."

"New ones?" Persephone asked. Eddie had debts the day she met him.

"New and old. They tend to mingle."

She felt sorry for him. Eddie moved in circles where 'you didn't want to owe people money' according to his sister.

"What do you want me to ask?"

"If anyone needs a stable lad. Temporary will do. Hard worker. Happy to befriend a pretty girl, if there's one that likes me, and take up a bedroom in the house..."

"Eddie!"

"Well, *you* did."

"That's different! But I'll see what I can do about the horses. Not here – I owe the Ballards too much already. But they may know a family that needs someone."

"They'd be getting a bargain. I do other work too – whatever's going. But horses are best. I grew up on a horse's back."

"I'll ask, I promise."

"Tell me tomorrow? Same time, same place?"

"You're a hard taskmaster, Mr O'Bryan!" She laughed, agreeing she'd do what she could.

It was only later that she wondered how hard it had been for a proud boy like Eddie to make such a request.

Times must be tough. But he'd carried it off with his usual style. And it was so very good to see him again.

⁘⌘ ⌘⁘

That night, dinner at the Ballards' table included Kitty's Great Aunt Violet, who lived on the top floor of the house and spent most of her life sewing samplers, and also the Clairmonts. This was not ideal. Bee had already given Persephone several haughty looks. But it was Persephone's only chance to talk to Frederick Ballard, who might be able to help with Eddie. She summoned up her courage between courses.

"I know of a young man…" she began, to sudden silence. She had forgotten that Persephone Lavelle's typical friends were artists – notorious and fascinating to the property developer and his family. Everyone turned to look at her and she coughed. "An old friend, a hardworking boy. He's looking for work with horses."

"With horses, my dear? To ride? Is he a jockey?" Mr Ballard asked.

"No. Not that. As a … a stable lad, I suppose."

Bee tittered. "Oh my *dear*, how exotic!"

"Not at all," Persephone mumbled.

175

Mr Ballard frowned, but Kitty leaned forwards eagerly. "Oh, Papa, weren't you saying only yesterday there was a problem with one of the grooms? I'm sure we could find him something."

"No!" Persephone cried out, "I didn't mean—"

"You might be right, Kitcat," her father agreed. "Some issue with a broken collarbone. I'll ask tomorrow."

"I—" She was too stunned by his instant generosity to say much. "Thank you."

Bee and her mother stared from her to Mr Ballard and back again.

"How charming," Mrs Clairmont said with a smile. "Aren't you *lucky*, Persephone? Your every whim satisfied by your hosts."

"I didn't want—"

"And Kitty... Now you will have another friend. A stable lad!"

"Did she say *stable lad*?" Aunt Violet queried tremulously. "A friend for Kitty?"

Kitty briefly caught Persephone's eye before staring at her plate, cheeks glowing. She loved to live her friend's life vicariously, but of course she wouldn't be consorting with the servants, and Persephone didn't want or expect her to.

Kitty didn't deserve Mrs Clairmont's sarcastic asides. She was too good for this tight-knit social circle. *Much* too good for men who had the gall to propose to other women. As so often, Persephone's thoughts turned to Arthur. He must be back in London soon. What would happen then?

Chapter Sixteen

Eddie O'Bryan was hired by Frederick Ballard the following week, with the minimum of fuss and the maximum kindness towards Persephone. His extravagant hospitality towards her made her feel that she was sinking into an ever-lower circle of Hell, but she couldn't help but be glad for Eddie. The gratitude in his eyes when she told him the news was palpable, though naturally he didn't admit as much.

She met him briefly at the gateway to the stables on a bright Monday morning, while he showed himself off in his new livery.

"The Ballards are lucky. So are their nags. I've a way with them."

"Oh, have you now?"

"You'll see," he said with a wink. "That black one there? The Friesian? There's speed in his eyes. The others don't know it yet, but I'll find it."

"I hope you do."

Why did young men always have to be so conceited? she wondered. Nevertheless, she hoped that his confidence was justified. It would be good if at least one of them could do right by this family.

That evening a messenger arrived to say that Lord Malmesbury had been held up by pressing diplomatic business in Milan, but would be arriving in two days' time. Once he had paid a visit to his mother, he would be honoured to call at Balfour House on Wednesday afternoon.

So he was coming at last.

Persephone wondered what on earth he had to say to Kitty. Would he rupture their understanding or would he make an official proposal now his first, secret one had been refused? She sensed he would not discuss his behaviour the night of the party – it did not cast him in a good light. But there was nothing she could do about it if he did.

The thought of it made her so nervous that she was determined not to be there when he came, though she would of course come back to comfort or celebrate with

Kitty afterwards. If she were being totally honest with herself, she was a little afraid of how he might treat her after the return of the emeralds. A man as powerful as Arthur Malmesbury would be a dangerous enemy. She prayed that she would never need to see him again.

⸙⸙

As Persephone half expected, Kitty was caught up in a crisis of hair and wardrobe after lunch on Wednesday. Persephone made an excuse when Kitty wasn't really listening. An old friend … an engagement to meet… She left the house in a hurry while Kitty was still at her mirror, keen to stay out as long as possible.

She decided to visit Effie. The Millais' house in Cromwell Place was one of the few places she was unlikely to run into Rupert and if Felix was there Effie would warn her.

He wasn't. John was in the middle of a painting and could not be disturbed, but Effie was thrilled to see her. They spent a happy hour discussing the relative merits of various palazzi on the Grand Canal, until the nursemaid arrived with a grizzling baby and Effie's attention was required elsewhere.

Outside, Persephone consulted her pocket watch and bit her lip. It was much too soon to return to Balfour House but she suddenly remembered the South Kensington Museum. She had visited it a few times when Rupert had been busy with his studies or his father. It was a new-built palace of wonders, crammed with architectural models, strange inventions and beautiful objects from around the world.

She spent a happy couple of hours admiring the exhibits there and wishing she had brought her sketchbook to copy some of them. She was rather jealous when she saw a young man draw just such a book out of his satchel. Persephone let him begin, then went to look over his shoulder to see what he was drawing. It was the copy of Michelangelo's statue of David, and it was very good. He turned round, aware of her presence behind him, and glared slightly.

"Oh!" she cried out, seeing his face for the first time. "Mr Whistler!"

It was the artist she'd met in Venice. How extraordinary! He wore the same unusual, low wide hat. His slightly drooping moustache was as elegant as ever. His sharp eyes gleamed.

"Miss Lavelle! I didn't recognize you without your hair!"

Persephone's hand flew to her bare neck. Kitty had insisted on playing with her hair that morning and had woven it into fashionable coils.

"I assure you, it's still there."

He grinned. "I'm glad."

"I still have your painting of La Salute."

"I'm glad about that too." There was a short pause. "And do you remember our deal?"

She thought for a moment. "Oh yes. You were to draw me, if ever I went to Paris."

"Spot on. But I fell sick and now I'm visiting my sister in London. Can I change the deal a little? May I draw you here?"

"I'm sorry you're not well," Persephone said.

"It's nothing drastic. My sister's cook is as good as any medicine."

"I'm pleased to hear it. And of course you can draw me. I'd be honoured."

He held out his hand for her to shake. "Excellent. There's a place near the river where I like to walk, if the weather's warm enough. Would that suit you?"

It would suit her perfectly. In fact, it was the most agreeable thing Persephone could possibly have hoped for. Whistler offered to pay, and the money she made would go towards making her independent of Frederick Ballard's charity. She gave him her address and he promised to send for her in a day or two.

After saying goodbye to him she positively danced down the road to the omnibus stand. Work! A little money of her own! And time spent with an artist, which was her favourite way to spend it.

But her high spirits dissipated as she neared Balfour House. Lord Malmesbury must have been and gone by now. What had been said?

Kitty rushed up to her in the hall before she had even removed her bonnet.

"Oh, Sephy! You missed him!"

"Oh dear," Persephone said blandly, scanning Kitty's face for signs of joy or distress.

"And by minutes. What a shame!"

"I'm sure you managed perfectly well without me."

"Not at all. I don't know what happened exactly but

it was a disaster!" Kitty said. "I was so looking forward to seeing him after so long, but he spent half the time nodding to Aunt Violet and the other half looking at the clock. He was bored, I know it."

Persephone was stunned. *Bored?*

"I wish you'd been there," Kitty complained. "I blame Aunt Violet."

"Why?"

"She kept asking him to repeat everything he said. After ten minutes in her company he started glancing at the door."

Oh, Kitty! Persephone thought, remembering his description. *"An attractive gas lamp."* It was not sweet Aunt Violet who bored him.

It occurred to her that Arthur simply did not have the courage to end what he had started. This surprised her. He was many things, most of them not good, but he had never struck her as fainthearted.

Kitty watched as she took off her shawl. "He's coming back on Friday. He asked after you, you know, and remarked quite sharply on your absence. You simply must be there next time, Sephy, I insist on it. It's always more fun with you."

As they headed upstairs, Persephone's mind was whirring. Arthur had asked after her? Why? And why had he come at all if he had nothing to say? The thought of Friday's visit terrified her. She couldn't bear the thought of them all sitting there in awkward silence. Did he want to punish her?

"What did you talk about today?" she asked Kitty.

"Practically nothing. I asked after his mother's health, which is apparently good. I hardly remember what else. Like I told you, Sephy – Aunt Violet spoiled everything."

They reached Kitty's bedroom, which was still stacked with dolls and childhood toys, now mingled with boxes for her jewels and displays of souvenirs. Persephone was thinking hard.

"We need a plan," she said, heading for the window seat. "What would you *like* to talk about?"

Kitty hesitated. Her face made it entirely obvious. *The wedding.* Persephone groaned inwardly on her behalf. This visit would be a nightmare.

As Kitty sat at her mirror, Persephone looked out towards the square beyond, remembering all her passionate discussions with Felix about colour and light, their mutual love of poetry, the sense that they would never run out of things to share and say. What sort of marriage was Kitty letting herself in for if she could not talk to her husband? What sort of husband would he be if he did not talk to her? Her guilt made Persephone want Kitty to shine more than ever.

"I'll think of something," she promised.

"Oh, *thank* you." Kitty sighed. "I know you will."

James Whistler sent Persephone a message asking to see her the following day. They met at a spot on Cheyne Walk, not far from Cremorne Gardens where she had gone with Felix and Kitty in the first heady days of knowing them both. She still thought of the place fondly.

Nearby was a coffee shop where men smoked cigars and played chess, and entertained women of uncertain virtue. Whistler asked her nervously if she minded going in. She didn't. It was warm and merry. She loved the smell of the cigar smoke, and the coffee, though not good, was drinkable. People stared at her, certainly – they usually did, because of her hair – but they were soon distracted by their own affairs. At times like this,

Persephone loved the freedom that being an artists' model gave her.

As they drank and talked, Whistler took a little notebook from his pocket and made quick character sketches of some of the people at nearby tables. He instantly captured the man with the bushy beard and the woman with the heavy eyebrows and extravagant hat.

"Where did you learn to draw like that?" she asked, looking over his shoulder.

"All over. I started in Russia, I guess."

"*You* were in Russia?"

"My father was an engineer back home. He went to build railways for the Tsar. I had a good tutor in St Petersburg but I learned the best stuff in Paris. *All* the best things are in Paris. If you go to the Louvre, it's full of Rembrandts. I sit and copy them. You pick up a lot of tricks that way."

Afterwards, they found a place for her to sit outside, on a bench overlooking the new park at Battersea, across the river. He drew her there for an hour and when he was finished they sat and sketched together – a nearby bridge, working barges on the water, a boatman repairing a sail.

Whistler was brilliant at capturing a scene or mood. He played with light and shade in ways she hadn't seen before. Felix had been all about drama. Whistler was the opposite of showy, but he made the paper glow. Somehow, at his touch, the working world in front of him became just as vivid as the legendary scenes she was familiar with.

It had never occurred to her before that a boatman – or an ordinary girl, simply sitting on a bench – might be a worthy subject for a picture. She had thought you had to be a character from Shakespeare or an ancient goddess to merit such attention. Now she realized that a great artist could make you look at anything. Look and see it differently. She wished she could stay longer to watch him at work, but it was getting dark and she reluctantly went home.

Chapter Seventeen

Friday morning dawned foggy, but inside Balfour House the gas lamps burned bright. The morning was spent with Bee and Maria, who made their feelings plain about being excluded from Arthur's second visit.

"I wonder if we shall ever get to meet him," Maria sighed pointedly.

Kitty laughed. "He has been in England less than a week! You'll meet him soon, I promise. He asked after Sephy particularly because he knows her."

At this Bee arched an eyebrow at Persephone with such a look of open suspicion and disdain that Persephone felt herself go cold.

"I wish you could be there too," she said sincerely. Much though she disliked them both, the more people that came between her and Lord Malmesbury the better.

After lunch, while Kitty changed into her spectacular cobalt-blue satin, Persephone spent time picking out her most unappealing dress. She put on a pale linen design that, without its jacket, made her resemble a large Regent potato. She then let Kitty put up her hair again, knowing Arthur liked it long, and resisted her friend's attempts to grease her lips or eyelashes. She wanted to fade into the background as much as she could.

Arthur arrived at three. A footman showed him into the winter parlour where Kitty was waiting with Persephone, her mother and the dogs. Persephone felt her heart palpitate.

"Lord Malmesbury, madam."

He came in, smiled at each of them in turn, and bowed. Today he wore a tight-waisted morning coat and low-cut violet waistcoat that hugged his body and showed off his physique. His shirt studs were pearls surrounded by tiny diamonds.

"My dear hostess, how charming you look," he said. "That orange suits you."

Mrs Ballard blushed and giggled. "Come, Samson. Delilah. Let us leave these young people in peace." As she swept out of the room with the dogs at her feet, Persephone glanced across at the visitor. He was watching her unblinkingly. She could not read him yet.

"Come and sit here, Arthur," Kitty pleaded, patting the chair next to the one she'd chosen. "Aren't you pleased to see Sephy again? We'll have so much more to talk about today."

As Kitty looked down to arrange her skirts, Arthur's gaze at Persephone flickered for an instant. She braced herself for a glimpse of hatred or bitter disappointment – but his eyes were dancing again. Nothing had changed!

She felt unbalanced and quickly sat down herself. It was not Kitty he had called on. This was wrong. So very wrong.

Kitty, however, was oblivious. At Persephone's suggestion they had rehearsed that she would talk about her travels and, after a quick nervous glance at her friend, she played her part eagerly. She opened the conversation like an actress in a play. "I was thinking only yesterday, Arthur, how much I miss the shops of Venice. Don't you? Particularly the ones that sold the Murano pieces. We must have bought a hundred presents there."

Persephone's heart sank. *Not the shops, Kitty. Anything but shopping.* Arthur sat up straighter for a moment with the briefest flicker of surprise. He too glanced at Persephone, sensing her part in this. Then the mask descended.

"The shops? Dear Kitty, I don't know how we live without them. Do you remember that one down Calle dei Fabbri that sold the leather-bound diaries? Near where you bought your headdress? I long to go back and spend more time there…"

It was an act, and it was brilliant. Persephone sensed he was doing it for her benefit: *if you choose this game, then I shall play it.* For a full hour, he talked vivaciously about everything they had bought together, remembering details of an afternoon searching for hairpins that even Kitty had forgotten. Persephone saw how dazzling he must be as a diplomat – leaping into the other person's skin, understanding their passions, reflecting them.

Is that what he did to me in the boathouse? she wondered. But she didn't think so. This was a performance. Back then, alone with her and unmasked, he had been himself.

Sitting beside him in the parlour, Kitty was quite taken in, and more enchanted than ever. The new flow in conversation even gave her the confidence to ask a question they hadn't rehearsed at all.

"Um, Arthur?"

"Yes?"

"I know Mama has mentioned it, but she didn't fully understand your answer. Now we're in England, nothing holds us back, does it, from announcing…? I know you haven't formally…"

Arthur stiffened. Persephone felt her whole body tense too. She silently begged Kitty to stop.

But after a brief moment's thought he nodded. "You're right. When a man falls in love, he should tell the world. I have some family business to attend to. I'll be back in a fortnight." He paused to think. "Shall we announce it then?"

He smiled blandly. As he turned his head, the smile took in Persephone, sitting silently nearby, and she paled.

But Kitty was delighted. "Oh, Arthur! May I tell Mama?"

"Of course. I'm sure she'll be the soul of discretion."

"I doubt that." Kitty bit her lip. "You know Mama."

Arthur's smile widened. Kitty took it as fondness for her mother's foibles and grinned back gratefully. But Persephone's skin pricked with alarm. It was obvious that Catherine Ballard could never keep the secret of an engagement – it would be across London in an hour. She sensed he was playing games again. People might get hurt and he didn't care.

After he left, Kitty ran to find her mother. Persephone was desperate to get back to her room to sit alone and think, but on her way upstairs she was waylaid by one of the footmen.

"Excuse me, miss. You're wanted."

"Oh yes? Where?"

He lowered his voice. "Out the back, miss. In the stables." Persephone frowned. It had to be Eddie. But she couldn't just run to him every time he felt like conversation. The footman seemed to sense her hesitation. "If you please, miss…"

There was something in his eye. A warning. She thanked him, found her bonnet and shawl and went outside.

❧⁓⁓⁓❧

Two minutes later she walked through the gate of the mews. A groom looked up when he saw her and nodded towards a row of stalls at the far end of the cobbles, through the fog. Persephone felt a tingle of fear run up her spine. Ahead of her, the low building was nearly dark. She approached it with rising dread.

Getting closer, she made out Eddie in riding breeches, a pale figure in the mist, standing stiffly in front of an empty stall. He looked uneasy.

"Eddie? What do you need?"

He shrugged. "I'm just the lookout. You'd better come in."

"Eddie?"

But as soon as she reached the stall gate, another figure stepped out of the shadows. She gave a small shriek of surprise.

"Shh! Aren't you pleased to see me again so soon?"

Arthur wore a dark cloak, top hat and a darker smile. How different from his appearance in the parlour. In the gloom he looked like a phantom from a ghost story.

"M-my lord!"

"Arthur, please. Or Harlequin."

"I… I don't—"

"You thought you'd got rid of me in Venice but I'm like your friend here, Mister O'Bryan. He'll go fifty rounds without conceding. And may I say what an unexpected pleasure it is to see him. The finest boxer in London, and the most underrated. You know some interesting people, Persephone."

"What do you want?"

Arthur didn't answer her straight away. "Eddie, I think this is a private matter. Get out, there's a good boy." He extended a gloved hand to Eddie, and she realized there was money in it.

Eddie took the half crown with the emotionless face of the servant who finds distaste in his master's bidding. He flashed Persephone a questioning glance and walked into the yard.

As soon as they were alone, Arthur's slow, lazy smile lit up his face, as if no time had passed since he'd fastened the emeralds around her neck. She stared at him.

"You seem surprised," he said conversationally. "Don't be. I entirely forgive you for returning the necklace. But it's yours, whenever you want it. My proposal still stands. I trust you've had enough time to consider it."

She tried to breathe, to tell him no, and found she couldn't. The shock of seeing him here, his sheer audacity in mentioning the emeralds after what he'd just said to Kitty, his ... *enjoyment* of the chaos he was causing… It was all too much.

"Take a moment." He smiled. "I'll wait."

"But just now you said…"

"That when a man falls in love he should tell the world. And I think I should, don't you?"

There was silence as his meaning sunk in.

"It's the wickedest thing I've ever heard." Her voice was a whisper.

"Why?"

"Because of Kitty!"

"How can you say that?" He seemed genuinely surprised. "You must see how well it works for all of us. I get to live with the woman I want. Poor Kitty isn't saddled with a man who finds her dull. And you become my duchess."

"I won't betray her."

"Shh. Stop thinking about Kitty. I'm sure the gas lamp will find a perfectly respectable young wag to love her."

"I…"

"You haven't imagined it fully yet," he insisted urgently, coming closer. "Not the way I do, every night." He took her firmly in his arms – holding her hard enough to stop her breaking free, but not enough to hurt her. His eyes looked relentlessly into hers. "I love you. I mean it. Nobody sees you as I do. A thousand men want you, yet my spies tell me you are purer than you seem."

Persephone shot him a look of disgust. "I didn't save myself for you."

"But you want me, admit it."

"I don't," she assured him, trying to escape his embrace.

"Well, you will. Most girls do, I find. You heard what I told Kitty: two weeks, until I come back. Then we can put her out of her misery."

She stared at him, trembling. "And if I say no?"

He let go of her and shrugged. "Then I'll love you from afar, like Actaeon and Artemis."

"Actaeon was torn apart by dogs," she noted grimly.

He grinned in acknowledgement. "Well, yes, but he did get to see Artemis in all her glory first. It was worth it, surely?"

Persephone sensed she was getting distracted. "What happens to Kitty?"

"If I'm not devoured by my hunting hounds?" He seemed to consider it for a moment. "Then I'll make an honest woman of her. Why not? She's better than most of the girls I've seen so far. She adores me."

"You can't do that! You don't want her!"

His eyes hardened slightly. "Don't tell me what I can and can't do. That would be unwise." He put a finger to her lips. She felt the gentle pressure of his skin against hers. "Think about it. I've given you two weeks. That takes us to the nineteenth of March. I'll come to you in private the night before."

"I won't let you hurt her," she hissed defiantly.

He smiled. "Then say yes." He lifted his hand to stroke her hair. "Don't forget – Kitty's happiness depends on this too. You know what an estimable girl she is. She deserves better than a wretch like me. But you can save me."

He dropped his head, gave her a sudden, deep kiss on the lower lip and stood back to look at her. Persephone flushed. Her skin stung. She was speechless.

He smiled. "I'm depending on you."

He bowed and faded into the shadows. When she looked round, he had disappeared from the stall completely. Persephone didn't move. She stayed in the semi-darkness, hugging herself and shaking.

Nobody could save Arthur Malmesbury. Treachery was in his blood. She could still feel the burning where he had kissed her.

"You need to be careful with that one."

"Uh?" Persephone jumped at the sudden sound. Eddie stood framed against the light. She sensed from his knowing look that he had heard everything. "You were supposed to go away," she glowered. She wrapped her arms tighter around her body.

He shrugged. "I don't always do what people tell me. There's things you should know about him."

"I know enough."

Eddie shook his head. "Hardly. Look, I can't talk now. Meet me in The Lamb after dinner. Ten o'clock should do it. Say you've got a headache."

"Eddie! Keep out of this. And don't order me around!"

"I'm not. I'm just trying to warn you."

Boots and horses' hooves echoed on the cobblestones outside. A carriage was being called for. By Roly, probably, who was back from visiting his mistress.

"I don't need a warning," she said.

Eddie came closer. "You do," he insisted. It made her shiver again.

"Oi! O'Bryan! Come and help here!"

Eddie turned to answer the call and Persephone slipped away while the men were busy with the horses.

I'm no good with Eddie and secrets, she reflected. He was always the first to discover hers. But what could he possibly have to tell her about Arthur that she didn't already know?

Chapter Eighteen

Within an hour the whole of Balfour House knew about Lord Malmesbury's 'proposal'. Even the servants smiled. Persephone caught Kitty as soon as she could and dragged her into a quiet corner.

"You did tell your mother exactly what he said? That the announcement wasn't to be for a fortnight?"

"Of course I did." Kitty beamed. "She understands. But everyone knows that when the bride tells her mother, it's more or less official."

Kitty's hopes were like a steam train gathering speed. The potential for humiliation if they were derailed was unthinkable. Yet over dinner the talk was of nothing but wedding plans, and how delightful Arthur would be as a son-in-law. By the time it was over, Persephone didn't need to lie about having a headache.

The Lamb was a pub two streets away and mostly

frequented by local working men. As she put on her darkest, plainest dress and oldest shawl to head out, she felt as if she were travelling back in time. Looking in the mirror, she was a maid again.

Eddie was waiting for her in the saloon, at a table near the bar. He had somehow saved the only free seat in the crowded room. Being a well-trained fighter with a boxer's build evidently had its uses.

"You're late," he growled, pushing a glass of beer towards her. "Nearly half an hour."

"I'm sorry. It took a while to get away. So what have you to tell me about ... our friend?"

"I know him better than you might think."

"Yes. And?"

"He's a sporting man. Known for it. He takes risks. Big ones. With horses and fighters."

"Fighters? What d'you mean?"

Eddie kept his voice low. "He's famous across all London for his wagers. And he loves a boxing match. The bloodier the better, they say. He's got money on my next fight."

"Oh, Eddie! A prizefight?" She had always pictured him in backstreet brawls. This was something different.

Prizefights were big money. She had no idea he could box at this level.

"What d'you think I do? Ponce about the stables all day, hoping for a ride? Yes, a prizefight. They're fixing it up for ten weeks' time, when the other guy gets back from New York. He's a big man, Cale Robinson. They call him the Blunderbuss. He never loses, but Malmesbury's right – I can beat him. Malmesbury's seen me fight. Rumour is he's wagered thousands on me."

She gaped, and Eddie nodded in confirmation. "But that's good, yes?" she asked. She heard the tension in his voice, but didn't understand it.

"It's crazy, that's what it is. Enough for you and me to live on for a lifetime – ten lifetimes, probably. On one Irish boy he's seen fight for half an hour. He does it for the thrill. I've been asking around… Everyone has a story. Once, he bet a whole country estate on a game of cards. He likes to live on the rough edge of life and for a rich man, that's hard. So he pushes and pushes…"

Persephone looked at her glass. "You saw how he was with me. I don't encourage him. He won't take no for an answer."

Eddie reached out to take her hand across the table. He hesitated when their fingers met, then took it anyway. She felt his warmth, his solidity, the *safeness* of him. "I wouldn't entirely blame you if you said yes. You'd be a duchess."

"Viscountess," she corrected with a sardonic smile.

"He wasn't lying to you in that stable. Not from what I could hear. He wants you, Mary, he does. And he could give you all those things he said. But how long till he wagers it all away? Or gets someone's dander up in my world? Boxing's a dangerous place."

"I won't accept him. It's Kitty I worry about."

"I don't care about her. I care about you."

"You're very kind."

He glanced down at his hand, which was still enfolding hers. Awkwardly, he withdrew his fingers.

"You need to get away from here. From Kitty. From him. I know she's good to you, but—"

"I know. I'm thinking about how to do it."

"Couldn't one of your artist friends...?"

"What?" She looked at him with a challenge in her eyes.

He blinked, embarrassed.

"You know… Look after you. Take you in as a housekeeper or something."

"A housekeeper?" Her gaze grew sharper. "You know what that really means, Eddie O'Bryan."

"All right. I'm sorry."

"And anyway," she went on, ignoring his apology, "I can't leave Kitty right now. She's in danger."

"That's a bit extreme, isn't it?"

"Perhaps," Persephone admitted. "But it's how I feel. There's so much that goes on around her that she doesn't understand."

"And you think it's your job to explain?"

She shrugged uncomfortably. "I don't know. But I can try."

Eddie shook his head. "Don't. If *he* likes you, it will only cause trouble. Look after yourself."

"You too, Eddie." She got up. "I'd better go. Thanks for the warning. It's just what I needed."

Without knowing she was going to do it, she bent and kissed his cheek. She could almost feel the heat of his blush. It made her smile. How could a man who made his fortune beating other men to a pulp be so sweetly delicate?

The next day dawned sunny and clear, and Kitty suggested they went riding before lunch. Eddie brought the horses round and stood obediently while Kitty showed Persephone how to mount sidesaddle. With another groom in attendance, the girls rode to Hyde Park.

Kitty rode her favourite grey mare, Belle, a spirited Arab. She had asked for the most placid horse for her friend. Persephone had ridden bareback as a little girl, as many of the village children did, and she was naturally comfortable on horseback. However, doing it in Kitty's spare riding habit, a tall hat, several layers of petticoats and boots, with her legs hooked round a pommel... Well, that took some concentration. For a while she could only focus on staying upright. But with time she began to enjoy the open air, the steady sway of the horse underneath her and the light through the bare-branched trees.

Spring had taken hold in London at last. Purple and white crocuses poked up through grassy banks, and drifts of yellow daffodils nodded in the sun. The air was still cold, but not as sharp as it had been. It smelled of freshness and brown and green, and reminded Persephone of afternoons in the fields and lanes of her Kentish home.

Their horses walked side by side down the sandy paths of Rotten Row, while the groom followed on behind.

"Isn't this lovely?" Kitty called out, turning rosy-cheeked to grin at her.

Persephone nodded, moving her body in time with the horse. "Yes, it is."

"We must do it more often. I shall ride out all the time when I'm in the country. I may learn to hunt."

Since last night Persephone had been waiting for her chance. Now she finally had ammunition to warn Kitty about Arthur that did not involve embarrassing admissions of her own. "About Lord Malmesbury..." she began.

"Yes?"

"I heard something else... In Venice..."

"What?" Kitty asked mildly.

"He gambles."

Persephone turned to watch Kitty's expression. She didn't want to shock her too much while she was riding. But frustratingly, Kitty didn't seem perturbed at all.

"I'm sure he does. Roly's a *terrible* gambler. He does it all the time."

"Huge sums, though."

Kitty smiled. "Dear Sephy. Roly would too, if he could. Arthur's richer than … well, even than Papa. All the wealthy wager large amounts."

"But I've heard … at least two of his bets have been proper fortunes."

Kitty nodded vaguely and waved to a couple of fashionable horsewomen who approached them on the pathway.

"Did you see Amelia's riding habit?" she said as they passed. "It was the most exquisite thing. I must find out who made it. I'm sure Mama's dressmaker is not so talented. And I'll need a dress for the ball…"

"What ball?"

"The one Mama is holding for me, *finally*. For the day Arthur comes back."

Persephone nearly fell off her horse. "A *ball*?"

"Yes. Isn't it marvellous? It means we can make the announcement in front of all our friends. Oh look! There's Maria, up ahead. If we ride quickly we can join her."

Persephone, struggling with her horse, was left behind. By the time she caught up, Kitty was busy telling Maria her news.

"Officially it's for my birthday. A little early, but Mama couldn't wait. I'm so excited! She's never let me host a ball before. And it will be the perfect way of celebrating Arthur's return."

Maria sighed. "And I *still* haven't met him. Has he gone away again? Already? Why?"

Kitty shrugged. "I don't know really. He mentioned business…"

Maria turned her head. "Do you know, Persephone?"

"I… Me? No."

"But you must be privy to so many secrets. I'm sure *all* the men talk to you."

Persephone cursed the bloom on her neck. "I assure you they don't. I hardly talk to anyone."

"But when you do…"

The smug look in Maria's eyes actually reassured Persephone. She just meant to be insulting in a general way. Persephone hated it that she was right.

"Actually, you did hear something, didn't you, Sephy?" Kitty said, as they rode back the way they had come.

"In Venice."

Persephone's neck grew hotter. "What? I'm sorry?"

"About Arthur. You heard he gambled."

"Um, yes."

"Sephy was worried about him." Kitty smiled and shook her head. "She thought he might lose his fortune."

Maria laughed. "Ha ha! As if a man such as the Duke of Bristol could lose his fortune!"

"His son, at least," Kitty corrected her. She glanced back at Persephone. "You worry too much, Sephy," she said gently.

"I just want to be sure he's right for you," Persephone protested. Her head hurt. Her heart ached.

Maria peered at her. "I do believe you're jealous! Are you *fond* of him?" She grinned.

"No! Really I'm not!" The words were heartfelt. More so than Persephone intended.

Kitty's smile crumpled.

"I don't mean it that way," Persephone said quickly. "Of course I *like* him. Not as *you* do." And now she had said the opposite of what she wanted.

"You aren't familiar with people of great wealth as we are." Maria sighed. "Your mother was … what?"

"An opera singer," Persephone muttered. This was the story she told, although even an opera singer would have been embarrassing in these circles.

Maria shook her head. "You've known people such as Lord Malmesbury a month or two. We've known them all our lives."

Persephone raged inside. Maria was half right: she didn't know aristocrats at all, except from books and scandal rags, and most of the time their morals and behaviour were a foreign country to her. But she knew *people*, and deep down they were all the same. They were good and bad, and money just exaggerated that. Kitty had spent her life surrounded by the good. Persephone, who had survived a hundred beatings by her father, knew the other kind better.

Oh, Kitty, I've seen an Arthur that you could not begin to imagine, she thought. *He's a scoundrel and he wants to marry me. He told me secretly, while he was wrapping emeralds around me.*

But she couldn't say it. She didn't know what to say.

Anyway, by now the talk was of guest lists, supper food and flowers, and the moment was gone.

Chapter Nineteen

Several days passed in similar fashion. Persephone gently tried to open Kitty's eyes to Arthur's faults and was rebuffed. Whenever she mentioned his name Bee or Maria fixed her with quizzical stares, and even Kitty grew uncomfortable. The only solution was to tell the whole sorry truth and she still couldn't do it. Nor could she think of anything clever to foil Arthur's plan. But Kitty mustn't marry him. There had to be another way.

The following Sunday after church, Persephone had another appointment with James Whistler. By now there was less than a week until Arthur's return and she hoped this would give her a chance to clear her head. The American was waiting at their previous meeting place near Cheyne Walk. He grinned as she approached and tipped his wide hat to her.

"I want to paint you," he announced. "Properly. I have

visions of you in a pale dress, standing in a white room – white on white – with only your hair glowing… I was thinking of it all yesterday. I have the thing practically finished in my head."

They agreed that next time they would meet at his sister's house, where he had turned a room into a makeshift studio. For now, she sat on the bench by the river while he quickly sketched her, getting ideas for the expression he wanted.

"Don't talk," he insisted. "I need your face still."

"Then tell me more about Paris," she entreated. "I need distractions."

Whistler's lips twitched as he talked about nights out drinking with his friends, and girls who could dance the cancan, and taking sketching classes outside and learning to really *look*… He had a girlfriend back in Paris too – a fiery seamstress called Fumette who made his life difficult by the sound of it.

"I don't get to talk about all that so often with young ladies round this way." The lips twitched again. "But you understand."

Persephone smiled. She did indeed. This – excepting the cancan and the outdoor classes – had been her world too, for a while. She still missed it, despite the grandeur of Balfour House. Once they had finished, not knowing her full history with Felix, Whistler asked innocently what it had been like to sit for one of the notorious Pre-Raphaelites. Persephone carefully talked about Felix's colourful, chaotic studio and didn't mention their stolen kisses. Whistler laughed.

"Believe me, when I'm with Fumette we don't talk about paint!"

She was still thinking about their conversation as she travelled home in a cab. Normally, she was at her happiest at times like these, but today something slipped and she felt her mind unravel. Whistler and Fumette... The artist and his girlfriend... Living a bohemian life, drawing and loving... Doing as they pleased.

That should have been me.

She had once pictured sharing Felix's world so vividly. For all his faults, he was the man she had dared to imagine herself growing old with. It would have been difficult making a life together at first – Felix had no money of his own – but already clients were starting to fight over his paintings. She wouldn't have minded being poor with him anyway. But then came Mrs Lisle.

Persephone felt another headache come on. The cab's motion made her feel sick. It wasn't just being exiled from Felix's life that hurt so much. With a twist of the knife Mrs Lisle had insisted that Persephone could never tell him her reasons for leaving. And so he was left to assume whatever he wanted. God knew what he thought of her now.

The pain had eased, she thought, with time. But no. It stabbed as sharp as ever.

"Stop! Please!" she shouted up to the driver, who took one look at her and pulled up the horse.

"Let me down. Don't take me any further. I don't feel well."

He did, and she paid him with a shaking hand. The cab took off smartly, leaving Persephone at the corner of Belgrave Square. She was a mile from home, but she didn't care. She just wanted to walk, fast, as if she could somehow step away from Felix and all the love, regret and misery that came with remembering him.

The grand, stucco-fronted houses she passed were built for aristocrats like Arthur Malmesbury. As she strode along, her thoughts inevitably turned back to him and Kitty. Why did he have to hurt her like this?

Why couldn't he just be honest and let her go? He would find girls like Bee Clairmont queueing up to take him. Kitty would be free to find a man who shared her tastes and would adore her properly. Not a duke, perhaps, but a true lover.

Persephone knew she was being wildly romantic. Adoration was the stuff of myths and paintings and novels. In real life, true love could pierce your heart, as she knew too well. But she also knew what it was like to have a man wind his fingers in your hair and stare into your eyes, then close his own and kiss you until your lips were bruised. If you loved him, there was nothing like it. She wanted that for Kitty. A man who called you a china doll would never touch your body and your heart that way…

Slowly, as she approached Hyde Park, a solution appeared, like fog clearing.

The only obstacle between Arthur and Kitty was herself.

What if she said yes?

It would mean Arthur had won. Marrying the son of the Duke of Bristol could hardly be called a sacrifice, but it would cost what little was left of her reputation and all her self-respect. Arthur would be unfaithful, she was sure of it. He would continue to be seen with attractive 'cousins', and follow his own pleasure. But she had lost her chance of happiness anyway. Not loving him was an advantage. And if he loved her, he would look after her at least.

Whereas if he married Kitty he would be callous to her. Without attraction, he would humiliate and desert her. Kitty would be desolate. It couldn't happen. She mustn't let it.

Kitty would hate her forever, and how Persephone would live with herself she didn't know, but Kitty would be safe and free to marry a man who could make her happy. That was the most important thing, surely. If she could think of nothing better by Thursday night, she would accept him, for Kitty's sake.

There. The decision was made.

⋞⋙ ⋘⋟

Kitty was in a fitting for her ballgown with her new dressmaker when Persephone got back to the house, shaken but determined. It suited her that everyone was busy and that Kitty was in too good a mood to notice her bad one.

It had not taken Kitty long to track down the woman who had designed the riding habit she had so admired on her friend in Hyde Park. Madame Madeleine was short and round, with hair dyed vivid black and a simple, elegant way of dressing that managed to be unshowy while suggesting a mastery of boning and construction. And she was clearly delighted to be working for one of the most fashionable girls in Mayfair. She called herself a *modiste*, and adopted a slight French accent on some words, though it was quite clear from all the rest that she was a good East London girl. Persephone sympathized entirely; she had done something very similar herself. In fact, she quickly grew to like Madame Madeleine.

Kitty's dress was to be one of the *modiste's* finest creations. It had possibly the largest crinoline yet seen in London, with tiers of shell-pink muslin bedecked with French-lace frills and garlands of silk rosebuds. Additional buds from real flowers would be sewn at the last minute into special pockets made to contain their stems. The low-cut bodice's neckline and sleeves were designed to show off her bosom and delicate arms. To finish, there would be a delicate headpiece made of matching lace and rosebuds for her hair.

Although whether she would get to wear it, Persephone didn't dare think. If she followed her plan, the ball would be abandoned. Could she really put Kitty through such disgrace?

Meanwhile, all around them, the servants worked hard on getting the house ready to host the cream of society. She knew what it was like because she had helped prepare for parties as a maid – small ones, and even they had been exhausting. Everything must be taken up, cleaned and polished. Precious objects, packed away for safety, must be brought out and displayed. Furniture must be moved and stored to make space for proper dancing.

There was so much to do that even the stable lads were brought in to help with heavy lifting. She saw Eddie on the stairs, carrying a mahogany dining chair in each hand, with a black eye and a bruise on his cheek.

"What happened?" she asked in passing.

He saw the look of concern in her eyes and grinned. "Training. The other guy's worse."

The footman on the stairs behind him, struggling under a single chair, nodded eagerly.

"Young Eddie's not bad. Not bad at all. We've all got

a bit of a wager on him."

Eddie laughed. "See? I have my uses."

Persephone watched as he bounded down the stairs. His muscles bulged, even under his jacket. Fighting was a strange way to make a living, she thought, but she was glad he was good at it.

<hr />

Thursday came and seemed to last forever. Persephone spent most of it in the library, out of the way of the busy staff, reading a novel and willing herself to come up with a brilliant way of avoiding Arthur's ultimatum.

Night fell. The air grew cold, despite the fires. Frederick Ballard retired to his study and Aunt Violet to her rooms at the top of the house. Roly, who had managed to tear himself away from his mistress in Sussex, dressed in his most impeccable evening coat and went out on the town. Persephone slipped away to her bedroom while Kitty and her mother swirled around the house in agitation, checking on last-minute details.

Alone, Persephone paced up and down in her room, glancing at the clock on the mantel. No brilliant idea had come. All she was left with was her plan to accept

Arthur and she hated herself almost as much as she hated him. She expected him at her door or window at any minute, appearing as if by magic, as he usually did.

The clock struck midnight. Then one.

If she went through with it, she would have to leave Balfour House tonight. Another minute in the Ballards' company would be impossible. How she would miss Frederick's calm conversation at dinner, and Catherine's impetuous benevolence, and Kitty's ... everything.

Oh, Kitty.

But time had run out. Moving like an automaton, Persephone pulled her trunk out from under the bed and started to pack. She hardly saw the room as she flitted around it, picking up objects and squashing them in. She didn't want to think, didn't want to feel, didn't want to imagine tomorrow, and Kitty coming in, and the bed being empty...

One day, surely, she'll forgive me?

At last the trunk was full. Persephone stared at it. Silver moonlight cast shadows on the floor. The fire was dead, it was late and she was tired. She dressed for the cold night outside and lay on the bed, waiting.

Two o'clock came and went. Still there was no sign of Arthur. All she could hear was the ticking of the clock and church bells in the distance. At the first light of dawn, she finally realized he wasn't coming. Either he hadn't meant to, and it had just been an aristocratic whim, or he had changed his mind.

She sat up and looked at her feet, laced in their leather boots. All the preparations suddenly seemed ridiculous. Of course he wasn't coming. Dukes do not marry muses. She began to wonder if she had imagined the whole story. In the cold light of dawn, she saw herself for what she was: a country girl caught up by city dreams and nightmares. Thank God it was not too late.

Ahead of her, the bursting wicker trunk glimmered with a ghostly sheen. Persephone leaped out of bed and rapidly unpacked it, put everything back and stored the trunk where it belonged. Relief swept through her body like a draught of good red wine. How comfortable those pillows looked. She changed into her nightgown and fell asleep, exhausted.

Chapter Twenty

When she woke up, sunlight was streaming past the shutters. One glance at the clock on the mantel showed Persephone that she had missed breakfast. She dressed quickly and ran to find Kitty to warn her about Arthur's intentions – but how would she put it? That he had made a hideous promise to betray her and not kept it? That he might not come tonight? She wasn't sure. Only that Kitty must be on her guard.

Kitty was not in her room, however. Winnie said she had gone out riding with Bee. When she came back, Bee came in too and stayed to lunch. There was no chance for a *tête à tête*.

"I hardly slept a wink," Kitty said brightly, over cold ham and potatoes. "I was too excited. I know I look a fright but we have time to make me presentable."

"You look fresh as a peach," Bee assured her.

Kitty smiled. "Don't be silly. I haven't put a single cream on and there's a spot right here on the tip of my nose. Can you see it? It's there I promise you. I can feel it growing. A hundred and fifty people are coming tonight and they shall find me hideously disfigured."

Bee stayed on after lunch to give Kitty tips on her complexion, only leaving at half past three when the dressmaker arrived for final fittings. Persephone hadn't managed a moment alone with her yet and began to wonder if she ever would.

She was the first in the gold drawing room, where her pale turquoise silk party dress lay ready to be inspected. Persephone had made most of it herself, but one of Madame Madeleine's assistants had added a hem of rich gold embroidery, and gold linings to the trailing sleeves. She took it to try on and as one of the maids helped her into it she announced that Persephone "looked like a queen from a fairy tale."

Not long afterwards, Kitty arrived in her pink rosebud gown, which fitted and billowed like a fashionable masterpiece.

"Pearls or garnets this evening?" Mrs Ballard said while Madame Madeleine and her assistants fussed around Kitty's skirts. "You may borrow either."

"What do you think, Sephy?" Kitty asked.

Before she could reply, a girl in the uniform of a parlourmaid knocked and put her head around the door. "Excuse me, madam, Miss Kitty, Miss Persephone." She nervously bobbed to all three. "Miss Persephone is wanted downstairs."

"What for?" Catherine Ballard asked.

"A delivery, ma'am. Sorry to disturb you." She bobbed again.

"You'd better go and see what it is." Mrs Ballard sighed. "It will be deliveries all day today, I shouldn't wonder."

Puzzled, and still dressed in her turquoise finery, Persephone followed the housemaid downstairs. In the hall, a kitchen maid was waiting to escort her through the green baize door behind the stairs.

"Why are we going this way?" Persephone asked. Family, and she was 'family' now, never went beyond the baize door to where the kitchen and the servants' hall were located. It was an unspoken rule.

"Don't know, miss," the maid said quickly, with a nervous dip of her head.

Persephone's heart started beating fast. Wonderful smells of roasting meat and spiced wine were coming from the kitchen, but there was something wrong. And when something felt wrong like this she knew who was at the heart of it. A door in the kitchen corridor stood ajar. She sensed his presence in the room beyond, even as the maid paused and nodded in its direction.

"You're to go in there, miss."

"Must I?"

The maid's eyes widened. "Oh yes, miss." She stood and waited for Persephone to go inside.

The windowless room was in half-darkness when Persephone entered. It looked like some sort of office for a senior servant – a housekeeper, perhaps. A gas lamp on a table burned at its lowest level. At first the room seemed empty, but Persephone knew better now. She turned slowly to look behind the open door. And there he was, lounging in a dark corner. Arthur had a penchant for dark corners. They seemed to be his natural habitat.

"Hello," she said.

Arthur was still in evening dress, somewhat dishevelled. His eyes burned in his wax-pale face.

"I think you mean, 'Good afternoon, my lord'. Or good morning. Whatever damn time of day it is."

"Good afternoon, my lord." Persephone's voice dripped with disdain, but he smiled anyway.

"I was joking! Persephone, my darling girl."

He stepped forwards, as if to hold her. She stepped back just as fast. She didn't want to be seen with him, or locked in a room alone with him. Did he not have any clue how wrong this was?

"You said you'd come last night," she said coldly.

"I was busy. It doesn't mean I didn't long for you. Did you yearn for me too?"

No, I did not yearn for you. I slept soundly, thinking you had left me in peace.

She thought this with a fiery passion, but all she said was, "First the stables and now here? Do you always skulk in other people's houses?"

"Don't be so inhospitable." He pouted. "Especially when I came to give you this."

He held out his hand, which contained three stalks bristling with small, vivid green leaves. "Myrtle," he explained. "From the hothouse in Somerset. Venus's flower – for your corsage tonight."

Persephone took the stems, which she had no intention of wearing. She would throw them in the grate as soon as she got upstairs. "Was that all?"

"No." His hand had disappeared into a pocket. When he opened his closed fist in front of her, it revealed an open leather box lined with white satin. Glinting in the lamplight was a ring that featured the largest ruby Persephone had ever seen, surrounded by diamonds. "This too. My grandmother's ring. For my duchess."

Arthur sank unsteadily on one knee and kissed her fingertips. He reeked of wine and tobacco.

Persephone felt a wave of nausea. Seeing him so debauched, so unrepentant, she felt physically repelled. She had thought she could bear it for Kitty's sake, but the Arthur in her mind then was the witty, cultivated, dashing young diplomat. Now she faced the dissolute roué he hid so well.

"Last night I was ready to say yes," she said in a low voice.

"What difference can a night make?"

"Where were you?" she flashed at him. Every day with him would be like this, she realized, wondering what new mischief was in store.

His tired eyes lit up for a brief moment. "Somewhere I couldn't leave. Already she scolds me!"

"Look at you," she hissed. "You have no thought for anyone but yourself. You bring me here today, where the servants might see me…"

"They'll love it. A fellow drudge elevated to the Queen's bedchamber. I told you – it's your job to rescue me."

"I won't do it. Not now. Not ever."

She meant it. He stood up, trying to summon his old charm. "My darling! You don't know what you're throwing away!"

"I'm beginning to understand. But I beg you, don't do this to Kitty." Persephone sank to her own knees now. He seemed to like grand gestures. She held her clasped hands up to him. "Don't give her the ring, Arthur. Please."

Her words finally sank in. Arthur's jade-green irises seemed to splinter as he looked down on her. To her dismay, she saw the mask of politeness descend. He pocketed the ruby and gave her that empty smile.

"Not give Kitty the ring? Get up, by the way, my dear. Let me help you. That's better. Not propose to my dearest Kitty? On the day of our engagement? How could you ask such a thing? Not give her my grandmother's ring? You're a cruel friend, Persephone. I had thought better of you."

"Arthur! Please!"

"I must go. I have a lot to do before this evening. Please forgive me. I'm sorry to have disturbed you."

He pulled the door wide and quickly strode down the corridor, his steel-tipped boots pounding on the hard stone floor.

Persephone stood where she was for a moment, catching her breath. She felt as if she had escaped a dark forest where wild things lurked. And where Kitty now was heading.

Chapter Twenty-one

The ball started at nine, and the Duke and his family were due to arrive at Balfour House at eight thirty, to give them time to greet the Ballards in private. This would be their first meeting since negotiations for the engagement had begun.

Eight forty came. Vast arrangements of hothouse roses flooded the ballroom with their scent. Kitty stood at the doorway in her exquisite dress, waiting patiently. Only the slightest hint of anxiousness spoiled her smile. Persephone stood nearby, wishing herself a million miles away. She had tried to talk to Kitty several times, but her mother or the servants had never left her side. Now it was too late. Unless Arthur had finally decided to do the decent thing and was not coming.

Eight forty-five. The great gold clock on the marble mantel ticked resolutely on. Servants padded up and down the corridors, adjusting last-minute details of food and wine. Eight fifty. Eight fifty-one…

And then the sound of carriages arriving. The Duke of Bristol and his duchess stood on the doorstep, ready to hand their furs to the footmen. They walked through the hall and up the stairs with their retinue of relatives. Arthur was right behind his mother, followed by five of his six sisters. He looked as impeccable as ever in black diplomatic dress decorated with gold embroidery. His face bore no trace of the previous night's debauchery.

"Aha! Welcome, your graces. We were beginning to wonder where you were," Frederick Ballard joked.

"An issue with the horses," the duke replied stiffly, his accent so sharpened by aristocratic hauteur that it was hard to understand at first. "Soon rectified. I like this room. Gilding and whatnot. Amazing what good money can do."

"Thank you," Catherine Ballard said, curtseying to the floor. "Your grace."

"Where's the girl? Ah, the young Catherine! As pretty as you told me, Arthur. She'll breed fine specimens."

Kitty blushed a deeper pink than the fresh rosebuds on her dress. Persephone couldn't bear to watch and her eyes turned instead to the Malmesbury women, standing in a row next to the Duke. The Duchess and her daughters all wore the finest, palest silks, draped over extravagant hoops and adorned with metal thread. Their waists, in tight corsets, seemed impossibly small. White shoulders were shown off by deep ruffles and collarbones glittered with gold and precious stones. Their hair was woven in intricate coils and caught up with flowers. Wherever money could be spent to make them look fabulous, it had been.

But it was Arthur who fascinated Persephone most of all. She watched him solicitously greet Kitty, and let his lips linger on her hand. She saw Kitty's face light up with pleasure, and his features arrange themselves in similar delight.

Am I imagining this? she wondered. *Is he quite normal – and I'm the one who's moonstruck?*

Soon guests started arriving in a flood. Balfour House was full of music, light from a dozen chandeliers and dancing. Champagne flowed. Women swirled in the colours of exotic jewels. Men were stylish in white tie and tails, or dashing military uniforms, though none were as elegant as Lord Malmesbury.

He and Kitty went from room to room, their comfort as a couple making their 'secret' obvious to the few who didn't already know it. Kitty was constantly praised for her 'exceptional bloom' tonight, which was code in polite society for how obviously in love she was.

The whole thing was suffocating. Persephone couldn't bear it. Eventually she took refuge downstairs in the library, playing with the dogs. She knelt on the floor by the fire, rubbing their tummies and listening to their happy growls.

The spaniels were disturbed by a noise outside and went to sniffle at the door. It was pushed wide and two women stepped inside, closed it behind them and sighed. The dogs went back to the fireplace and settled down. The women were hidden from Persephone by a large armchair and a palm tree in a pot, as she was from them. But from their cut-glass voices, like their father's, she recognized them as Malmesbury girls.

"Phew. It's cooler down here. What's the matter, Sissie?"

"My bosom pad has shifted," the other one giggled. (This must be Arthur's sister Cecily.) "I can't tell if I've straightened it properly. Can you check?"

"Oh, Sissie! I can see it sticking out! Quick, let me…"

There was more giggling, and the sound of grunting and straining. Persephone tried not to laugh herself and prayed for their sakes that they wouldn't see her. The embarrassment on both sides would be extreme.

"There. That's better. Is it comfortable?"

"Of course not. Lisette laced me much too tight tonight. I can hardly breathe. Can we stay here a little, do you mind?"

"If you like. Do you want to sit down?"

Persephone held her breath.

"I couldn't possibly in these hoops, could you? Let me lean against the door. That's better."

Persephone breathed again. So did Sissie, apparently. She became more conversational.

"And so at last little Arthur is settling down."

"She's a pretty thing. You can see why he chose her, I suppose. Despite the lack of breeding. He won't leave her side tonight. He seems besotted."

"Arthur always runs his own course. And at least she lives in reasonable style. Have you seen the quantity of champagne? Even Papa is hardly so generous."

"Well, new money is money I suppose."

"I was still surprised he picked Kitty, weren't you?"

"Not particularly. She chased him halfway around Europe."

"True, but even last week Mama was sure he had his eye on someone else."

"Oh, Sissie! Who?"

"You know Arthur. He wouldn't say. But she could feel it. 'A mother knows her son', she said."

"Perhaps he'll keep the other one as a mistress. Poor Kitty. Do you think she knows?"

"Look at her – so wide-eyed. I doubt it. Although of course she's hardly a cloistered nun."

"What d'you mean?"

"You must have heard the gossip, Lizzie. Driving around town all hours of the day and night with only her brother for company. No decent chaperone…"

"I thought her aunt—"

"Only sometimes. And of course, she will insist on consorting with that artists' model."

"Oh yes! Ma'mselle Lavelle! Who knows what gutter *she* crawled out of?"

"Well, if Kitty will court scandal—"

"She'll be ripe for Arthur!"

"Sissie! You're positively cruel!"

They opened the door again and wandered off upstairs towards the ballroom and the dancing, still laughing. Persephone stayed where she was, stroking the dogs again and staring ahead blindly. Kitty was nothing but kindness and yet these young witches were to be her new family. Persephone knew that Arthur might be unkind ... but all of them? The dark forest grew darker.

A gong sounded loudly from the top of the stairs. Dancers and gossipers stopped what they were doing and headed towards the noise. Reluctantly she joined the crowd gathering in the hall. Frederick Ballard stood above them at the head of the stairs, flanked by his wife and children. Arthur stood a few feet away, sharing asides with a dapper young gentleman who looked almost his twin but for his thin nose and thick moustache. The guests waited expectantly. Eventually there was quiet.

"Your Graces, Lords and Ladies, honoured guests..." Mr Ballard began. 'You're all very welcome here tonight. I can't tell you what a pleasure it is for Catherine and me to see so many friends here, together, on such an auspicious day."

There were some calls and clapping, and a little whisper went around the crowd at the word 'auspicious'. "Yes, yes. And auspicious it is, because… Well, you all know that Catherine and I have been blessed with two fine children. Roland –" catcalls and whistles from the crowd, presumably Roly's friends – "and his lovely sister Kitty."

Cheers and applause.

"Kitty is our only daughter, and how very lucky we are to have such a beautiful girl of such fine character."

Cries of 'hear hear' from some men in front of Persephone.

"I always said any young man would be lucky to have her … and that lucky young man has come along. Kitty, my dear, step forwards."

Kitty did, blushing fiercely.

"Kitty, I am pleased and honoured to say, has accepted the hand of Lord Arthur Malmesbury, only son of his Grace the Duke of Bristol, who is our guest tonight, and they will be married in the summer."

Whoops, laughter, more applause.

Arthur stepped forwards too, bowed briefly to the crowd and turned to Kitty. He took her hand in his and kissed it tenderly.

"Kitty, Lord Malmesbury … may you be very happy."
At this, Mr Ballard paused to rub something out of his
eye. Pink-cheeked like his daughter and overcome with
emotion, he seemed to lose his train of thought. His
wife nudged him. "So let's raise a toast to Kitty and
Lord Malmesbury."

He raised his champagne glass and everyone
followed. The servants had been busy in preparation
for this moment so most of the glasses were full. The
whole house seemed to echo to the sound of raucous
congratulations.

Even from the back of the throng, Persephone could
see something change in Kitty's blue eyes. She stopped
staring down at her skirts and beamed out at the crowd.
She had made her parents happy and her girlhood was
complete. She could be a wife and mother now, which
was all she wanted. She glowed.

Persephone felt something crack inside her. Not
at Kitty's happiness – which she wanted more than
anything – but the shifting sands it was built on. She
looked away, and in doing so she caught the eye of a
nearby footman carrying a tray of champagne glasses.
The knowing glance he gave her, based without a doubt

on her assignation with Arthur earlier today, made her flush to her core.

She took a glass from his tray and downed its contents quickly. When Kitty caught her eye and beamed more brightly, Persephone smiled back with all the encouragement she could muster. Kitty, delighted, nudged Arthur and pointed Persephone out in the crowd.

The look he gave her was endless black.

Chapter Twenty-two

The wedding was set for June, making it a short engagement. "But June is the nicest month," the Duchess observed. And Catherine Ballard liked to point out that "the two young people have already spent so long in each other's company".

As far as Persephone was concerned, Kitty might as well be going to the scaffold. Arthur was the most devilish man she had ever met. And yet everyone adored him. Bee and Maria alternated between looks of intense jealousy at Kitty and triumphant glances at her 'artistic' friend, whom they had suspected of trying to ensnare him.

Mrs Ballard started an epic project of letter-writing to let all her friends and relations in every part of the country know the good news. Every day cards and presents arrived at Balfour House. It was impossible to move in some of the smaller rooms for flowers.

Then there was the wedding itself to plan. This was complicated by the fact that the Duke had mentioned in passing at the ball that it was 'always nice to marry on the family's Somerset estate. The church, you know, in summer...' The Duke, in the Ballards' eyes, must never be questioned. All Catherine Ballard's detailed plans for a London wedding in the Grosvenor Chapel had to be abandoned, and mid-June was only twelve weeks off. There was a mountain of work to do.

This turned out to be a role Kitty's mother was born for. Every day new lists were written of necessary purchases and activities, parties that must be attended, and new acquaintances made. The list of 'necessities' for the wedding itself got longer by the hour, from bonbons for the bridesmaids' baskets to special off-white livery for the footmen of Kitty's carriage.

The only person who seemed immune to her mother's whims and schemes was Kitty herself. So anxious and self-absorbed before the engagement, she was now quite serene. Persephone noticed it privately, but Winnie was the one to point it out, as they prepared to go for a drive with Aunt Violet.

"Anyone would think you'd been married a hundred times, Miss Kitty. What's got into you, to make you so calm and peaceful? It's not natural in a young bride."

Kitty glanced at herself in the mirror. "It's true. I do feel calmer." She quickly appraised her face and hair, and turned back without a second glance. "It's because it's real. It's actually happening."

"Why ever wouldn't it be?" Winnie asked.

Kitty bit her bottom lip.

"What?" Persephone insisted.

"Nothing."

"Out with it!" Winnie teased. "You can't fool us, Miss Kitty."

Kitty sighed, and fiddled with the soft silk recticule she had chosen. "You'll think me ridiculous."

"I never would," Persephone promised. Winnie agreed.

"Well, it's too silly and I know it, so don't mock me – but when I was nine, my governess took me to the circus. There was a fortune-teller in a little tent in the corner of the grounds, and my governess loved that sort of thing. She was always pouring out the tea and checking the leaves for signs... Anyway, she went in to have her fortune told so of course I went in too.

It was dark inside, and smelled of … I don't know what, but there was smoke and scents of spice and something sharper. And the woman was old and hunched over her table. She was wrapped in scarves with gold hoops in her ears – everything you'd expect. I told you not to mock me, Sephy. After she'd muttered a few sentences to my governess, she motioned over to me. She took my hands in hers and put them on the ball.

"My governess leaned over me. 'What is it?' she asked. 'What do you see?' And the woman shook her head, but my governess pressed her, and she said, 'You will be unhappy in love, my little one. Tragedy for you. He's not for keeping.' That's all. My governess begged her for good news, but she wouldn't say another word. She simply took the money and shooed us away.

"I didn't run to Mama when I got home. I was very quiet. But I thought about it often. From the day we arrived in St Petersburg right up until the ball I never really dared… I always imagined something might go wrong. It was almost as if there was a curse on me."

She looked at them, embarrassed.

"Then Arthur didn't propose in Russia, or even in Venice. I know I pretended I didn't mind, but it rankled. I could feel the prophecy coming true. But it didn't. Papa made his announcement at the ball, and Arthur stood beside me, and suddenly it was all so real and I realized what a silly dupe I'd been. It was just smoke and mirrors that day in the tent. He *is* for keeping."

Kitty shook her head at herself and held up her right hand so the ruby caught the light.

"Oh, Miss Kitty, you poor, dear thing. You should have told me!" Winnie scolded. "I could have comforted you and told you to wipe it from your mind. Those women are quacks and fakes, all of them."

"I'm sure they are. But there was something about her…"

"Well, it's over now."

"Sephy, you're smiling." Kitty turned to look at her. "I told you not to tease."

"I'm not," Persephone insisted. Though she *had* been smiling at her friend's sweet innocence. In fact, she marvelled at the story and found it more than a little unnerving.

Kitty's newfound serenity was so lovely that Persephone could not bear to shatter it straight away. Which was why she kept quiet about Arthur's latest secret declaration for several days. However, the bitter truth must be told eventually and the longer she left it the worse it would get.

They were alone together in the parlour one morning. Kitty was working on a miniature of Arthur, the spaniels at her feet. Persephone sat opposite, sewing a bonnet for Harriet's baby. She put it down. *Now. Do it. Just say the words.* Her throat was parched. She called for a glass of water and drank it down. *Do it.*

"Kitty…"

Her heart was beating so fast she wasn't sure if she'd spoken aloud. But Kitty looked up with an eyebrow raised. "Yes?"

"Kitty. Something happened before the ball. I must tell you. Arthur… Arthur and I…" Persephone swallowed. *Do it.* "Arthur asked me… That is…"

She had been staring at a corner of the pattern on the rug at her feet but now she forced herself to meet Kitty's eye. To her surprise, Kitty was half-smiling as if she knew what was coming next.

"Go on," Kitty encouraged her gently.

Persephone took another breath. "Arthur asked me to marry him."

There it was, in the room at last. She braced herself for some kind of explosion. But Kitty's composure remained unruffled.

"He offered me the ring," Persephone blurted into the unexpected silence. "Before he gave it to you."

"Oh, Sephy." Kitty sighed. Her face was wreathed with pity. "He said this might happen. Poor you. You should have told me."

"Yes." It was a whisper.

"Poor Arthur too. It was the most terrible misunderstanding. He warned me you might have taken it the wrong way. You see, he knows you love him..."

"What?"

"And it's obvious, dearest. You talk about him all the time – even Maria said so. But I understand and I see you try to fight it for my sake. Anyway, he explained that he was joking with you one day, and you got quite carried away imagining life as a duchess. He admitted the game went too far and he worried you had got the wrong idea, and he was sorry. He is so very upset about it, honestly. I told him to apologize to you directly, but he's too shy."

Persephone's mind was a whirl. *Arthur? Shy?* Did Kitty know him at all?

"No! That's not what happened!"

"I assure you, Sephy, it is. He told me – after the ball."

Kitty's voice was sharper now. This was the spirited girl who was prepared to fight for her fiancé. Persephone scrabbled in her brain for evidence to prove that she was right and he was wrong. But what was there? Eddie, in the stables! He had heard everything. But Eddie was her friend. How easy it would be to accuse him of lying in her favour. What else? The myrtle? She had burned it. Nothing else. Nothing.

Arthur was brilliant. *Imagining life as a duchess...* She had done that – after he first proposed. He twisted the truth like a master, and worked fast while she had waited. She felt as if she was in a hall of mirrors.

"He knows you love him... It's obvious..."

For a moment, she almost believed him herself.

"But Kitty—"

"Enough!" Kitty stood up and shouted the word. And Kitty never shouted. "I know it must be hard for you, but I will marry him. You must be glad for me. There. It is said. Now, neither of us will speak of it again."

"Excuse me."

Persephone stood up shakily to go but before she could take another step Kitty swept out of the room, leaving her staring, desolate, in her wake.

Chapter Twenty-three

Any other girl would have thrown her out then and there, but Kitty was made of sterner mettle. It wasn't just that she felt a loyalty to their friendship that Arthur would never understand. She was also fed by an inner certainty that seemed unshakeable. Persephone thought it came from Kitty's life of love and luxury. Nothing had harmed her yet, so nothing ever could. Kitty trusted Persephone to 'master her emotions', her fiancé to behave impeccably, and herself to manage the situation with finesse. After her outburst in the parlour she was true to her word and no more was said.

Persephone's first thought was to take any position she could find and go anyway. Living here, watching the engagement run its course, was agony. But if she left, Arthur would win for good. She had eleven weeks to prove what kind of a man he really was behind the mask. Surely there was time?

Arthur treated Persephone as if nothing had passed between them, and she found it chilling. To her relief, when he visited Balfour House Bee and Maria generally made sure they were there too, but when Persephone was unlucky enough to join them he met her with the politeness of a palace courtier. They barely exchanged a word.

To Kitty, he was always playful and charming. He bought her a puppy – a King Charles spaniel she called Ruby, in honour of her ring. Persephone noticed that Kitty spent more time fussing over the puppy than Arthur, but he didn't seem to mind. He never asked how the wedding preparations were going. The ceremony didn't seem to interest him in the slightest. Kitty didn't show signs of noticing this at all.

Given his brilliant act, Persephone soon realized she had little to learn from his visits. She would have to find another way to defeat him. Meanwhile she took Harriet out to lunch on her cousin's day off. She went on a trip to Oxford with Effie, and out to the theatre. She accepted Rossetti's offer to sketch her. Anything, anything to get away.

She was posing for Rossetti at his studio in Blackfriars when the grand Sara Prinsep came to call. Rossetti abandoned his drawing of her as the poet Petrarch's sweetheart, Laura. Persephone was grateful, as Rossetti had recently acquired a pair of bright green parakeets and she had been distracted from her enigmatic, literary pose by their disconcerting squawking.

"Persephone!" Sara said, entering the studio in a swish of silk and cashmere. "What a delight! It's *months* since I've seen you."

Their mutual greeting was warm. Mrs Prinsep was one of the finest hostesses in London. She knew 'everyone', from artists to politicians, and entertained them all at her house in Holland Park. Persephone had been there before, the night she dressed up as a Nubian maid, and had adored it.

"You must come again," Sara said resolutely. "In fact, I'm having a little tea party on Saturday. Come to that. My son Val is putting on some theatricals with Mr Thackeray. I promise they'll be a delight."

"Thank you." Persephone hesitated though, and Rossetti spotted it. His face broke into an impish smile.

"Ah! When I saw you there last, you were having a

little *tête à tête* with someone. Who was it? Oh yes: Rupert Thornton. And Felix Dawson was in the garden with my Lizzie. Oh, what a tangled web we weave…"

Persephone flushed scarlet. "I wasn't deceiving!" She was horrified Rossetti might think so, though he had a reputation for doing as much himself.

"Don't worry, my dear," Sara Prinsep cut in, putting a hand on her arm. "Mr Thornton won't be there. And nor will Mr Dawson, I'm afraid. I simply cannot abide his simpering girlfriend. Am I terrible to say so? Gabriel, I don't know how you put up with her. The girl looks like an angel with that mane of bright hair, and has not a single word to say for herself."

Persephone beamed at her. Here was another true friend! "I'd love to come. I read Mr Thackeray's *Vanity Fair* last winter. It was quite thrilling."

"Wasn't it? You see? The new girl might as easily mistake him for the chimney sweep. I'll send you an invitation. Gabriel, you'll be there, won't you?"

"I wouldn't miss it for the world," Rossetti said with a bow and a wink at Persephone.

Back at Balfour House, Maria Hope was in the hallway, putting on her bonnet. She gave Persephone a superior smile as she swept past. In the parlour, Kitty looked up, startled, when Persephone came in.

"Winnie told me you were in here. Are you all right?" Persephone asked.

"Yes, I suppose."

"What happened?"

"Madame Madeleine came. To talk about my wedding dress."

"Oh, my goodness!"

A romantic, fascinated by fashion, Persephone forgot the wedding for a moment and just thought about the dress. For herself, if the day ever came, she would want something understated and unusual, like the fur-trimmed cloak the bride on Torcello had worn. However, she was more interested in what other girls chose. And Kitty's would no doubt be the best that money could buy.

"It wasn't lovely at all," Kitty grumbled. "Mama had a million ideas, all of them contrasting. If I wore everything she suggested I'd be as big as an air balloon. Maria and Bee came to help too but they spent the afternoon fiddling with lace and dreaming of their own weddings. Particularly Maria, who's marrying Samuel in September. I had forgotten what it's like choosing things without you. You always give me the best advice…"

"No! Stop it!" Persephone earnestly protested.

"It's true. I'm the vainest creature in the world and you never complain, or fight me for the glass. You stop me being too extravagant. I simply *must* have you here when Madame Madeleine comes back on Saturday."

"Ah. Saturday…"

"Don't tell me you're busy. You *can't* be. Mama has every other thing organized already, down to the strawberries for the fruit cup. The dress is the one true thing I care about."

Persephone crumbled. She owed Kitty so much. "Of course," she agreed.

"Oh, *thank* you! You know, while you weren't here, Bee and Maria said some rather horrid things about you. They said you were trying to use me, and I know it's not true. If anything, I'm using *you* for your company. It struck me that you never say a bad word about them in return. You're twice the lady they are."

"Please! Stop! Stop!" Persephone was laughing now. Kitty was the world's kindest creature. *If I could die for her, I would*, she thought. But her eyes strayed to Kitty's right hand where the ruby ring glittered on her engagement finger, and she felt trapped in a web of lies.

She could not carry on like this. She needed to find someone who would understand and keep the secret – and perhaps even help find a way through. There was only one person she could trust.

Eddie cut a distinctive figure in the saloon bar of The Lamb, hunched over a small table under the window, his cap sat rakishly as ever on his head. It was late. Persephone was supposedly asleep in bed, but the bar of the pub was better. Especially with Eddie there. She was glad he had got her message.

Then she noticed he was deep in conversation with a young woman who sat beside him. She stopped in her tracks and flushed with confusion. Was Eddie in *love*? She had never thought about him that way and the idea unsettled her for a moment. But as she approached she saw the woman's skinny pale face and strong work-worn hands.

"Annie!" She rushed over to embrace her friend.

Annie O'Bryan stood up and looked her up and down. "It's a long time since I've seen you, *Persephone Lavelle*! Look at the flesh on you! You're a proper lady now."

"Just what your brother said. I'm not a lady and never shall be!" Persephone grinned. "I haven't seen you in an age! How's everyone in St George's Square?"

"Oh, nothing changes. The mistress is unhappy. The master's busy with his work. The children are growing. Alice is becoming quite a beauty, bless her."

"And Mrs Green?" Persephone had been very fond of the cook.

"Ah." Annie sighed. "She's leaving soon. She's met a man! She's so old it's hardly worth the bother, as I keep telling her. She's more than forty. But he keeps an inn and she'll cook for his customers. And I…" Annie faltered and stopped. She and Cook were best friends. Persephone knew how devastating it must be to lose her. She hugged Annie again.

Annie sat down and patted the place beside her. "I can't stay long. But my brother says you might be in a spot of trouble." She lowered her voice so she could hardly be heard. "That Lord So-and-So, Eddie's guessing."

"You've told her about him?" Persephone stared at Eddie, who nodded solemnly.

"Only what I know. You can trust my Annie. She's silent as the grave. Come on, drink up and tell us everything."

He pushed a glass towards her. Persephone took a sip of beer while she considered what to say. Keeping her voice not much above a whisper, and mentioning no names that might be overheard, she told them the whole story, from the first rejected proposal to the recent twisted lies. Annie and Eddie listened, fascinated and appalled.

"Well?" she asked at the end.

"Well what?" Eddie said.

"What can I do?"

"You can leave," Eddie said simply.

His sister nodded.

"But she needs me. I'm the only one who can warn her."

"You've tried that, you say."

Persephone's shoulders sagged. "She thinks I'm a fantasist. I need proof."

"Look, you've done what you can. It didn't work. Stay out of it. I told you last time."

"But Kit— The *friend*. What of her?"

Brother and sister shared a glance. They shrugged and looked back at her.

"She's rich enough. She'll manage," Annie said.

"She won't! He'll betray her in a heartbeat. It will kill her."

"Nonsense," Eddie said. "It happens all the time. The man mistreats his wife. She learns to live with it. It's how it's always been."

"Not for me!" Persephone said hotly. She flushed to think of her own family, because that was exactly how it had been. "If I can stop it, I will."

Eddie reached out across the table and placed a big strong hand on her arm.

"Don't! It never pays to interfere with grandees and their golden girls. You'll be the one to suffer."

Persephone appealed to Annie. "You can't agree?"

"I most sincerely do," Annie declared. "This is between him and her."

"But—"

"She wants to marry him. Think of what she'd be

losing. Don't spoil it with romance."

"But Kitty's different!"

Eddie let go of Persephone's arm and folded his own. "Promise me. You'll do nothing more."

"You're always asking for my promises."

He glared at her. "That man's bad news. If you just knew—"

Annie cried out with a catch in her voice. "Oh, Eddie!"

Persephone stared at her. "What? What don't I know? Is this about the bet?"

Eddie shook his head warningly at his sister, but she spoke up anyway. "He's a wicked fool. He's got Eddie into a world of trouble. Ruined him, maybe."

"How could betting on Eddie ruin him?"

"Quiet, Annie," he glowered.

Annie fell silent but Persephone sensed a new, dark shift in the atmosphere. Even with the worries she already had, it alarmed her. "What is it? Come on. I'm not leaving until I know."

Eddie sighed. "All right. But outside. I'm not talking here."

They left their beer on the table and walked out into the night. A cold grey mist was sidling through the streets, and both she and Annie stayed close to Eddie, grateful for his reassuring presence and steady step.

"What is it?" Persephone asked again.

"You're to tell no one. I'm serious this time. Swear on your life."

"I swear," she agreed, startled. "On my life." She held her hand over her heart to prove it.

Eddie steeled himself to talk. "They want me to throw the fight," he muttered.

"Who do?"

"The gang who run my end of town. The Whitechapel Boys. If there's sport or gambling, they've got their fingers in the pie. You don't argue with them, ever. You do as they say, or else."

"What do you mean, exactly … 'else'?"

"A knife, usually. Or a sharpened buckle. Sometimes they take a finger or an ear…"

"Stop it! Stop it!" Annie cried out.

"She asked me!"

Persephone's stomach churned. "What's it got to do with Arthur? Is he involved with them?"

"Not exactly. But when he wagered that fortune on me, they took the bet. They gave good odds, 'cause compared to the Blunderbuss I'm supposed to be a nobody. If I win, they have to pay him fivefold and naturally they don't want to do that. So I must lose."

"Is that a terrible thing?" Persephone tried to be optimistic. "It's just one fight. You might lose anyway."

He stopped and stared at her. "You're asking a boxer, a man who lives for the fight, if it's a terrible thing to lose on purpose?" he growled. "To throw the contest? To trash your reputation?"

He was shaking with fury – not at Persephone, she thought, but at the very idea of what he was being asked to do.

"I'm sorry," she murmured.

They stood on the narrow pavement on the corner of a square while he tried to compose himself. A passing carriage splashed them with mud from a puddle in the gutter.

"I hate it here," he grunted finally, with passion. "What's a man to do? How's he to survive? Bad men and rich men running the town. I've a mind to go away…"

"Don't, Eddie! Please!" Annie said, clinging to him.

"*You* did," he answered, turning to her. "You were the

first to leave home. You should understand better than anyone."

Annie looked up at him with tears running down her cheeks. "You're all I've got."

Arthur had done this. With his reckless bet, he had caused this misery. Persephone felt suddenly desolate. For Annie, for all of them.

"And you." Eddie turned to her. "For your own good. Promise you'll be careful."

Persephone nodded. So far Arthur had outwitted her at every turn. She had no weapons left in her armoury anyway.

Chapter Twenty-four

When Saturday came, Persephone thought wistfully of the theatricals at Little Holland House. She longed to meet the great William Thackeray and see Sara Prinsep again. However, it wasn't to be.

At half past four she and Kitty met Madame Madeleine in the gold drawing room, where the contents of several trunks had been laid out on every available surface. The elegant dressmaker stood in the middle of the room, surrounded by fabrics and trimmings.

"You remember my friend Persephone?" Kitty asked.

The *modiste* nodded and looked uneasy. Before, when she had come to fit Kitty for her ballgown, she had arrived with an army of assistants but this time there was only one.

"I think we agreed on the ivory duchesse satin," she began. The girl beside her lifted a bolt of the material from a trunk they had brought along. "And the Venice lace..."

Several fashion-plates from the latest Paris magazines were laid out to be admired. Kitty poured over them with an expert eye.

"I'd look a fright in all those puffs, but they're so pretty. I like the train on that one, but it's rather grand. I don't want to be a *grand* bride. Oh, look at those *engageantes*! I love the lace but I don't want long sleeves in June..."

Persephone sat quietly and listened. She had a thousand things to say, but Kitty did not need distractions. Besides, Catherine Ballard arrived and quickly threw the viewing into disarray, loving everything Kitty had dismissed and clucking at what she had liked.

"Don't forget the bridesmaids, Kitty. They can look pretty enough, but you must outshine them. Oh, and I found this. I put it aside for you this morning. Would you like it?"

She picked up a slim bundle of creamy-white fabric from the side table next to her and handed it to Kitty, who peered at it curiously and shook it out. It seemed to hang in the air for a moment, like a wisp of smoke. Then it draped itself to the floor.

"Your veil, Mama?" Kitty asked.

Her mother nodded fondly. "I have the dress too, of course, but it's old and out of fashion. But this, I thought..."

Kitty's eyes were glistening. The veil was made of very fine net, plain at the top but appliquéd with cascading lace decoration of increasing complexity.

"Can I try it on?"

She stood very still as Madame Madeleine stepped in to arrange the net around Kitty's face, pinning it to the crown of her head where her coils of hair were thickest. The assistant rushed forwards to position a large glass in front of her. She and her mother looked at each other with tremendous love.

"I hope you'll be as happy as I was," Catherine Ballard murmured.

Kitty simply nodded.

"What do you think, Sephy?"

Kitty turned round so Persephone could see the full effect. Watching them from her chair, she thought they looked like two Renaissance angels with their porcelain skin and golden hair. The veil added a bridal glory to Kitty's face. With orange blossom in her hair it would be perfect.

"Oh look! You're crying!" Kitty said.

Persephone wiped her eyes roughly and tried to pretend she wasn't.

Mrs Ballard smiled, complicit. "I know! Exactly!"

But you don't know, Persephone thought. *That's the whole problem.*

Perhaps she was wrong to keep thinking of romance when a grand society wedding was supposed to be a transaction, but she couldn't help it, and nor could Kitty, it seemed.

Before Persephone could find the breath to speak, Mrs Ballard had turned back to Madame Madeleine. "Another thing… I had a few more thoughts about the trousseau. We haven't ordered enough travelling clothes or evening gowns. I didn't have nearly enough when I got married."

Madame Madeleine paled.

"Are you all right, madame?" Kitty asked. "Can I send for a glass of water?"

"Quite all right," the dressmaker said. But now that everyone was looking at her, it was clear she wasn't.

"What is it?" Kitty pleaded.

Madame Madeleine looked on the verge of tears. "I'm very sorry. I had wanted to save you the news. Two of my seamstresses have left me."

"Oh, why?" Kitty asked in alarm.

"One is to be married herself," the dressmaker said with a moue of irritation. "The other is sick. I'll find others and train them, of course. But those two were my best girls. They made the frills and silk flowers for your last dress, Miss Ballard. Hands like that are hard to find. Without them I can't get it all done on time. I'm so sorry."

Kitty tried to look encouraging but couldn't. As she'd said, this was the one thing she truly cared about. "I'm sorry too. I'd been looking forward to having everything made together. And by you and your lovely girls."

"So had I," Madame Madeleine said dully.

Persephone hated sitting silent in the corner when she knew that she could help. "I sew," she said.

Kitty swung round. "Oh, Sephy." She smiled sadly.

"The frills on your ballgown, and the roses," Persephone persisted. "I could have made those."

Mrs Ballard tutted. "Those girls are *real* seamstresses, Persephone. They don't do it for fun, as we do."

"I mean it. My mother taught me, and she was taught by her own mother, who was a seamstress to a Lady Adeleide, in Kent." Persephone paused for a moment, thinking of the life story she had invented for herself. Would an opera singer have had a mother who was a seamstress? Too late – it was the truth. "My grandma made all Lady Adeleide's clothes for years. She knew all the stitches and pattern tricks. They said she had magic in her fingers."

Here at last was a chance to do something, to keep her mind busy while she tried to keep Kitty safe.

"But … *engageantes* … rosettes … embroidery…" Madame Madeleine's bleak look encompassed all the finer elements of sewing.

Persephone knew how hard it was to make such delicate pieces to the highest standard. Stitches must not show. Every one must be precise. The fabric must be unmarked. It did indeed demand 'magic fingers'. She had them.

"Let me try."

❦

And so she found herself on trial to help make a dress that she thought should never be worn. Madame Madeleine gave her some sample sleeves to sew, and silk embroideries to complete. If she passed the test, every stitch would bring Kitty closer to Arthur! She was quite mad.

Kitty watched her start on it that evening, with little Ruby snuggled peacefully in her lap.

"You're such a marvel! It's quite unfair that you have such looks *and* talent, you know. When I'm married, we'll find a nice house to set you up in. I'm sure Arthur has a tenancy you can take. Until you're married too, of course. Which won't be long."

"I assure you it will be. I have no intention of marrying."

"Don't be ridiculous! Every woman must marry. What else would we do? And any man would be lucky to have you, Sephy. We just need to find the right one."

I found the right one, Persephone thought. *And I abandoned him because I had to.*

Once she produced her sample lacework and embroidery, Madame Madeleine was astonished by the quality of her work. "If you help me, I think we might just finish…" Broken with gratitude, she offered to pay Persephone the same rate as her regular seamstresses. Persephone's head started to spin at this point.

She had only offered to help to take her mind off her own troubles.

"I couldn't possibly…"

"How gracious—" Madame Madeleine started to say.

"But you must!" interrupted Kitty. "I insist. How wonderful!"

And so now, here she was, sewing for profit, for a day she prayed would never come.

⁂

She was working on a chemisette for a bridesmaid the next time Bee and Maria came to call.

"Did we see you out in the rain last Thursday night?" Maria asked, sipping her tea. "Mama and I were returning from a *wonderful* soirée in the barouche. You were on the corner of Berkley Square, talking to two unsavoury individuals. We should have stopped, but Mama was rather afraid."

"That wasn't me," Persephone said, remembering who she had been talking to and why. Berkley Square was not far from The Lamb. She also remembered the carriage that had splashed her. Maria arched a skeptical eyebrow.

Bee looked down and noticed what Persephone was

sewing. She watched her as she threaded lace flowers and seed pearls to gossamer fabric.

"My goodness! Are you working for the *modiste*?"

Persephone pursed her lips and nodded.

"I must say, I admire your skill. But –" she lowered her voice and leaned forwards – "you know only harlots sew for money."

Persephone flushed scarlet. This was accepted wisdom in some circles.

Bee looked at her with mock concern.

Kitty, who was busy playing with the new puppy, hadn't heard her. Maria did though and giggled. She adopted the same false, pitying look. "Yes. You see how it must look for Kitty. Having a *tradeswoman* in her house."

"What are you talking about?" Kitty asked, standing up with Ruby cuddled in her arms.

"Oh, only how very *workmanlike* Persephone is," Maria said. "We were admiring her industry. I do believe she must have earned a shilling while we've been talking!"

"I hope she has," Kitty observed. "Madame Madeleine was quite overwhelmed with all the work we've given her. If it wasn't for Sephy's nimble fingers you would have no dresses at all."

The other girls looked aghast at the idea of wearing anything Persephone had made, and hid it badly with tight smiles. If only they knew how she longed to flee this place even more than they wanted her to go.

❧❦❧

The next day Persephone left early for her sitting with James Whistler at his sister's house on Sloane Street. Time spent with him was the perfect antidote to her life at Balfour House. He had no interest in marriage at all, only travel and art. He was teaching her to see colour quite differently from before. Felix had always sought out the brightest, sharpest, most vivid pigments. Whistler taught her, by contrast, to appreciate subtle differences in tone and shade.

This time he stood her by the grand piano and, using his sketches from before, made a quick painting of her in oils. It was small and simple, depicting her pale moiré dress against the black piano. The portrait wasn't a pinpoint accurate portrayal, as Felix would have made. This was rougher, using hardly any colours. The effect was almost black and white, apart from her red hair and a hint of crimson on the carpet. Persephone wasn't sure why she loved it so much, but she gave him a heartfelt hug when he promised to give it to her.

"It's yours as soon as it's dry. I guess you don't have many pictures of yourself."

"I gave the last away."

He smiled. "I can do others."

But when she encountered him by chance, after church on Easter Sunday, he announced there would be no more painting. He was going back to Paris.

"I miss the damn place. And, as my sister keeps reminding me, I'm better now."

"You're leaving soon?"

"Next week. Come to lunch before I do. I can give you the portrait. Will Tuesday do?"

When Tuesday came she paid great attention to her outfit, choosing her amber velvet dress, and carefully brushing her hair. Outside, the cool March spring had turned to rainy April, and even the sand on the roads was soggy. She decided to take an omnibus but as soon she left the house she spotted a cab loitering nearby. Delighted by her luck, she hailed it and climbed in, calling "Sloane Street!" to the driver.

They set off at a clip, heading south down Park Lane

before turning west towards Chelsea. Persephone settled back against the cushions, watching the few pedestrians who were braving the wet weather. But then she noticed the cab heading straight past Sloane Street and on down the Cromwell Road. She called up to the driver.

"You've made a mistake."

"No, miss."

"We've passed the turning."

"That's not where we're going."

"But I told you!" The driver simply ignored her and carried on. Persephone looked back in alarm. "Where are you taking me?" she shouted. No answer. Her breath came short and shallow. *Am I being kidnapped?* "Stop! Stop!"

He didn't listen. If anything, he drove the horse a little faster. He turned left down a street she didn't know. Her heart was hammering now. Her hands were clammy. What if he took her into the countryside, alone? Or down some alleyway where gangs were waiting? Persephone searched around for a weapon to defend herself. For once, she cursed her long, loose hair. If she had worn it up, she would have had a hairpin. She could have jammed it into him. As it was…

But as she looked desperately out of the window, ready to holler for help, she noticed the familiar frontage of a pottery. Next came a workhouse and beside it a market garden. She knew *this* street. A right turn took them past a terrace of cottages and then the carriage turned into a wider road with taller villas, painted gentle shades of pink and blue.

This was Walton Street. Where Felix Dawson lived. Now panic turned to sheer confusion. The carriage slowed down, but her heart kept pounding. First, the wide house ... then the low house ... and the sky-blue villa she knew so well. The horse whinnied and slowed to a stop.

"We're 'ere, miss," the driver called down.

"I see," Persephone said in a low voice.

"'e said to deliver you safe and sound. Right up to the door."

She stayed where she was, but the front door was already opening. Felix must have been looking out for her. There he was on the steps. Collar-length hair, gently curling. Dark velvet jacket. Necktie trailing from his pocket, kingfisher-blue.

He was walking towards her, hand out to help her

down from the carriage in the rain. The next thing she knew, he was holding her hand to steady her and she was close enough to kiss him.

It was all she had longed for. What would Mrs Lisle say if she saw her now? Persephone stood back, trembling.

"What do you want?" she asked warily.

"How lovely it is to see you too," Felix said without smiling. "To paint you, since you ask."

"To *paint* me?"

"It's what I do."

"You were the one who had me kidnapped?"

"It's a long story," he said. He nodded to the cab as it pulled away. "That was someone else's idea. I said you wouldn't fall for it, but you did. Shall we go inside?"

She didn't feel she had much choice. The door to the house was open. Furious with herself for being so careless, she let him lead the way.

Chapter Twenty-five

Felix took her through the hall and up the familiar stairs. It was so strange to be here again. Persephone felt lightheaded as she reached the top floor and stepped into the studio. Nothing had changed. Instantly she was transported back to last summer. The smell of turpentine, the light from the tall window, the mess everywhere, the canvases, the bowl of bright spring flowers on the trestle table where he kept his paints and brushes. It was as if she'd never been away.

Felix walked ahead of her, towards the table.

"Can I pour you anything? Wine? A beer?"

"Why am I here?"

"As I said, to be painted. You like being painted, don't you?"

The disdain in his voice broke her heart. They had been so loving once.

"I … don't understand. Why now?"

He picked up a pencil and absent-mindedly jabbed the fleshy part of his thumb with its point. He looked older than when she had seen him last summer. She still wanted to touch the moles on his cheek. She knew him so well that she easily saw beneath his coldness. He had suffered as much as she had. The pain of the jabbing pencil seemed to ease his mind a little as he talked.

"I've received a commission. One I can't turn down. The client wants a painting of you in a … particular situation. Life-size."

She stared at him.

"What client?"

"I'm not allowed to say."

Her mind started racing. Rupert had been the first man to think of her as a 'stunner'. He had offered large sums to buy the last painting Felix made of her, and was bitterly disappointed not to get it. Was this his way of trying to win her back?

She shook her head. "I can't do it."

Felix gave her a tormented look. "You must!"

"Why?"

"It will change everything. I'll be free of her…"

Persephone gaped. "Do you mean Mrs Lisle?"

"I do. I hate her. She thinks she owns me."

"I hate her too," Persephone agreed with feeling.

Felix looked surprised at this but didn't comment on it. "Then help me. The money's spectacular. I said no at first. Twice in fact. But each time he doubled the sum. This will set me on my own course. I'll give you some of it…"

In his talk of freedom, the frost between them started to melt. Here was her old love, united with her in a common hatred of the woman who'd kept them apart. Something he had said bothered her. She felt it rub in her brain, like grit in an oyster, but there were too many other things to think about. Should she risk Mrs Lisle's wrath? What would happen to Harriet then? But Felix was so close, so familiar and desperate. She had missed him so very much.

"I … yes … perhaps."

"Oh, Mary!" It felt strange to hear her old name on his lips this way. She couldn't look away from them. Lips that had kissed her, over and over… He was closer now, but hesitating. "There's only one thing."

"What?" She was breathless. As always with Felix, it

took an effort to keep her body under control.

"He wants you ... naked. Like a Venus." He swallowed.

Silence. The room swam around her.

"Naked?"

"Yes. Wearing a crown of roses. Lying down, as if on an old-fashioned bed. We could keep the room warm, I promise. I'd make sure you were comfortable..."

"Naked?"

She walked unsteadily to the nearest chair – covered as usual with Felix's unwashed laundry – and collapsed on to it. The thought of them together ... here ... him looking at her... She had dreamed about it so often. Felix had captured her face, her arms and hands so beautifully before, and the shape of her under her dress. If he could capture *all* of her ... could turn her body into art... She knew he wanted to. Artists did it all the time. She had wanted it too, but he had never even seen her in her stays. This would be like the *Venus of Urbino*. It would be her deepest, darkest secret come to life. No wonder 'the client' had offered so much money.

Of course. The doubling of the money. The Venus.

She saw it clearly now. Rupert could not afford such lavishness. Nor was he so depraved that he would enjoy the idea of her old almost-lover painting her this way. Only one man would think of it.

"Mary! Let me get you something. You look as if you're about to faint."

Felix rushed around, finding a glass and filling it with water. She took it in trembling fingers and drank it slowly.

"So you know Arthur Malmesbury?" Her ragged voice came out as a growl.

"Hush! It's a condition of the commission that we don't talk of him, ever."

"He still thinks of me?" she wondered quietly.

"I suppose he must." Felix raised an eyebrow, as if it were amusing.

"He's marrying my best friend."

"He has ... unorthodox tastes. He said you might enjoy it. I'm to paint you Titianesque, surrounded by silks and furs. He can provide them. He wants you to wear an emerald necklace. It will be called *The Emerald Venus*. He made me promise not to..."

"What?"

"To touch you." Felix looked down.

If Arthur had seen *Persephone and Hades*, he would

know the rumours about her feelings for Felix, and his for her. How that tingle of thwarted passion would please him as he looked at her naked body later, laid out for him on a canvas. The glass finally slipped from her fingers. It landed with a dull thud at her feet.

"And you said yes?"

"I couldn't say no," Felix protested feebly. "The money will keep me for a year. Me … us…"

"And you thought I would agree?"

She felt sick. It wasn't so much the thought of posing for such a painting, but to do it for *her best friend's future husband*? Felix thought she would accept? That her body – something no man had ever yet fully seen – was such a commodity? What *did* he think of her?

As she glanced up she noticed an unvarnished painting beyond the pedestal, propped up against the wall. It depicted a girl in medieval dress, standing next to a stream in a wooded glade. At her feet was a knight in silver armour who looked asleep or dead.

"Ignore that," Felix said hurriedly. "It's not finished."

His anxiousness made Persephone look harder. She saw it suddenly and plainly. Under the new stunner's long blond hair, green eyes stared back at her. Her own eyes.

The full lips were *her* lips. But what an expression on that face! The painting was really of her, but the stone-hard look in the eyes was one she did not recognize.

"What is it?" she asked.

"It's just … a piece I was working on."

"What's it called?"

"Nothing. Nothing."

"All your pictures have a name. What is it?" Her voice was steely.

"Nothing!" he insisted. But she strode towards the painting, knowing he was lying. He sighed. *"La Belle Dame sans Merci,"* he admitted. "From the poem by Keats."

Persephone didn't take her eyes from the scene. "I remember it," she said. "From the book you gave me. The beautiful, merciless lady who lulled kings and princes to their doom."

"I…" He gulped and hesitated. "Yes."

She turned to look at him. "So that's who I am?"

He went pink in the face. "You left me!"

"You don't know *why.*"

"I do! To live with that … buffoon. Who could pay for your dresses."

"You really think I valued *dresses* over you?"

"Why else would you go?"

"Ah, yes!" she shouted. "What other reason could there be? I left for money! I left for dresses! I left for another man! I sold myself to him!"

"Well? Didn't you?"

Felix had moved in closer now. They were barely a foot apart, facing up to each other, breathing heavily. Persephone's eyes raked his face. She still loved the look of him, the way he lived, the things he made – but how could she love him, if he could think such terrible things of her? She thought she could bear his contempt, but to paint a *portrait* of it...? And not once to question that she might have higher motives for what she had done?

My God! The pact!

"I made a vow never to see you again," she said, her voice quavering. "I must go."

She turned and ran down the stairs.

"Mary! Mary!" he called after her. "Come back! What do you mean you made a vow? Explain!"

"You don't need an explanation!" she shouted back at him. "You already think you know everything!"

"Please! Tell me! I need you!"

She flew down the hall, past the startled maid, and out into the street. She had gone halfway down it before she paused, gasping for air.

"Mary!"

What would Mrs Lisle do to Harriet if she found out? It was raining harder than before. He was still behind her, running to catch up. Persephone picked up her muddy skirts and ran faster and faster, until she reached the end of the street. Glancing back, she saw that he had been held up by two burly dustmen who saw her running and blocked his path. On and on she dashed, hardly stopping, until her legs ached and her arms ached and every part of her was soaked, and her heart felt ready to burst.

By now, Walton Street was far behind. She paused against a lamp post to catch her breath. Looking around, she realized she was not far from Bee's house in Kensington. Instinctively, she had run north, in the vague direction of Balfour House and Kitty, not east to Sloane Street, where Whistler was waiting for her.

She could not turn back now. She would send a note to Whistler later, apologizing and saying goodbye. In the meantime, she needed to get home. She found another cab and huddled in the corner, shaking.

He thinks I'm nothing but a harlot.

He would have stripped me bare and laid me down...

She felt dizzy at the idea. And more dizzy at the thought of Arthur Malmesbury greedily gazing at the painting later.

So Arthur still wants me. In his own perverted way.

As she began to calm herself a little, she saw the scene in a different light. Felix was weak to agree, but it was Arthur who organized to have her kidnapped and who had commissioned the painting. He was the one at the root of it all. She began to wonder if his obsession knew any bounds. This thought plagued her until she was halfway to Mayfair. Only then did another thought strike her.

Where would he keep such a painting?

Not where Kitty could see it, certainly. Why pay so much money for such a thing if you could never look at it?

Persephone dimly remembered a story Felix once told her about Renaissance patrons who had secret rooms built in their palaces precisely for enjoying art they dared not show in public. Did Arthur have such a place? If so, what else was there?

Chapter Twenty-six

Eddie was not in the stables when she went to find him, having changed out of her wet clothes. She asked if a fellow groom could let her know when he returned. She went to her bedroom and took up her sewing, but her thoughts ricocheted between fury at Felix and fascinated horror at Arthur's twisted imagination, and she had to unpick almost as many stitches as she made. She was grateful to be interrupted an hour later by Winnie.

"Eddie's back, miss, if you want him."

"Thank you, Winnie." Persephone looked up. The girl was hovering, clearly keen to say more. "Yes?" she said, putting down her needle.

"He's got a reputation, that one," Winnie went on, encouraged. "He's the one they ask now if the grey mare's sick or the stallion's in a bad mood. A fine figure of a man, if you don't mind me saying."

"Of course not. Is he your type then, Winnie?"

"Oh *yes*, miss. I like a man with a bit of muscle. He's a fighter too, did you know?"

"I did."

"I've got most of my savings on him for the big fight. They're all saying he'll take it easily. You should put some money on him too."

"Oh!" Persephone caught her breath. Winnie's savings? How terrible to think of her losing it all in one moment. The other servants had placed bets as well. She longed to warn them what was coming – but it was too dangerous, and anyway, it was too late.

She stood up with a sigh. "Thanks for the tip, Winnie."

Eddie was at the back of one of the stalls, in his shirtsleeves, wielding a heavy spade as if it were a toothpick. He didn't hear her approach. Persephone coughed.

"Hello."

As he looked up and saw her, his face fell. "Oh. It's you. Don't come any closer."

"Why?" she asked.

"Because you'll get covered in horseshit. Why d'you think?"

She looked down. It wasn't just hay he was shovelling. That would explain the smell. "Don't worry," she said. "What animals do doesn't bother me."

Still, he looked surly. "Did you have to come here? Can a man not have any peace?"

"But…" She was stung. After her showdown with Felix, she was in no mood to be talked to this way. "What have I done?"

Eddie shovelled away for a minute. "It's what *I* do," he said, straightening up. "Shovelling their muck. Cheating, because of their grand wagers. No life of my own."

She saw that he was ashamed to be seen like this. He usually hid it well, but today she had caught him at a low moment. "It will get better. There will be other fights…"

"You think so? After this one? Who'll fight me then? What life do I have here? I've a good mind to go to America. I've got cousins in Chicago. A man can make something of himself in America."

"I'm sure you could," she said, "but don't go. Don't leave Annie. She needs you."

"And so do you, I gather."

She nodded reluctantly. "Yes."

He leaned against his spade and sighed theatrically. "What is it, then? What must I do for you this time?"

It was true: every time she saw Eddie it was to ask for something. She dropped her gaze. "I need information," she admitted. "About the man we both know."

He shrugged. "I've told you everything."

"He asked … for a painting of me. In a … certain situation. The question is, where would he put it?"

"Of you? Why couldn't he put it anywhere?"

She thought how to describe the nature of the commission and blushed to the roots of her hair. Eddie somehow guessed the worst of it.

"The rogue!" he growled. Did all men's imaginations run so easily in the same direction? It made her blush all the more. She folded her arms across her chest and looked at him pleadingly. "But I'm not asking anybody anything else about him," he insisted. "D'you know what'll happen if his people find out I'm digging around? It's a fool's game. Besides, I told you – stay out of it."

"If you won't, I will. Tell me who to ask." He shook his head, but Persephone stood her ground.

"I mean it. Tell me."

"They'd eat you alive."

"Let them try. He has a secret place, I'm certain. I'll find it, however I have to."

"Ah, Mary." Eddie sighed. "You'll be the death of me. All right. I'll see what I can discover. I'll send word via Winnie if I hear something."

"Thank you, Eddie!"

She wanted to go to him and kiss his cheek, but the pile of horseshit between them stood in the way. Instead, she curtseyed. He waved her off. "Be gone with you, woman!"

On her way back, Persephone found herself thinking about the casual way he had mentioned Winnie. How friendly were they? she wondered. She reflected that Winnie could do a lot worse than a young man like Eddie, regardless of what he shovelled or how it smelled.

❧ ❦ ❧

Winnie found Persephone in the parlour, alone, sewing the next morning. She held out a letter.

"From Eddie," she explained. "He's had to take a horse to market. He said you'd want to read what's inside before he came back tomorrow. He taught himself, you know. To write."

Glancing up, she saw an unmistakable look of love in Winnie's eyes. Winnie was a warm-hearted girl with a pretty face and a smart way of dressing. If he was interested, Eddie could do worse than a girl like her.

The letter was brief, which was lucky because Eddie's writing, while painfully neat, was also hard to decipher in places.

To M

I write this with hessitachun, because if Certain People find it there will be trubul. So burn it in the fire without deelay. But you shuld know that there is not a room as we disscused, but a hole House. It is near the Dairy. The number of Annie's house minus 19. It is sicrit from the famly and used for Plesure. Pleese burn this.

Your humbul servant
EOB

Persephone read it three times. Each time, she was more unsettled by what she understood.

Arthur kept a secret house for pleasure? A whole *house*

he had not told Kitty about? She imagined the Venus portrait hanging there and shuddered. Were the walls full of pictures of naked mistresses? What else didn't Kitty know?

It took a while to work out the address. Persephone watched the letter turn to ashes in the grate as she thought it through. She reasoned that the 'Dairy' must mean the Grosvenor Dairy, which was nearby in Mount Street, on the way to Hyde Park. She knew there were other dairies but she was not familiar with them and if Eddie was not more specific, that was surely because he knew she would guess this one. As for the number, the Atkins family, who employed Annie in Pimlico, lived at Number Sixty-three St George's Square, so this must be Number Forty-four.

She must go and see it. Today.

Kitty was getting ready for a fitting for some of her trousseau dresses. Persephone complained of a headache, saying she needed some fresh air. Or 'The Eddie O'Bryan Patented Excuse', as she thought of it now.

"You don't look well," Kitty agreed. "You go. I have a lot to discuss with Madame Madeleine anyway. Would you like Winnie to go with you?"

"No! Thank you."

Whatever Persephone was about to discover, she needed to do it alone.

Chapter Twenty-seven

Ever since she had read of it, the secret house had been unfurling in Persephone's imagination. By the time she got to Mount Street, a mere four streets away, she half expected to see a circus, with strongmen outside and tigers prowling. But no. All was calm. Two dairymaids walked along with wooden yokes on their shoulders. The street smelled of cow, but otherwise looked ordinary. Either side of the dairy, the tall grey Georgian houses were models of restraint and respectability. Number Forty-four did not stand out from its neighbours in any way.

Persephone stood contemplating it for half an hour. The house sat there, quiet and undisturbed. Persephone began to wonder if Eddie had got his information wrong. Would Arthur really have the audacity to keep an address so close to the Ballards' home? It could just be the home of some innocent, law-abiding family. But then her attention was caught by a smart barouche barrelling up the street. It was going so fast that it took a moment for the driver to halt the horse. A gentleman in a frock coat and top hat got out and walked back along the street a little way. Persephone held her breath as he stopped at Number Forty-four, almost opposite where she was standing.

She caught sight of his face briefly as he glanced around before going up the steps to the front door. She knew him instantly from his high-bridged narrow nose and thick moustache. He was the young man who had been standing next to Arthur when the engagement was announced. They had seemed to be best friends.

Here was her proof.

He knocked at the door and was ushered inside. After that, the house returned to stillness and silence. Eventually, Persephone gave up watching and made her way home.

⁂

For three full days Persephone agonized about what to do. Simply telling Kitty about the house in Mount Street was pointless – she would never believe her, and if she did it would just make Persephone seem more obsessed.

She thought of Eddie and Annie's warnings about staying out of it, and perhaps they were right, but the black look Arthur had given her on the announcement of his engagement still haunted her. She would fight him however she knew, and whatever it cost.

That evening Roly Ballard passed her on the stairs after dinner, dressed to the nines.

"Are you still here?" he asked coldly.

"For as long as Kitty needs me," she replied with equal froideur.

"Huh."

Without another word, he descended the staircase and put on his evening coat. Persephone watched him go out and realized that she had seen him head off at this time of night before. It sparked an idea.

"Where does Roly go?" she asked Kitty, as they sat at their sewing the following day.

"To play cards," Kitty said absently, threading a needle for her embroidery. "At his club, I think."

Quite often, Rupert had left Persephone in her apartment at about this time to go gambling or carousing with his friends. She decided to take a gamble of her own and hope that Arthur was a creature of similar habits. If they could catch him going in or out of Number Forty-four, it would be so much easier to convince Kitty to ask questions. Surely, if Eddie could find out so easily that Arthur owned it, then Frederick Ballard, with all his contacts in property, could do so too? He might even know someone who could tell them what was inside.

Persephone set aside the lace border she was sewing. She felt her heart beat faster.

"Kitty dearest, do you mind finishing dinner early tonight?"

Kitty frowned. "Why?"

"I'd like to take you somewhere. Not far. It's a little adventure. I know how you love them." Persephone cursed herself for using the word this way.

Kitty brightened instantly. "Really? How exciting! Oh, it takes me back to the old days. You and Felix and Roly and me in the carriage... I shan't be able to do any such thing when I am married."

"Exactly. One last trip. There's something I want to show you."

"A new venue? Like Cremorne Gardens?"

"Not exactly. We shall have to slip out of the house. And dress darkly so we can't be seen…"

With every word Kitty's eyes grew wider. It made Persephone feel more wretched than ever to be tricking her this way. Kitty took great delight in planning the best way to leave the house, avoiding busy passages used by servants preparing dinner. But she drew the line at borrowing one of Persephone's plainer dresses to disguise herself.

"I shall wear my midnight blue shantung skirt with a black cloak over it. And my black bonnet with velvet trim. No, the grossgrain. The brim is larger. Oh, Sephy! I haven't had this much fun in ages!"

<hr/>

Persephone wore her darkest green dress to dinner and sat there feeling like Judas at the Last Supper. Kitty feigned a headache during the dessert course and as soon as it was over, her mother encouraged her to go to her room with a tincture and lie down. The two girls left the table together and Kitty had to suppress her giggles as they went upstairs.

After a smooth escape from Balfour House, they

found themselves walking arm in arm through the streets of Mayfair. Kitty was still giddy with excitement.

"You look transformed! I would hardly know you, Sephy. You're a mistress of disguise!"

"Hardly." Persephone had simply thrown her old shawl around her shoulders and tucked her bright hair as well as she could under a large bonnet borrowed from Aunt Violet's impressive collection in the hall. However, she certainly looked more disguised than Kitty who, despite her best efforts, glowed with her usual vitality, her rich skirts and golden coils of hair glinting under every streetlamp.

They didn't have far to walk. Occasional strolling couples passed by, and groups of workmen heading home. The dairy was closed up at this time of night and Mount Street was much quieter than before. They could hear the pounding hooves and grinding wheels of the distant traffic on Park Lane. Above them, the night sky was clear and the moon was rising.

Kitty grinned. "Isn't this thrilling? Where are we going?"

Persephone guided her past a few more buildings. "We're here." She stopped opposite Number Forty-four.

"Here? But we're nowhere. This is just an ordinary street."

"Not exactly. Wait and you'll see."

They were standing between two houses on the other side of the road, in a dark spot between two gas lamps. Persephone's heart was racing. All her energies had been focused on getting Kitty to this place but now they were here, she was already starting to regret her decision. How long could she make Kitty stay? If Arthur didn't appear on cue, how would she explain?

Kitty pulled her cloak around her. "I'm cold. I didn't realize it would be so chilly."

"I'm sorry."

"Must we stay here long?"

"I... I don't know."

But Kitty gasped and clutched at Persephone's arm. "Look!"

Someone had opened a shutter in a house opposite and thrown open the window behind. Golden light spilled out of it, and laughter.

"A party! How lovely!" Kitty beamed at Persephone.

A carriage stopped a few yards down the road and two girls clambered out of it. They paid the driver and teetered on high heels across the road, their colourful cloaks billowing behind them in the breeze. They knocked at the door of Number Forty-four and were shown in. Kitty was entranced by the activity. But these were not genteel young women. Persephone felt a sense of foreboding.

"Kitty, wait!"

But Kitty was already walking across the street. She called behind her.

"Are we invited too? I shouldn't really go without a chaperone…"

Persephone ran to catch up. "No!"

"Then why…?"

Persephone grimaced. "It's Arthur's house." The truth came in a rush. "He keeps it secretly. I thought you ought to know. I wanted you to see—"

"But how…?"

Kitty's question was cut off by a man in workers' tweeds brushing roughly past them and running up the steps. He knocked at the front door and it was soon answered. A footman swore at him as he handed over a small package wrapped in waxed paper.

"You shouldn't be up 'ere! It's downstairs for the

likes of you!"

"I can knock anywhere I like. Wot I got's like gold, see? 'e'll lick your boots for this."

"Don't be disgusting! Get out of 'ere, g'wan."

The footman shoved at the man, who staggered down the steps with a curse. He bumped into Kitty, who had drifted even closer towards the house and now cried out in alarm.

From the open doorway the footman stared down at her, and Persephone not far behind.

"Two more of 'em?" he muttered. He turned behind him. "Oi! 'arold! There's two more!" Then he turned back to them with a glare of annoyance. "You ladybirds! You coming in or wot?"

Persephone flushed with humiliation. They had been mistaken for ladies of the night! She pulled at Kitty's arm, but Kitty stood her ground.

"Is this –" her voice shook with emotion – "the h-house of Lord Arthur Malmesbury?"

He laughed. "'ark at 'er!" he said. "Plum in 'er mouth. A right proper lady! Yes, this is the place, miss. Your *ladyship*, I should say." He gave a mock bow and motioned her inside.

"No! Don't!" Persephone called out.

She would have turned and run, but she couldn't leave Kitty behind. Poor Kitty, who had no idea what a 'ladybird' was and didn't understand what she was being taken for. Kitty looked back at her briefly, confused and frowning. It was as if she wanted answers but didn't trust Persephone to give them. Her blue eyes hardened.

"Yes, I'll come up," Kitty said firmly.

"Come on then. I can't 'old this door open forever."

She walked up the steps with Persephone at her heels, She undid her cloak and bonnet and handed them to a second footman who was waiting inside.

The second man stared at Kitty's face and hair. "My word!" he said, nudging his colleague. "She's the spitting image, that one. Where'd 'e find you then?"

"Lord Malmesbury is … a friend," Kitty said uncomfortably. She wasn't used to being questioned by servants.

"I bet 'e is!" He gave her a broad wink. "Come along then."

He took Persephone's shawl and bonnet too, and guided them up towards the lights and laughter. A maid, laden with empty champagne bottles, passed them on the stairs. She too stared at Kitty.

"Oo! Blimey! Just like the fiancée from the big 'ouse. Saucy! And the other one. Like 'er friend!"

She bellowed with laughter.

These were like no servants Persephone had ever known. They were clearly accustomed to visiting tarts. And they thought she and Kitty were specialty girls, chosen to look like Arthur's fiancée and her companion! It was not 'saucy' – it was obscene. Was *this* how Arthur lived? Kitty would never bear it. She must not see…

"*Kitty!*" she called out desperately.

Kitty turned back, scared and still confused, but the footman urged them on and they were led through one silk-clad chamber and then another, until finally they came to the source of the party. Here the room was lit by a hundred candles and the air was hot. The walls were red and cast an unearthly glow on the company. Several half-dressed women looked up from games of cards and Ouija boards. Another was playing a jig on the violin, wearing nothing but stays and pantaloons. She stopped as Kitty gasped in shock.

Persephone looked past Kitty's shaking shoulders as her friend stood in the doorway, struggling to breathe.

In the middle of the room, Arthur lay on a low daybed, draped with two young women who were feeding him fruit and wine. A third was embracing him like a long-lost lover. He wore an unbuttoned shirt and breeches. His hair stuck to his head, damp with perspiration, and his eyes were glazed. Several small glass vials lay broken on a table beside him. He seemed feverish, but he smiled at the sight of Kitty. That slow, unfurling smile.

"Ah, Kitty-kitty-kitcat. Hello, Mrs Malmesbury. Did I invite you? I don't remember. Have a grape."

He did not seem remotely troubled by her presence. Persephone quickly saw that he was too far gone in his drug-induced haze for that. Kitty stared. She grabbed at the doorframe with a white-knuckled hand to steady herself.

It was worse, so much worse than Persephone could ever have imagined. This was the ninth circle of Dante's Hell: treachery. Arthur's. Hers. She blamed herself entirely for bringing Kitty here.

"Kitty!"

She rushed towards her friend, but Kitty threw her off. Though deep in shock, she flung Persephone backwards with the strength of a stevedore, so her body hit the wall. That's when Arthur saw her. Through the fog of laudanum and wine, he lit up like a beacon. His face was transformed.

"Persephone!" He threw off the girl who had been embracing him – a small, dark-haired creature in lace-trimmed knickers – and held out both arms to her. "My darling! Come to me!"

The dark girl slumped to the floor as Persephone was grabbed by strong hands, dragged forwards and placed on Arthur's lap. He enfolded her resisting body in his arms and buried his face in her neck. "My lovely lovely lovely girl."

Persephone sat there, trapped, and turned to look wretchedly at Kitty. "I'm so sorry!"

Kitty hadn't moved from the doorway. Her lips formed a round 'O'. Her breath came in noisy gasps. "You… You…"

"I tried to tell you…"

Kitty held up a hand to stop her. The other girls were beginning to work out what was happening and grinned at each other in pure delight. Kitty's voice was not much more than a whisper, but everyone was listening.

"Harlequin… Columbine… From the very beginning. It was you."

"No! It wasn't. I promise!"

"I should have seen. You took him from the first."

"No! *Honestly*, Kitty!"

Persephone struggled to get up and run to her again, but Arthur held her close. He was nuzzling her ear. Her stomach churned.

"You tried to put me off…" Kitty's voice was dreamlike. "And all the time…"

"I told him no!"

But all Kitty saw was her best friend and her fiancé, his arms around her, murmuring tender words and phrases…

Persephone saw at once that all was lost. She had brought Kitty here. Kitty assumed she knew everything and that this had been her intention.

Kitty held the back of her hand to her mouth. She was still breathing too fast. Persephone thought she would faint, but she didn't. Kitty turned and ran, and as she did, she started screaming: short, high-pitched screams that sounded down the stairs, through the hall and into the street outside.

As the cries faded, Persephone turned back and slapped Arthur as hard as she could on his hot, sweaty face. He smiled. "Do that again!"

She had been about to, but stopped. Tears flowed.

"I'll never see her again!" she howled at him.

His smile didn't waver. "You can if you want to. I won't stop you."

"Nor will *you*, you idiot!" She was tempted to hit him, even if he enjoyed it, but one of the women, sensing her impulse, held her back.

"You've 'ad your fun. You'd better go," she said in a calm, tired voice that suggested she was used to managing violence.

Arthur let go of her. As the woman led her away by the wrist she turned to face him.

"May you rot in Hell."

He smiled up at her. The endless black behind his eyes made her unsure whether to fear or pity him. "Oh, I will."

PART III

SHADOWS ON WATER

Chapter Twenty-eight

Persephone moved out of Balfour House that night. Catherine Ballard was too busy comforting her daughter, hysterical with shock and grief, to notice her go.

Image after image flashed through Persephone's head of the moments she should have told Kitty everything she knew, whatever the cost. That first time in Venice, when they officially 'met'. The island of Torcello. The night of the *Carnevale* party... Anything would have been better than this.

At her message, Eddie came with a cart to the tradesman's door and helped her take her things away. This time her trunk contained her sewing box and scraps, and the few things she had brought from Venice. She tucked Whistler's painting of La Salute under her arm.

They travelled east through the dark empty streets to Spitalfields, where Eddie's lodgings lay.

"You're in luck," he said. "There's a woman in my building who moved out a little while ago. I say moved out – she died. But the rooms are clean, there's a few sticks of furniture and the rent's not bad."

"I can pay," she told him. "I have money saved."

"Of course you can!" Eddie smiled. "I can't see you relying on anyone for a while."

"Not ever," Persephone said firmly.

"So tell me. What happened?"

She described the full catastrophe at the house in Mount Street, blaming herself at every point along the way. "I shouldn't have taken Kitty... I shouldn't have told her the house was his..."

Eddie showed her little sympathy. "I told you. Keep out of grand people's problems. You wouldn't listen."

He only softened when Persephone got to Kitty's reaction, and her own sense of loss at seeing her friend in pain. "She'll never forgive me." Persephone was crying freely now.

"She won't," he agreed. He put a comforting arm around her as the cart trundled past the law courts, towards the distant dome of St Paul's. "God knows what you saved her from, but all she'll see is what you cost her."

Fifteen minutes later, they were there. Spitalfields was old London, like Mayfair, with rows of tall Georgian houses but these ones were packed together, narrow and tight. They were black with soot, plain, and almost jostling on to the pavement. There were no grand squares here, only places to live and work – and drink, if the pub on the corner was anything to go by.

The house where Eddie lived had been divided into three dwellings to maximize the rent. Eddie was at the top and Persephone would take the two rooms at the bottom. There were bare boards on the floor, no curtains at the windows and only plaster on the walls. The fires had not been lit in a while. Both rooms were damp and freezing. The few chairs and tables left behind were old and broken.

Persephone looked around in wonder as moonlight streamed into the larger workroom at the front through broken windowpanes. There, in the corner, her chair would go, near the window. She would fix the shutters and mend the table. That's where she would work, she could see it all now. And behind was another room to wash and sleep. All this was hers and hers alone!

For the first time in her life, she was free. She sank to

her knees in thankfulness.

"Mary! Let me help you!" Eddie was at her side in an instant, assuming something was wrong. He brought her to her feet again, but she gently pushed him away.

"I'm quite all right." She smiled shyly. "And thank you."

"For what?"

"For this."

Eddie stared at his feet. "It's nothing. I owed you."

"You've paid your debts. I owed you from the time before."

He shook his head and laughed. "Look, nobody owes anything. Agreed?"

She nodded.

"I'll get your things in. Then you need to sleep."

She lay on the narrow, lumpy mattress on the floor that night, looking up at the ceiling, which had collapsed in one corner and threatened to do so in another. Her thoughts turned to Kitty for the hundredth time. She pictured her dearest friend lying between her lace-edged, linen sheets, consumed with utter desolation, and knew with every beat of her heart who was the lucky one now.

The engagement was broken off the next morning. From his position in the stables, Eddie got to hear the gossip pretty fast. He told Persephone the news as soon as he got home.

"Did they say why?" she asked.

"They said a relative had died and they were respecting a period of mourning."

"Which side? His or hers?"

"It wasn't clear. Everyone knows it's an excuse. Half the servants seem to think he was carrying on with someone and the other half think *she* was. It's not pretty."

Persephone shook her head sadly. "I suppose the half that think it was him assume the 'someone' was me."

"No, they don't, actually," Eddie said.

"Oh? But didn't they see Arthur meet me in the housekeeper's room?" She still stung at the thought of it.

"Yes, two of them did. And they saw him leave quickly afterwards with a flea in his ear. They got a pretty clear idea all right. Servants aren't as blind as you think."

She managed a laugh. She hadn't thought herself so blind when she was one of them. "That's good. Thanks, Eddie." It was a big relief, in fact. Losing Kitty's good opinion was bad enough. Persephone was over being thought ill of for things she hadn't done. But still … there were things she *had* done. "Is Kitty out of her room yet?" Her voice was low and thick with regret.

"No. She's still there," Eddie said. "The doctor's been and gone. She'll only talk to the dog, Winnie said. Not even those hoity-toity friends of hers can visit. Her mama's mad with worry. But she'll mend. It's only heartache."

"I know heartache," Persephone reproved him. "There's no 'only' about it."

"Maybe Kitty won't forgive you, but you should forgive yourself, Mary."

She half-smiled and nodded.

"Promise me," he said.

"Not another promise!"

"You usually break them! I mean it this time."

He wasn't joking. Persephone shook her head. She had done everything wrong and Kitty was suffering for it. She couldn't forgive herself.

Eddie put his big arms around her and held her awkwardly for a while, patting her back as if she were one of the horses in the stables. He murmured into her hair. "You did what you had to do. Be proud of yourself. I'm proud of you."

She clung to him and cried into his shoulder like a child. He waited patiently until she was all cried out, with puffy eyes and a sore throat from sobbing. Then he stood back to look at her.

"And to think... They called you a stunner."

She tried to glare at him but ended up smiling, which was his intention. "To think, they called *you* a..."

"A what? Something too terrible to say?" he asked.

She didn't answer at first. *A fine figure of a man*, she had been thinking. But she didn't want to inflate his already excessive opinion of himself.

"Yes, definitely," she lied.

He laughed. "Probably deserved." Looking around the shabby room he asked, "D'you want me to help you with the furniture? I've some time this evening."

She shook her head. "I'll fix it. It won't take me long."

"And how will you do that?"

She looked up at him scornfully. "I'm a country girl. I can do anything."

She wasn't boasting. Or at least, she was, but there was truth behind it. She was used to working hard. After he went, she spent the next few hours mending the shutters and the table, cleaning the grates and getting the lodgings the way she wanted them. The labour cleared her head and gave her a measure of peace. By midnight she was filthy and exhausted but there was a glowing fire in the bedroom grate. She lay down on the narrow bed feeling happier than she had any right to be.

Chapter Twenty-nine

Persephone would gladly have never visited the West End again but she needed to see Madame Madeleine. She had been working on several pieces for Kitty's bridesmaids. The expensive fabrics belonged to the *modiste* and she felt honour-bound to return them. So she accompanied Eddie on his next trip to work at the stables.

Madame Madeleine's establishment in Fitzrovia was a large, well-proportioned house, with bay trees either side of a matching green front door. Persephone smiled to see it, thinking of the comments about sewing from Bee and Maria. Here it paid for the smartest house on the street.

With the wedding cancelled and so many part-finished dresses not needed suddenly, Persephone half expected to find the dressmaker and her assistants in shock and tears.

But instead, the workroom on the first floor was bustling with activity. Madame Madeleine greeted her dressed in her working smock with a scarf full of pins around her neck. "Thank you for these, Miss Lavelle. I'm sure we'll find a use for them. I'm so sorry about your friend."

"Thank you," Persephone said quickly. "I see you're busy. Has Kitty decided to keep some of the dresses?"

"Oh no! The poor girl wants never to see them! And I quite understand. But her mother is an admirable woman. She's agreed to pay for what we've done so far, which is more than many would. And I have to admit, I'm busier than ever."

"Oh?"

"Kitty's wedding-dress design caused quite a stir. All her friends were talking about it. Now several girls getting married in the summer want something similar. I've been turning work away for days."

Looking around the workroom, Persephone saw new designs and patterns littering the tables. She also saw what Madame Madeleine was too delicate to mention: jackets and skirts from Kitty's trousseau being carefully picked apart so that they could be remade for another client, another time. Little would be wasted and

Madame Madeleine's reputation was assured. Not everybody would lose from Kitty's tragic situation.

"I can give you more work if you want it," the *modiste* said, seeing Persephone's keen eye taking in every detail. "Plenty of it."

"I'm afraid I couldn't." Persephone had betrayed her friend quite enough. Remaking her trousseau for someone else was beyond the pale.

Madame Madeleine eyed her sharply. She lowered her voice so the nearest assistants couldn't hear. "I could pay you more per piece. Significantly more. It's hard to find hands like yours."

"Thank you, but no. I wish you every success, though."

"Well, tell me if you change your mind."

Persephone left the house deep in thought. Her initial refusal had only encouraged a higher offer. Was this how one negotiated? Were her sewing skills worth so much?

By the end of the day she had visited three other well-known *modistes* and got trial work from two of them. Her rent for this month was already saved and next month's was assured. The pay was not good but it was better than a maid's wage, and more reliable than a model's, and her rooms were cheap. If she continued to sit for her favourite artists too she would even be able to buy the occasional luxury. On the way home she bought herself a hatpin in celebration and a posy of spring violets to put on her mantelpiece.

❦

In Mayfair she had felt disapproving eyes on her busy hands but back in Spitalfields she was at home. The streets were full of silk weavers and seamstresses. Needle-sellers passed from door to door; gossip at the butcher's was all about the next import of Indian gold thread or Venice lace. Some of the larger houses spoke of their success. The women dressed well, like Persephone, in skirts and jackets they had made themselves – perfect copies of some of the best West End designs.

Two women shared the rooms on the floor above her. They were not fine seamstresses but shirtmakers – a mother and daughter called Jane and Eve Ellis, who helped Persephone find the best source of thread and thimbles. They liked to visit her workroom and talk, while they admired her 'fuzzy' painting of the white church on the mantel and the graceful way she had arranged the simple furniture.

"And them flowers, miss," Eve said eagerly. "They're beautiful."

Persephone had thought that perhaps, here among working people, she might revert to being plain Mary Adams – as she still was to Eddie – but the Ellises insisted on calling her Miss Lavelle.

"It wouldn't seem right, you being one of us," Jane Ellis said. "With ... the way you are."

"What way is that?"

Jane couldn't put her finger on it. She didn't mean to be unkind. "Your voice, your style, the things you know. It's different for you."

"I don't think it is."

But Jane wouldn't be persuaded, and her daughter agreed. "Besides, I like to tell my friends I know Miss Persephone Lavelle."

Eve, who was a year older than Persephone, ran her hands lovingly over the delicate lace pieces she was sewing.

"How I'd love to work with these. Will you teach me?"

"Of course," Persephone said, grateful for the girl's company.

In the days that followed, while Eddie worked in the stables by day and trained for his prizefight by night, she too worked all the hours she could, by daylight and gas light, until her fingers seized up and her eyes saw stars.

She didn't feel so different from the Ellises then, but her 'magic hands' still set her apart. Eve Ellis was a keen worker, but she didn't have the knack for the stitches that Persephone had. Her seams were uneven and fabrics often got dirty in her hands. Persephone tried to be kind, but found herself becoming increasingly impatient as she unpicked yet another piece of embroidery. There was only one person she knew whose fingers could fly across a piece of silk the way hers could. They had been taught together by their mothers. Her cousin Harriet.

If only she were here, Persephone found herself reflecting for the second time one morning, as Eve spoiled a satin rosette by pulling on it. The last time she had seen Harriet was two weeks ago, on her afternoon off, when Harriet's head had fallen on the table halfway through their dinner at a local chop-house. She was too exhausted even to eat. She wouldn't talk about Aileana, either. Though she lived and worked in a grand house, Persephone worried about her.

If I could just take care of her myself, she thought. Then she looked around her busy workroom and suddenly all her fears and hopes crystallized into one beautiful idea. *I need her. And I* can *take care of her. Who is to stop me now?*

Eve looked up from her sewing. "Why are you laughing? Is it my rosette?"

"Not at all," Persephone said with a smile. "Though it does need work. I'll show you later. Wait here – I'll be back."

<hr/>

She wrapped up warm against the crisp spring breeze and walked two hours across London to Chelsea. Summoning all her courage, she went up the path to the big grey house on the King's Road. This was where Felix's painting of *Persephone and Hades* was almost certainly hidden, if indeed it still existed. It was the home of the dreaded Mrs Lisle.

As she rounded the corner to take the path to the tradesman's door, she heard voices behind her. She looked back to see the darkly dressed widow walking down to the front gate arm in arm with a much younger girl, to whom she spoke affectionately. Persephone flattened herself to the wall. Her heart beat like a piston. She watched as they reached the gate and melted into the passing crowds. They hadn't noticed her. Only then did she dare breathe.

She paused for a long moment before knocking, smoothing her hair and pinching her cheeks. By the time a man in a footman's apron answered the door she at least gave the appearance of calm.

"Yes? What is it?"

"I've come for Harriet, the laundress," Persephone said with a cocky assurance she didn't feel – though she was glad to know that Mrs Lisle was no longer at home.

The footman peered at her. "'arriet? I didn't know as she was going anywhere."

"Oh yes. It's all arranged."

Persephone had thought about what to say on the way. If she showed any fear or hesitation, she would be turned down and might not get to see Harriet at all. Her cousin's next day off was two weeks away and she couldn't wait that long. Sheer brazen nerve was better.

"I'll go and find 'er," the footman said, frowning.

When Harriet came to the door five minutes later, she was a picture of confusion, but she threw her arms around her cousin in delight. Persephone felt how desperately thin she was, how her bones stuck out, and noticed how the lines on her face had deepened this last year.

"I've come to take you away," she whispered. "And Aileana too. You don't have to come if you don't want to, but—"

"Oh!" Harriet's hand flew to her mouth. "Wait here."

Harriet gave her a desperate look. Without another word she fled back inside, leaving the door open. Persephone stood where she was, fearing that a senior servant would come to shoo her away at any moment, or, worse, that Mrs Lisle might return and somehow catch sight of her at the side of the house.

However, a few minutes later her cousin was back, dressed in a shawl and shabby bonnet, with her baby wrapped in a blanket in one arm and a basket covered by a napkin over the other. Persephone hoped the basket contained all her most precious things, because she wouldn't be coming back.

"I'm sorry," Harriet said. "I had to get Aileana. I'm ready."

"Then let's go."

She led the way down the path, across the road and down a quiet street. No sign of Mrs Lisle, or anyone she knew. They walked quickly, too happy to be in each other's company to speak at first. Persephone took them to an omnibus going in the right direction and paid for their tickets. Harriet stared out through the window.

"Where are we going?"

"To my house in Spitalfields."

"You have a *house*?"

"Well, part of one. There's enough space for you and Aileana, if we squeeze. You don't mind squeezing, do you?"

Harriet's thin face was torn between shock and joy. "I *love* to squeeze. We don't mind, do we, baby?"

She looked into the wide blue eyes of the child in her arms, who gazed back uncertainly. Harriet frowned and her own eyes formed tears.

"What is it?" Persephone asked.

"It's nothing."

"It's not nothing! You've been saying that for weeks and I see how unhappy you are."

Harriet hesitated. "You've been so kind. You've been

my angel, Mary, and none of this … I don't want…"

Persephone gave her cousin a stern look. "Let's get this clear. The only thing you owe me is the truth. But that much I need. I can see it's bad. Tell me."

"Oh, Mary!" Harriet broke down. "She is a cold, hard woman. The menservants she treats well, but the butler likes to give the girls a beating, and she lets him. She hardly feeds us, either. But she loves the baby. She took her from me the week after she was born."

"What?"

"She said she was the prettiest thing, and that when she adopted her niece she never knew her as an infant and now was her chance. She had a cradle set up in her bedroom so she could watch her. The wet nurse came in to feed her, and so my milk would stay I had to sneak in when she was out and wake the baby. I hated to do it. I hardly had any milk to give her. But it was our only time together. Even so, she hardly knows me. Look! She's scared of me."

Harriet stroked her daughter's head and wept. Persephone tried to assure her that the baby was frightened only of the omnibus, not her mother, but the child grizzled and would not be comforted.

Persephone saw how much emotion her cousin had been holding back these last few months and cursed herself for not noticing properly before. She cursed Mrs Lisle more though.

"That monster! She *promised* me! She vowed to look after you. I did everything she wanted…"

For a while, her fury was boundless. She wanted to go back to the house and wait for the widow, to find something sharp and deadly, and plunge it into her cold, black heart. All the sacrifices she had made! Her love for Felix destroyed! And all for nothing. Harriet had been in torment, and that was exactly what Persephone had moved Heaven and earth to avoid. Was a rich woman's word worth nothing?

<hr/>

The back bedroom in Spitalfields was warm with bodies that night. Persephone borrowed a second mattress from one of her neighbours and padded a drawer with blankets and soft cottons as a cradle for the baby. By day, the workroom was busier than ever. Harriet, though frail from lack of food and overwork, had still lost none of her talent with a needle. While

Aileana slept beside her, she cheerfully helped Persephone with her tasks. When the baby was awake, she played with her and sang her Kentish lullabies. At mealtimes Persephone set the table with kidney puddings and gypsy tarts and all her cousin's favourite foods. Harriet's milk came back more strongly with each feed and gradually the little girl's wary gaze became more trusting.

Persephone loved to watch them together while she worked. She began to understand why the Renaissance masters so often liked to paint the Madonna and child, like the ones she had seen in Venice's endless churches. She didn't want a baby of her own, she realized, and wasn't jealous. But she was moved by their growing bond and wanted Aileana to have the best of everything.

The house thrummed with activity. For the next few days Persephone was in and out, seeking new commissions for herself and Harriet, and zealously working on them at home. Eve Ellis did what she could – more often than not helping with the baby. And Eddie was busier than all of them, rushing between the stables in Mayfair and his training in the East End. The big fight was only a week away and though Persephone dreaded it, she hoped he would soon bounce back after his enforced defeat.

Then Eddie went away. For the final days he was to be held in a secret location by the Whitechapel Boys, who didn't want any foul play to destroy the fight – until their own foul play in the closing bout, of course.

"Don't come and watch," he said, shouldering his bundle as he came to say goodbye.

"I wasn't intending to," Persephone admitted. The idea of seeing a man she liked being pummelled by a famous fighter held no appeal for her at all.

"I'll see you when it's over."

Unable to think what to say because her heart was too full, she flew to the mantelpiece and grabbed the posy of forget-me-nots that was sitting there. She slipped them into his pocket where they nodded delicately, looking fragile against the tweed.

"Thanks," he said gruffly. With a lopsided smile, he doffed his cap at her and was gone.

Chapter Thirty

The day of the fight came at last. It was due to start at two o'clock, on open land nearby in Bethnal Green. Thanks to the fame of Eddie's opponent, they needed plenty of space for the expected crowd. Persephone didn't want to think about it – the very idea of the Blunderbuss terrified her.

To take her mind off it, she decided to go to Mayfair to collect new embroideries to sew. Picking up a panel for a countess to wear at Court, Persephone found herself thinking that the sleeves on the dress in question were cut too low and the taffeta used was too light for such a design. *I could have made it better*, she remarked to herself, not for the first time.

But today, back out in the street, her thoughts went further. *Why not?* Dressmakers were not born with fine houses like this one – they earned them. They found and trained their assistants. *I could do that, given time.* Why only make the extra pieces when the true artistry, the joy of it, came from the original design?

Kitty had exquisite taste but not all the *modistes'* designs were as fine as the ones she had worked on with Madame Madeleine. Often, Persephone's artistic eye was offended by a flounce too many, a sleeve too wide, or a colour combination that jarred when it could have been harmonious. Without really knowing it, she had often longed to be the one in charge, making things that were truly beautiful.

As she walked back east, she started to plan a new business. She knew how her clients lived and how to please them. Just as Kitty knew what suited her best, Persephone could tell instinctively what fabrics and what proportions worked with each woman's complexion and shape. All of them wanted wide skirts and she had noticed that some crinolines, made of watch steel, were lighter and easier to wear than others. She could combine her artist's eye with her skill at making patterns. She was sure, given time, that she could create new looks that would make her clients stand out in a crowd without collapsing under the weight of their clothes.

It might take years to achieve what Madame Madeleine had done but she was young – she had time. Now she understood how the business worked, and had connections with some of the best weavers and textile designers in Europe. Her mind buzzed with possibilities.

Back in Spitalfields, she could hardly wait to explain her ideas. Harriet was waiting for her there, with Aileana in her arms, and Eve Ellis too, who had come downstairs for company while her mother was out. In the middle of the room stood Annie, ashen-faced.

"Oh thank God you're here!" Annie said. "I was about to go back, but I wanted to find you…"

"Go back where?" Persephone asked in alarm. "Oh Lord. Eddie."

The fight must have started. She felt sick.

"Is it over? Is he safe?" Annie looked so stricken that she began to imagine terrible things.

"No. He'd gone nearly twenty rounds when I left," Annie groaned. "But … the damage… I can't bear it. Come with me, please."

"To watch?"

"Please! It's not far to go. I—" Annie broke down again.

"Of course I'll come," Persephone said, putting down her basket. "Where is he? Take me."

"No, no!" Eve Ellis leaped to her feet, tipping over her stool. "You mustn't!"

"Why?" Persephone asked.

"Not like that!" Persephone frowned at her, but Eve stood her ground. "I know these crowds. They pass this way often enough. Men drunk and excited, keen for blood. It's no place for a pretty girl in your finery."

Persephone thought of the crowd of men in Venice and gave an involuntary shudder. But Annie started to keen with despair. "I must go back. Who knows what's happened."

"I'll come, don't worry."

"Let me help you then," Eve begged.

She was not a fine seamstress, but Eve was an excellent judge of costume. While Harriet consoled the waiting Annie, she took Persephone upstairs and searched rapidly through her mother's mending pile. The Ellises also altered clothes for neighbours, and in the pile she found stout cord trousers, a coat and belt, and best of all a large tweed cap with a broad brim that Persephone could use to hide her hair.

In minutes, she was transformed. She was an urchin, whose nose and chin only peaked out from under her hat. Her feet were encased in too-large boots, which chafed her skin, but gave the impression of a growing boy.

Downstairs again, she showed herself to Harriet and Annie. "Will I do?" she asked.

"Even I would not know you!" Harriet declared.

"Then I'm ready."

❧❧

She ran with Annie through the streets of Spitalfields, heading north towards Bethnal Green. As they went, Persephone noticed more and more groups of men and boys heading in the same direction, calling out to friends what they had heard: that there was a 'show worth seeing'. She picked up her pace, outrunning many of them, with Annie close beside her.

"It may be over soon," she said to calm her friend. She was almost glad now that Eddie had been told to lose. The frenzied atmosphere in the gathering crowd was alarming.

"It should be by now," Annie panted. "They told him to last fifteen rounds at least to make an event of it."

Fifteen rounds. It sounded a lot, but the fighters did not normally stop until one or the other was incapable of standing. Back in Kent, though she rarely watched, Persephone had heard of worse. But then she remembered what Annie had said. "Hadn't he done more than that when you left?"

Annie nodded. "Eddie won't give up," she said. "Though the other man's a brute the size of a bear."

"Then we must go faster."

They reached the road leading to Bethnal Green, where every person seemed to be heading for the same place. The crowd gathered them up and they were propelled along down Paradise Row to a patch of common land where hundreds of men were gathered. The air was thick with baying shouts. Annie flinched with every boo and roar. The match was still in full-spate, but Persephone despaired of getting close enough to watch it.

"Come on. This way," Annie shouted.

She elbowed her way forwards and Persephone followed in her wake. Groups of gentlemen in top hats and frock coats jostled alongside dockers in shirtsleeves and bowler hats. Every one of them was hollering for his man. After much ducking and shoving, Annie managed to get to a place where they could see the makeshift pen set up in the middle of the open ground. The two fighters were held in a clench in the middle of it, stripped to the waist and wearing tight, pale knitted drawers stained red with blood. Young boys, not more than nine or ten, stood close to the ropes, keenly watching. Persephone noticed a small group of women nearby and dragged Annie closer to them.

"Oh, thank the Lord! He's still standing!" Annie cried. She turned to Persephone and buried her face in the warm old felt of her baggy coat.

There was nothing for it but to look, and there he was: broad, brave, open-hearted Eddie, who had always looked out for her, held up it seemed by his opponent, his face raw, his body bruised.

"Oh, Annie!" The words were out before she could stop them. "How many rounds have they gone?" she asked the woman nearest her.

"This is number thirty-eight," the woman said. "Though there won't be many more, I'm thinking. That Irishman's taking a beating from the Blunderbuss. I dunno how 'e's gone this far."

"Thirty-eight?" Persephone wondered why he still stood in the ring. The other fighter had stepped back and was punching Eddie's chest and arms with his bare fists. Eddie seemed disorientated and exhausted, but tried to defend himself. Why not take a hit now and be done with it?

"What's his plan?" she muttered to Annie, who by now was staring grim-faced at the ring.

"He's a stubborn mule. Won't give in, doesn't know how. He'd go a hundred rounds if he could."

The Blunderbuss grappled Eddie again and threw a punch to the side of his head. Persephone swore she could hear it land. Eddie fell to the ground and the round was declared over. His seconds dragged him to his chair in the corner. One man tipped his head back and poured water over him from a bottle while another mopped up the mess with a sponge. Eddie's face was a bloody pulp.

Unable to bear it, Persephone turned her eyes back to the crowd.

A small group of gentlemen opposite stood out for their smartly tailored coats and shiny silk hats. Also, they were shouting and gesticulating more violently than most. In their midst, one stood quite still. Under the tallest, shiniest hat of all she spotted Arthur, and clinging to him was a pretty, dark-haired young girl. With each thud and thump, his friends turned to him in delight or despair. But Arthur's expression hardly changed. He looked strangely euphoric. Persephone wasn't sure, but his eyes seemed unfocused. This was the same Arthur she had met in the red room – drugged up, dazed and happy, almost oblivious to the bloody fight in front of him.

"You know 'im, sweet'eart?"

Persephone looked round. The woman beside her was looking down at her. Clearly, at close range her disguise was not as good as she hoped.

"Know who?"

"Lord Mount'em. That's what we call 'im. On account of 'is 'ouse. Ah! I see you do!"

Persephone pursed her lips. The woman, now she looked closer, was not the kindly, motherly type she had assumed and nor were her friends. They had red-stained lips, and wore lace-trimmed chokers under their shawls and petticoats designed to show under their skirts. These were ladybirds. And so it was no surprise that they should know Arthur. But she even knew the house on Mount Street. He was famous for it! Kitty would have been shamed through the whole of London.

"'e's got a lot riding on this fight, I'm told," the ladybird went on.

"I was told that too," Persephone admitted.

"You know 'im well?"

"Not as well as you, I imagine."

The woman laughed. "That may be true!" She took a drag on a cigar snatched from the fingers of one of her friends. "Count yourself lucky. 'e's got a reputation. The things 'e does… You wouldn't want to know…"

"What kind of things?"

The woman shrugged. "Like I said… 'e likes 'em young and willing."

Persephone looked across at the girl beside Arthur, who indeed seemed almost childlike and vaguely familiar. Had she seen her in the red room? She had the same glazed, euphoric look as Arthur and seemed caught in the same spell. But Persephone's attention was soon dragged back to the ring. Time was nearly over and the next round was being called. The Blunderbuss stalked around the ring, black-eyed but unbowed, raising his fists to the crowd in promise of victory.

"Not much longer," the ladybird said, then shouted loudly, "Come on, Blunderbuss! Kill 'im! You can do it!"

Annie buried her face in Persephone's shoulder.

The next rounds were harrowing to watch. The Blunderbuss seemed to have taken Persephone's new companion literally. He stormed around the ring, hitting and punching, grabbing and throwing without respite. He was taller than Eddie and broader still, with more muscles than Persephone had ever seen on a man. His eyes glittered with intent as he blocked and jabbed, and his strength seemed superhuman.

Looking at those eyes, Persephone saw something that frightened her: a strange, excited detachment that reminded her of Arthur. There was something in his blood, something chemical. Not laudanum, she thought, but something else that gave him his prodigious energy. The referee often had to step in to reprimand him for an attack of illegal savagery. Eddie was mad to keep fighting him. She willed him to give up.

But Eddie would not. He took every punch and throw, and hit back when he could. He somehow survived another round, though only one of his eyes was open enough to see, and his knuckles were raw and weeping. There was a shift in the crowd as time was called. The tension rose to a new level. They sensed they didn't have much longer to wait.

As the forty-fifth round began, the excitement in the air was palpable. The Blunderbuss seemed to have decided that the time had come. He went in for the kill with a blur of arms and fists. Had nobody told him he was destined to win anyway? Eddie took one blow, then another. He feinted, ducked, blocked and recovered his breath. The flurry of blows coming at him grew thicker and faster as the Blunderbuss circled, ready to deliver the coup de grâce. Eddie planted his feet wide, held his fists up ready, and punched back at his opponent's face.

One punch, so hard it caught the Blunderbuss by surprise. He rocked back on his heels and nearly lost his balance. For a moment, he looked around, confused. Then, furious, he went in for another attack. Instinctively, Eddie hit him with a left hook to save himself. It connected with his opponent's jaw. The crowd heard the crack of bone on bone as the Blunderbuss's head snapped backwards. He spun on his heel and hit the ground, eyes closed.

The round was over. Eddie stood in shock while the referee started to count the thirty-second break. This time, it was the Blunderbuss's seconds who rushed forwards to pull him back.

The crowd went wild. Depending on who they had wagered on, half swore at him to wake up and the other half crowed that he couldn't. After twenty-eight seconds, he opened one eye and looked around. The cheering was intense. His seconds helped him struggle to his feet.

"Come on!" the ladybird muttered beside Persephone. It was clear where her wager lay.

"What must he do?" Persephone asked.

"'e's got eight seconds to come to scratch. Come ON, Blunderbuss!"

"One, two, three…" The referee held up his fingers to the chanting crowd. The Blunderbuss stood up unsteadily and staggered forwards. His seconds watched him helplessly. Eddie, meanwhile, was back at his mark, waiting. It was impossible to tell if he was poised to deliver another blow, or ready to fall himself. There were no certainties in this fight any more.

"Five … six … seven…" the ladybird murmured.

The Blunderbuss stood still, turned to his corner with unseeing eyes, and fell to the ground again, out cold. The mob erupted.

"O Lord! 'e's done it!" the ladybird shouted, astonished, as Eddie stood alone in the centre of the ring, until the referee and umpires came to join him. The Blunderbuss lay still and silent.

"Eddie! My Eddie!" Annie tried to rush towards her brother, but was held back by the cheering crowd.

His two seconds went to the centre of one of the ropes where two handkerchiefs, one red, one blue, were entwined. They untied them and presented them both unsmilingly to their fighter. This seemed to be his prize. For a moment, Eddie looked too shocked and bloodied to know what to do with them. Then he raised one exhausted arm in victory. His expression was tense. If anything, he looked afraid.

Persephone's first emotion was pure relief. *He's alive!* But instantly she thought of the bet and its consequences. He was in as much danger as ever. She followed Annie as she pushed her way through the crowd to try to reach him.

Looking up into the ring, she saw Eddie's seconds

glowering at him and noticed the shiny, sharpened buckles on their belts. What now?

At last she and Annie managed to fight their way to the side of the ring. Here, shirtsleeved men tried to hold her back, but she would not let them. Wearing breeches was so liberating! She could move and shove past resisting bodies without fear of catching her petticoats.

But Annie, in her maid's dress, was ahead of her still, already forcing her way through the stunned officials, between the ropes and into the ring. Before anyone could stop her, she was at Eddie's side. He took one look at her and fell to his knees. She caught him and lowered him to the ground. Only willpower had been holding him standing. His nose, bent at an angle, was clearly broken. One eye was a slit and the other was invisible under a shiny mass of pink flesh. Annie knelt beside him and stroked his hair, murmuring to him as if he was a little child.

Persephone was pushed forwards by the crowd of excited men behind her, and found herself next to the brother and sister as the ring was overwhelmed. As she bent over Eddie to see how bad the damage was, a lock of copper-coloured hair spilled from her cap. Quickly, she gathered it up and stuffed it back inside – but not before Eddie, through his slit of an eye, had noticed.

"Mary!" he gurgled, with the hint of a smile. Then it faded. "I'm sorry."

"What for?"

"For winning."

"He would have killed you!" She remembered what he had told her not so long ago. Bending further down, she said into his ear, "You did what you had to do. I'm proud of you."

And though his face and chest looked more like raw meat than the man she knew, and the stench of the ring was vile, she felt a sudden urge to kiss him. She wanted him to know he was loved. Such a thing was impossible here and now, but she put a gentle hand on his heart. He put his own hand over it. It took all her strength not to weep as he closed his eyes and the men with sharpened belt buckles stepped in to carry him off.

Chapter Thirty-one

Perhaps the Whitechapel Boys had plans to spirit Eddie away and dump him in the river. They had been known for worse. But a cheering crowd accompanied him all the way back to his lodgings, carried on a stretcher by six strong men. It would have been almost impossible to take him anywhere else. They even called a doctor, who spent an hour by his bedside instructing Annie on how to look after him.

Annie stayed there late into the night, though she knew she risked getting the sack for it. Persephone gave her fresh cotton to use as bandages and heated some water for her on her little stove. There wasn't much more she could do so she prowled around her rooms, trying not to think of Eddie and thinking of nothing else.

"Do go to bed," Harriet pleaded with her. "You must sleep!"

"I'm sorry, Hattie. Ignore me."

"How can I? You'll wear the floorboards out. Come and lie down."

Persephone tried laying on her mattress, still in her clothes, but it only made her mind race more. Something was wrong. She could feel it… Eventually she sat up.

"I can't bear it. I can't be still unless I know he's safe."

She went upstairs, clutching a candle, and told Annie of her nameless fears. Annie didn't contradict her, but merely nodded. Beside them Eddie tossed and turned in his sweat-soaked sheets, moaning in his sleep.

"I know it's mad, but can we…? Will you help me move him?"

"Where to?"

"Just downstairs. To my rooms. I just think… I'll feel better if he's there. With you and me watching over him."

Together, they lifted him and between them the two women somehow carried him down two flights of stairs. Eddie groaned with every step. Persephone hated making him suffer more, especially for no obvious reason. At the first landing, she almost turned back, but Annie gave her courage. The other girl was as spooked as she was. As gently as they could, they moved him into the small back room, where they laid him out on Persephone's bed and covered him with a blanket. He shivered for a while, then slept again.

"I'll stay with him," Annie said.

Persephone and Harriet moved into the workroom, finding floorspace where they could. Little Aileana slept on beside her mother in the drawer that was her cradle. Eventually, Harriet started to snore, but Persephone stayed wide awake. She had seen and heard too much today to push her thoughts aside.

She was still awake when the church bells struck four in the morning. A few minutes later there was the sound of hobnailed boots on the cobblestones outside. She couldn't tell exactly how many men – maybe four or five. As they came along the street she held her breath, praying for them to pass quickly by, but they didn't. Instead, they stopped dead outside the front door.

There was a flurry of knocks, delivered by a hard stick of some kind. Nobody answered. Another knock, and then the sound of a shoulder to the door.

This. This was what she had known would happen.

With a splintering of wood, the door gave in easily. Boots ran up the stairs. She pictured Jane and Eve Ellis in the room above her, clutching each other in terror in the dark. Even as she did so, Harriet came to lie beside her. They held on to each other. When the baby woke from a fitful sleep and cried, they held her too.

Then the boots were on the stairs again. They paused at the Ellises' door. It was opened and there was shouting. A minute later, her own door flew aside. They didn't even knock. Two men were in the room – two shadows – grunting and breathing hard.

"Where is 'e? Where's 'e gone?"

Harriet drew in her breath and screamed long and loud, clutching the baby to her. Persephone had to admire the powerful noise she made. Baby Aileana, not to be outdone, wailed even louder than her mother.

"Get out of here!" Persephone shouted above the noise.

And, after a shattered second, they did.

Persephone leaped up and closed the door behind them. She put her back to it and sank down to the floor. For a while, there was just the sound of her own panicked breathing, and Hattie comforting the baby, until Annie put her head round the inner door.

"Have they gone?"

"Yes," she said.

"Oh Lord."

At daybreak, they ventured gingerly upstairs. The rooms were a wreck. In chalk, the gang had scrawled a warning message on Eddie's door. Two simple words: DEAD MAN.

Except he wasn't. They felt fear and defiance in equal measure as they hugged each other on the stairs.

Annie had to go back to Pimlico or there would be no job to return to.

"Promise me you'll—"

"Of course," Persephone said. "Trust me."

All day Persephone tended to her patient while Harriet and the Ellises got on with their work. Twelve hours later, under cover of darkness, dressed in skirts and petticoats, a large figure in an ungainly bonnet stood ready to be spirited away. Persephone thought, for a moment, of Roly – who had looked similarly strange once in his disguise. But then it had been a joke, and now it was life and death. Eddie didn't say where he was going. Persephone didn't want to know. It would be too dangerous for both of them.

"Tell me when you're safe," she said as he prepared to go to the waiting hansom.

"No," he said. "If you don't hear from me, it's good news."

She sighed. Eddie was right. Even sending a message would be highly risky. But she hated the thought of his silence.

It was extraordinary how quickly he had recovered – seemingly by an effort of will. Though his face was a swollen lump of bruised and bloodied flesh, he could walk unaided and had insisted on dressing himself. He could even laugh at himself in his washerwoman's attire.

"Don't I look the fancy man?"

"You look a fright," she told him.

"Kiss me for luck."

She did, on his thickened lips, though she worried even kissing him might hurt him. But she so badly wanted Eddie to be lucky. And yes, she wanted to kiss him. So when he bent his head for a second kiss, she gladly gave that too. And a third, which was soft and gentle and lasted long enough for her to forget where she was.

This surprised them both. He stood back, startled. She blushed and fiddled with his bonnet ribbons.

"You'd better go."

He nodded. But when he came in for a fourth kiss, she laughed and gently sped him on his way. Forty-five rounds in the ring. If she didn't stop it, who knew how long such a goodbye could last?

Chapter Thirty-two

Persephone blocked the fight from her mind eventually, but she wasn't so lucky with the kisses. The feel of them kept coming back to her in a rush, even as she was busy explaining her new business plan to Harriet, or heading west to pick up piecework to sew.

She was thinking of them – and those ridiculous ribbons – a week later as she travelled to Mayfair to collect veils to embroider with lace edges for two new brides. With the fabric safely packaged in her basket, she looked at her pocket watch: ten o'clock and no more appointments until twelve thirty. A thought struck her, prompted by the veils.

Kitty always liked to go riding at eleven, if there was nothing else to do. By the sound of things, she hardly had an active social life these days. Betting on the charm of the bright May morning, Persephone strolled the short distance across Park Lane to Rotten Row.

The park hummed with the sounds of summer. Children playing with hoops crashed into nursemaids pushing their younger siblings in perambulators. Young men took to the boats on the lake, while older ones played chess at nearby tables. Women in smart new summer jackets walked up and down, hoping their outfits would be noticed. There was plenty to keep Persephone amused while she positioned herself behind the largest horse chestnut tree along the route the riders usually took. She didn't mind waiting, or getting strange looks from young boys who thought she was playing a game.

After less than half an hour, her wait was rewarded. Kitty appeared in the distance, accompanied by a manservant, riding Belle, her favourite horse. She was, as always, dressed in the height of fashion – pink candy stripes and a smart black riding hat – but her signature joy was gone. Persephone's heart contracted. *She still isn't better. Broken hearts take time to mend.*

It would be especially hard for Kitty this week. According to the *modistes*, news had just come out that Arthur was courting a young German princess. They had gossiped about little else this morning, hoping to be picked to make the Malmesbury family's wedding clothes, if not the bride's. She was 'quite handsome', apparently, 'in a German way', and very rich. Arthur had bought her a diamond tiara with his winnings from a sporting bet, it seemed, and it was assumed they would be married by the end of summer. Persephone did not envy her. One day she would discover what kind of man she was married to.

Another group of riders came by and Persephone remembered from the old days how everyone who was 'anyone' would call out to Kitty and vie for her attention. No longer. This group gave her curt nods and moved along smartly. The wound their pity caused was obvious. Kitty tried to hide it but her brave smile told the story.

Soon after she passed Persephone's hiding place a stylish young man in a pale wool jacket stepped forwards to greet her. Kitty pulled up her horse. He spoke a few words while an elegant greyhound waited at his heels. Kitty must have said something about the dog, because he grinned and patted the beast. They talked some more. He raised his hat and she went on her way. Persephone saw how he looked after her until she was out of sight, and smiled.

It was time to go home.

Two more weeks passed without news of Eddie. She prayed he hadn't gone to Ireland because the Whitechapel Boys had thought of that. All the pubs were full of talk of the men they had despatched to look for him there. She thought of him with every stitch she made and was grateful that Harriet diplomatically never mentioned him.

Meanwhile, Aileana grew bigger and stronger. The notes detailing Persephone's business plan grew thicker every day. Shillings were saved in a precious jar. The workroom was piled high with fabrics to sew, and *modistes* throughout West London queued for Persephone and Harriet's favour. Half the ladies in Court, it seemed, would soon be wearing dresses with *engageantes*, flounces and ruching by the cousins from Spitalfields.

Harriet worked day and night without complaining, but one day, as she fell asleep at her needle, Persephone realized that her poor cousin needed a break.

"You should go to the theatre or Cremorne Gardens. Get some fresh air and see some dancing. God knows you've earned it. I've kept you here for an age – I'm sorry."

"I couldn't go without you," Harriet protested. "And then who would mind the baby?"

This was easily fixed. Eve would look after Aileana while they both went out. They deserved an evening of pleasure. On her travels, Persephone had seen a poster advertising a balloon flight – by a woman – from Vauxhall Gardens.

"We have to see it, don't we? Can you imagine? A woman flying high in a balloon, right over London?"

Harriet could not, and to be truthful nor could Persephone, even with her vivid imagination. What would happen when the balloon came down? Would it crash on to houses? She was fascinated and scared, and desperate to watch.

They dressed in lilac and plum poplin skirts and perfectly tailored jackets they had made themselves between commissions. Eve pronounced them "as beautiful as actresses", which apparently was a compliment. They giggled as they put on their matching bonnets and headed out of the door. Persephone felt almost giddy. She had never set out for an evening of pleasure designed by herself before. She was quite surprised she knew how to do it.

The sky was still bright when they left Spitalfields. The sun would not set for another hour. They bought hot eels, pickled whelks and ginger beer from various street vendors along the way. They walked when they needed to and took an omnibus when they could. Persephone felt that she owned London tonight. True, there were whistles and calls from groups of men, but she ignored them. She had always been taught that women didn't leave the house unaccompanied unless they were working. But it was amazing what you could do, and enjoy doing, if you simply tried.

Harriet was too transported by joy to speak. For a long time, when she was pregnant with the baby and afterwards when Aileana was given to Mrs Lisle, she had thought she would never be happy again. Yet here she was. Persephone could feel her fizz, like the ginger beer in its bottle.

In this spirit they wandered west to Vauxhall.

They paid their entry into the gardens and began to look around. As always, Persephone concentrated on the clothes – the choice, cut and colour of each outfit, male and female. Did it work, did it fit, was it exciting? Could she have made it better? Almost always, she could. Did it give her ideas? Often, it did.

Then she noticed wide black skirts sweeping through the crowd at a little distance. Black was an unusual colour for this place. Black reminded her of...

"Oh!" Harriet gasped and grabbed Persephone's arm.

The widow.

She had turned round. Persephone saw her oval face now, and her dark neat hair. She was walking with a companion, who was hidden by a portly gentleman ahead of them. But even before he moved out of the way, Persephone knew who she would find. The dark curling hair, the bright necktie – pink this time, chosen with an artist's panache – the linen jacket for summer, the perfectly picked camellia. He turned and saw her. Mrs Lisle had seen her too. Harriet pulled on her arm.

"Quick! Let's go!"

Persephone's first instinct, equally, was to turn away. But Felix called out to her.

"Please! Mary... Persephone!" He looked angst-ridden.

Last time, she had run fast and hard, but she remembered that last time, lives had depended on it – she'd thought. Those lives were safe now, safer than they had ever been in the house in Chelsea. Harriet was standing right beside her. Why run?

Persephone had not forgotten Mrs Lisle's cruelty to her cousin. She turned to Harriet and quickly murmured to her to wait nearby. And then she walked forwards, slowly.

"Good evening, Mr Dawson. Madam." She curtseyed with all the sarcasm she could convey.

Mrs Lisle gave her a furious stare that said everything. *I told you to stay away from him.*

Persephone's cool look back was equally transparent. *Try and stop me.*

Felix saw them exchange glances and looked uncomfortable. Everything about him was awkward tonight, she realized: his posture, his expression, the way he held his arm out for his mistress-patron to hold on to tightly. She remembered what he'd said: *I hate her now. She thinks she owns me.*

Interesting.

Unaware of the distance they were supposed to keep, Felix reached out to her. "Persephone, please… You said things last time… I didn't understand. What did I do?"

Persephone's feelings towards him, if not his mistress, had softened since their last meeting. "I made a pact," she said simply. "I wasn't as heartless as you thought."

She glanced at Mrs Lisle, who gave her a warning look.

Persephone raised her chin and gazed back at Felix. "If you knew me, you might have guessed that I loved you more than life, but someone was keeping me away." The hand holding Felix's arm gripped tighter. "You know how desperate I was to save my cousin…"

"Was that her there with you just now?" Felix asked.

"Yes."

"Then she was saved?"

"Yes, she was. Eventually."

Here Mrs Lisle smiled very slightly. "*I* saved her." Her voice was low and proud and cool, just as it had always been.

"And blackmailed me," Persephone elaborated. "The price for Harriet's safety was you, Felix."

His beautiful brow furrowed. "How?"

"She thought you loved me – and she didn't want you near me. I wasn't to see you, contact you or explain." Persephone's words were thick with emotion now. "I couldn't refuse."

Felix stared at the woman beside him. "Is this true?"

"No, it's not true! None of it! She's lying like the little tramp she is."

"But you just said you saved her cousin…"

"Out of charity! I adopted my sister's daughter. This was the same."

"It wasn't," Persephone sputtered. "It was anything but charity. You wrenched a baby from her mother's arms. You worked Harriet half to death while you kept Aileana for yourself. And for this, you let Felix think I left him for money—"

"Enough! I'm not going to stand here and listen to this from you!" Mrs Lisle was white with fury.

"Yes, that's enough," Felix said. He was quite calm. He turned to his mistress. "I always wondered what you were capable of. I admit I was too lily-livered to fight it. Keep your artist-brothel. I'll be gone by morning."

"No!" To Persephone's shock, Mrs Lisle turned to her with tears in her eyes. "Tell him it's not true.

Explain how I helped you."

"You tried to break me. You almost broke Harriet too. I owe you nothing."

Felix was already detaching the older woman's hand from his arm. It gripped him like a claw.

"Please! Please!" she begged, turning to him. It was astonishing how quickly she had sunk from pride to desperation.

His look was cold and haughty. It reminded Persephone, in fact, of *La Belle Dame sans Merci.* He stood back as she reached for him, and nodded to Persephone.

"I'm sorry. For everything."

"So am I," Persephone said.

"I assume it's too late. I wish…" He hesitated.

She wished he hadn't agreed to Arthur's hideous commission, that she hadn't seen the cruel portrait, that he had helped her when she needed it with Harriet. And, undependable as he was, that she didn't still love him.

"I wish you well," she said, holding out her hand.

"Goodbye." He kissed her fingers and walked off swiftly through the crowd.

Mrs Lisle stayed where she was, hunched over with grief. Pleasure-seekers in the gardens stopped to turn and stare. They seemed to expect Persephone to comfort the weeping woman. But she thought of all her broken dreams with Felix, and the time that Harriet had lost with her little girl, and felt no shred of pity at all.

Harriet was beside a nearby stall, waiting. It didn't take long to find her.

"What happened? I saw him leave. What did he say?"

"It doesn't matter," Persephone said. "He knows the truth. Now let's find the balloon."

They walked arm in arm towards a gap in the trees, where the vast, striped red and blue balloon was tethered. A woman dressed all in white stood in the wicker basket underneath it, with a top-hatted man beside her. Soon the tethers were released and the balloon started to rise into starlit sky. The passengers in the basket waved and members of the crowd waved large flags back at them in celebration.

Harriet grinned. "I can hardly believe it! Are they really leaving the earth? Where are they going?"

"Who knows?" Persephone said. A part of her was rising with them too, drifting high into the air and sailing over London. "Do you care?"

"Not really." Harriet laughed. "Isn't it beautiful?"

Chapter Thirty-three

By now, Eddie was a legend across East London: the Irishman from nowhere who had defeated the Blunderbuss and made a fortune for many an astute gambling man. Half the men in Spitalfields wanted to shake his hand. Persephone too had unfinished business with Eddie O'Bryan.

Seeing Felix again had stirred up emotions whose strength she had forgotten. She had kissed two men in her life now, and somewhat to her horror she wanted to kiss both of them again. What sort of woman was she? But Felix was out of her life now and, a month on, Eddie's whereabouts were still a secret. She wondered if Winnie was secretly giving him consolation, and the thought did not please her as much as it should.

And then, one morning in early June, a woman knocked on the door.

"Let me in. I've got some mending for you."

"We don't take in mending," Persephone called out, half-dressed. "You need to go upstairs."

"I don't. This is for you."

There was something compelling in the woman's voice. Persephone pulled her shawl around her and opened the door carefully.

"Yes?"

The woman held out a tweed cap, in perfect condition, and said nothing. Persephone recognized it instantly as Eddie's. She ushered the woman inside.

"Tell me everything."

First, the woman made sure the door was firmly closed behind her and the shutters at the windows were fast. The room was nearly dark and her face was lit only by the candle in Persephone's hand. It was an old face, pockmarked and haggard. The hair above it was a vibrant orange, and Persephone suspected a wig. The black-ribbon choker at her neck suggested her profession. Persephone had never entertained a tart before. "Will you sit down?" she asked, unsure what to do.

"No. I'll not stay long. I've got a message. Not to be repeated, ever. Swear it."

Persephone knew what was at stake and didn't argue. "I swear."

"'e wanted to write, but it's too dangerous. No paper, nothing to say what I'm about to tell you. If you tell a soul, 'e's dead, you're dead. We're all dead. Got it?"

"Yes."

"All right. Now listen." The woman had been speaking in a quiet voice before, but lowered it to a whisper. Persephone had to lean in to hear. "'e couldn't stay in England—"

Persephone gasped. "He's gone?"

"Quiet! Let me tell the story. They were tracking 'im down. They 'ad spies everywhere. So 'e's took a boat to a place where they'll look after 'im. You'd know it, 'e said. 'e wanted you to know 'e's safe, 'cause you won't 'ear of 'im again in this city. And 'e said 'e'd miss you." The woman paused and almost smiled. "Ackshally, 'e said you'd miss 'im."

Despite her sadness, Persephone laughed. "Yes, he would say that." She tried to smile her gratitude. The woman had taken a great risk coming here today. To her surprise, the visitor put a sympathetic hand on her arm.

"'e 'ad to do it."

"I understand."

The woman's hand rested where it was. Persephone felt her sisterly solidarity. At least, Persephone was thinking that's what it was and the woman echoed her thoughts when she coughed and said, "By the bye, did you know Ruth Vincent?"

At this name, Persephone's eyes pricked with tears. A popular ladybird had been found dead in her bed in Petticoat Lane two nights ago. All the streets of Spitalfields pulsated with the story. It was laudanum, the doctor said. Too strong a dose. And her arms were laced with cuts and bruises.

The visitor saw Persephone's glistening eyes. "So you were a friend?"

Persephone shook her head. "No. But they said she was at the prizefight. A pretty, dark-haired girl with a rich client..."

"That's the one. 'e was 'er favourite."

"I saw her there."

Ruth must have been the girl who had been hanging on to Arthur that day. And thinking about it, she was sure Ruth was the same girl she had seen lying on him in the red room – the one he threw off to make space for her… She felt an icy chill run through her at the memory.

"She loved 'im," the visitor said. "Silly sweet'eart. She was too young for 'is games. 'e was the one wot liked to give 'er the stuff. But you know as 'ow 'e'll never pay."

Persephone nodded. "I do."

"We're 'aving a little ceremony for 'er. Tomorrow. By the river. It would 'ave been 'er sixteenth birthday. 'er dad was a waterman, see? She loved that river. 'er life it was, as a child. D'you want to be there?"

"Yes. Yes I do."

"Good. Come along. First light. St Katharine Docks. Bring a flower for Ruth."

"I will."

"Right. I'm off." As she turned to leave, the woman caught sight of the tweed cap in Persephone's hand. It seemed to remind her of something. She cocked her head and fixed Persephone with sharp eyes. "Wot we was talking about before… You were the only one 'e wanted told, except 'is sister. Thought I'd mention it."

Persephone nodded thoughtfully. "Thank you. I'll see you tomorrow."

After she'd left, Harriet crept out of the little back

room, holding her sleeping baby.

"What was that about?"

Persephone told her about the ceremony for Ruth Vincent, torn between grief and fury. They held each other and the baby for a while, grateful to be safe.

"And Eddie's gone away," she added softly. "To America, I think. You must tell no one."

"Of course. What will you do?"

"Nothing. What can I do?"

But Persephone was never a girl to sit and do nothing. She was utterly restless. She couldn't sew, couldn't concentrate, couldn't think. In the end she put on her walking clothes and went to Pimlico, where she called on Annie.

Persephone was glad that Eddie hadn't kept his sister in the dark. Annie grabbed her bonnet and they spent five minutes walking by the river at the southern end of St George's Square. In the warm weather a considerable stink came off the water. In some ways, Persephone reflected, Eddie was well rid of the city.

"You've got cousins in Chicago, haven't you?" she asked Annie.

"How did you know?"

"Eddie told me."

Annie nodded. "They're doing grand. He'll make his fortune and come back a lord!"

"They don't have lords in America, Annie!"

"Don't they? What do they have?"

"I'm not sure... Just rich men, I think. Generals and railwaymen and presidents."

"One of those then. You watch him."

⁕⁕⁕

Persephone walked the long way back to Spitalfields and as she did so she found new plans forming – even bolder and brighter than the ones she had before.

So Eddie was off to America.

He had told two people where he was going, or at least in such a way that they could guess. Two people – not three. Persephone felt sorry for Winnie back at Balfour House. But he had not given her the message and selfishly, Persephone was glad. By now he was probably in Chicago and if he had sent his friend to tell her, she assumed he wouldn't mind if she joined him there. Surely that's what he really meant by taking such a risk?

It was a lot of assuming. The thought should have scared her but it didn't. And if she was wrong, and he wasn't there, it was not the end of everything. She could look after herself, especially somewhere like America, where the streets were paved with gold if you worked hard enough to find it. In London she would always be the girl from Kent, the 'tradeswoman' that Bee and Maria so despised, but in Chicago she could be anyone.

Or she could go to Paris. *All the best things are in Paris.* They made the most elegant dresses there – of the kind she longed to design. She didn't speak the language but she could learn. James Whistler had talked about the Louvre. Perhaps Felix might be tempted to go one day and study the Rembrandts. He would spy her in the street, dressed finely, and she would show him to *her* studio, like Madame Madeleine's, where a dozen girls would be busily working. She refused to depend on him again, but to be with him as an equal… That was a different matter. And if he still needed a patroness, what about her? What a dream it was! Except, it felt not so much a dream as an ambition.

Chicago or Paris? It was hard to decide. With each street she took towards the City she became more tempted by them both, so that by the time she reached the steps of St Paul's it seemed obvious to go up them and pray for guidance.

Inside, the vast cathedral soared above her. There was poetry in its graceful arches, and joy in the sunlight that flooded in and scattered across the floor. Nostalgia too, in its gold mosaics, which took Persephone back to that other cathedral in Torcello, infinitely older and smaller, but praising God with the same intent. It was not an answer to her prayer exactly, but it helped.

Back home Harriet wept when she explained her decision, but by then she had made up her mind. She could go to one place, then the other. Why not? She would settle wherever success lay.

"You'll be safe. That's all I wanted," she said gently to Harriet. "You'll have all this, and Eve will help you. You're so much more patient at teaching her than I am."

"That's true." Harriet laughed through her tears. "You're a terrible teacher."

"But you aren't. Eve can earn so much more here, doing this, than mending with her mother. Soon you'll have a roomful of assistants. You'll be a Spitalfields *modiste*!"

"Don't tease me! But they don't have Court ladies in America, do they? What will you do?"

"They have rich ladies who wear fashionable clothes. I know what rich people want. In fact, one day I shall be one of them! If Eddie can do it, so can I."

"Oh, Mary!"

"I can. Why not?"

"You're a girl of seventeen."

"Did no seventeen-year-old ever get rich one day?"

"Not that I know. And no girl, certainly."

"Then I shall be the first." Persephone puffed out her chest with mock pride, but then she was serious again. "Don't make me stay. I know this is the right thing."

Harriet sighed. "I know too. Nothing can stop you, 'Persephone Lavelle'. When will you go?"

"Soon. When I've bought my passage." Persephone picked up the gurgling baby who sat on cushions at her feet and rubbed noses with her playfully. "You haven't seen the last of me, little one."

This was not like running to Venice. Then she had been running away. Now she had much to stay for but she wanted more. In her mind, her life was mapped out. The work would be tough but wherever she went, dress by dress, she would enrich herself until she owned the world. She did not need the likes of Arthur Malmesbury to give it to her.

Before she left, though, there was one important ceremony to perform.

Chapter Thirty-four

Early the next morning, Persephone stood in the dim, pearlescent light, surrounded by women old and young, looking out on the River Thames. The tide was low, and a small breeze whipped up little waves beneath them. Snatches of voices were carried on the wind, but most of the women were silent. They stood shoulder to shoulder, looking east towards Tilbury, where the river flowed towards the sea.

Ruth Vincent had been buried yesterday in a pauper's grave. Her resting place would not be marked, but her life would be. These women came to honour her: a young girl, doing what she could to survive, doing nobody harm. Her only mistake was to let a particular rich gentleman take care of her.

Who knows what had happened that night? Had he left her or hurt her? Was it an accident or an overdose? Either way, he walked away from it untroubled by consequences. Persephone thought of the bottomless, dead look in Arthur Malmesbury's eyes and shuddered.

Strangely, her thoughts turned to the sobbing, beseeching Mrs Lisle. Once, that woman had owned her – had dictated everything she could and could not do. Escaping from her clutches had seemed impossible but now here she was: free. Mrs Lisle was the one in chains of her own making. Now it was *she* who was condemned never to see Felix again.

There could be justice, Persephone thought. However dark the future seemed, light seeped into it. If Mrs Lisle could be defeated then so could Arthur Malmesbury, one day.

I'll do what I can, she promised Ruth. *Give me time.*

The sun was rising. The sky ahead of them was glorious pink, flecked with pale grey clouds. The air was warming. Soon the summer stink from the river would become unbearable. They must be quick.

"For Ruth," somebody said. She raised a single long-stemmed red rose and threw it into the river. Another joined it, and another.

Persephone had intercepted a cart heading for Covent Garden that morning, and held a bouquet of summer flowers: lilacs and lavender, sweet peas and pale pink roses. Fresh and sweet-smelling; the wedding flowers Ruth would never have. She threw the bouquet hard, tossing it out into the current as far as she could. The stems broke apart and floated separately away, delicate petals carried by the waves, on and out to sea, mingling with the reds and blues and yellows of the other flowers thrown by the group of women around her.

We won't forget you. We won't forget.

Persephone looked up and stared towards Tilbury and sea. Sixteen months ago, she had sailed up this river as Mary Adams, riding the *Queen of the Thames,* ready to make her mark on London. Now, she pictured other seas and the new boat she would soon take.

The women seemed grateful for her presence, but they stood a little apart. With her fancy clothes and West End ways she was, and was not, one of them. The wind had caught her hair that day last year. It did again. Copper trails whipped around her face. She pulled them aside and gazed at the horizon.

The sun rose higher in the sky, which turned from pink to blue. *Celeste* or *azzurro*? Persephone shook her head and smiled. What colours did they call the sky in America?

Historical notes

I have moved Titian's *Assumption* back from the Accademia, where it was to be found in the nineteenth century, to the Frari, where it was originally hung and where readers can see it today. The painting was the pride of the Accademia's collection in the 1850s, but I have cheated with its position because it can best be appreciated from its original spot, and because I would like to give readers a sense of how you might experience seeing the painting for yourself if you go to Venice (please do!) – as I did, in my student days. I still remember being amazed by the glory of that painting the first time I saw it. It's a golden image that stays with you forever.

You might also want to visit the Uffizi Gallery in Florence – one of my favourite museums – where you can still see the *Venus of Urbino*, although be warned: Mark Twain called it "the foulest, the vilest, the obscenest picture the world possesses", and not fit for public display. Or perhaps the Musée d'Orsay in Paris – another of my favourites – where you'll find Manet's *Olympia*, painted in 1863 and based, in part, on the Titian. This is perhaps the type of picture Felix would have painted for his secret patron, if Persephone had let him. We shall never know.

I have also cheated a little with Whistler, who was too ill to visit Venice in January 1858 and in fact didn't go there until much later. However, he did visit his sister in London that spring, and liked to etch and paint in the outdoors. He didn't meet his famous red-haired model and mistress, the Irish Jo Hiffernan, for another year, or paint the pictures of her I so love until the early 1860s. But I like to think Persephone might have inspired him. Do look out for his *Symphony in White: No. 1* and *No. 2* paintings of Jo. They're monochrome, haunting and beautiful, and the ones I had in mind while I was writing.

Acknowledgements

As always, thanks to Jenny at ANA, for being a great agent and sounding board, and to all the team at Stripes. To Paul for another stand-out cover, and Lauren and Charlie for telling people about it, and everyone behind the scenes. And once again thanks to Katie Jennings for being such a great editor to work with, even when we were down to unwanted commas. To Alex, Emily, Sophie, Freddie and Tom, for putting up with me being mentally in nineteenth-century Venice. To all my online and in-your-face writing friends (you know who you are) and this time, the Royal Literary Fund for taking me under your wing and making me a Fellow. Thank you.

A huge thank you to Professor Laura Lepschy, whom I first met when I was nineteen and who sent me off on an art history course to Venice. It was a special chapter in my abiding love for Italy. There I got together with Joe Iuliano, who opened my eyes to so much art. As with the last book, I hope this one inspires readers to get out their own pencils or watercolours and to discover paintings that they love. Art is a chance to see the world through someone else's eyes, and that is a great gift. Of course, so is a book...

Places to go and see the Pre-Raphaelites and their world:
Birmingham Museum and Art Gallery
Tate Britain, London (which is also home to some lovely Whistlers)
Manchester Art Gallery
The Walker Art Gallery, Liverpool
Leighton House Museum, London
The Victoria and Albert Museum, London
Kelmscott Manor, Kelmscott, Gloucestershire
Red House, London
Buscott Park, Faringdon, Oxfordshire
The Oxford Union, Oxford

And if you get the chance, do visit the Accademia Gallery and the Peggy Guggenheim museum in Venice. Or indeed anywhere in that beautiful city. I recommend going in winter, as Persephone does, when it is cold and damp and atmospheric. Wrap up warm, and picture her in a gondola.

Sophia Bennett

Sophia Bennett always wanted to be a writer. Her first book, *Threads*, was published in 2009 and sold around the world. Since then she has written several acclaimed books for teens including *Love Song*, which won the Romantic Novel of the Year 2017. Her favourite subjects are art, music, fashion, travel and adventure, all of which make it into her stories. Sophia lives with her family in London and escapes from them to write in a shed at the bottom of her garden. When she isn't there, you can generally find her in a gallery somewhere, soaking up the art. You can also find her at her website: sophiabennett.com.